What the critics are saying:

"...I believe that Ms. Windsor has far exceeded the others of this series; The Captain's Fancy had no limits and swept the reader way with its depth, action, emotion and the fire between the characters." ~ *Tracey West, Road to Romance (Reviewer's Choice Award)*

"An epic futuristic romance full of white hot passion and true love..." ~ *Courtney Bowden, Romance Reviews Today*

"...Flaming hot and grabbingly emotional...THE CAPTAIN'S FANCY is a rare and special treat. A wonderful read.... Definitely recommended." ~ *Ann Leville, Sensual Romance*

"The Captain's Fancy is highly erotic and sensuous, heartwarming and at times, heart-wrenching. I stand in awe of Ms. Windsor's gift and am extremely thankful she chose to share it with the world." ~ *Sharyn McGinty, In the Library Reviews*

"...Well-conceived and well-written..." ~ *Jean, Fallen Angel Reviews*

"With her unique story line and writing style incorporating action and suspense with dynamic characters, sensually erotic love scenes and sweet romance, it's no wonder Annie Windsor is one of my favorite authors and on my auto-buy list, without a doubt." ~ *Brenda Lee, Romance Junkies*

Arda: The Captain's Fancy

Annie Windsor

THE CAPTAIN'S FANCY
An Ellora's Cave Publication, April 2004

Ellora's Cave Publishing, Inc.
1337 Commerce Drive Suite #13
Stow, Ohio 44224

ISBN #1419950932

ISBN MS Reader (LIT) ISBN #1843606755
Other available formats (no ISBNs are assigned):
Adobe (PDF), Rocketbook (RB), Mobipocket (PRC) & HTML

Edited by *Martha Punches*
Cover art by *Christine Clavel*

Warning:

The following material contains graphic sexual content meant for mature readers. *Arda: The Captain's Fancy* has been rated *E-rotic* by a minimum of three independent reviewers.

Ellora's Cave Publishing offers three levels of Romantica™ reading entertainment: S (S-ensuous), E (E-rotic), and X (X-treme).

S-ensuous love scenes are explicit and leave nothing to the imagination.

E-rotic love scenes are explicit, leave nothing to the imagination, and are high in volume per the overall word count. In addition, some E-rated titles might contain fantasy material that some readers find objectionable, such as bondage, submission, same sex encounters, forced seductions, etc. E-rated titles are the most graphic titles we carry; it is common, for instance, for an author to use words such as "fucking", "cock", "pussy", etc., within their work of literature.

X-treme titles differ from E-rated titles only in plot premise and storyline execution. Unlike E-rated titles, stories designated with the letter X tend to contain controversial subject matter not for the faint of heart.

Also by Annie Windsor:

Arda: *The Sailkeeper's Bride*
Arda: *The Sailmaster's Woman*
Cajun Nights
Equinox
Legacy of Prator: *Cursed*
Legacy of Prator: *Redemption*
Redevence: *The Edge*
Vampire Dreams

Arda: The Captain's Fancy

Prologue
Council of Worlds, Tower on the Tor, Old Earth
Time Before Time

"I cannot kill *Barung*." Arda's *Ord'pa*, the most fearsome and renowned executioner in the civilized worlds, shook his head. The black of his unfettered hair seemed deep and endless in contrast to the startling silver stripes on his taut cheeks. "He is too powerful. The energy he stored during his rising would disperse and destroy us all. Perhaps the known universe with us."

The expression he wore, of burden and seriousness beyond measure, was shared by Kaldor, First Priest of Kaerad, the eldest among the three. Kaldor sat at the Tower's round table, a table Earth's kings of men would one day hold dear. He used the circular structure to keep a healthy physical distance from his two fellow Council members. Kaeradi were empaths of the first order, telempaths, in fact. Not only could flesh-contact with an incompatible bring great pain or even death to the Kaeradi, but the projection of that pain could kill the innocent who touched them as well.

Kaldor had a physical look similar to the *Ord'pa*, to the Ardani in general, but without the universe's living substance etched into his flesh. He had instead a great golden stone set into his chest just above his heart. Gold was the color of a spiritually transformed leader, of a mystic who had achieved the highest disciplines. Gold was for the fire that lived in stone, and it was this gold flesh-rock he touched in a gesture of weary defeat.

"So." He sighed, sitting back. "We have contained the evil by a combination of our strengths, but we cannot destroy it."

"I refuse to accept that." Myrddin of Perth, and now of Earth only since Perth was no more, stood and went to gaze out of the tower windows. Avalon stretched before him, bright, sparkling, and new. All that was good in this world frolicked on the verdant fields, both those with deep magik and those with the younger, wilder variety bred of this planet alone. Perthling, Ardani, Kaeradi, or halfling mingled with the lesser-developed humans of this world — it mattered not. All were welcome. All were joyous and free to be what the universe called them to be. Earth had fulfilled its promise thus far, as a haven for those fleeing the darkest necromancer ever to rise to power in the universe.

Barung. Lord of the Dark. Eater of Light. Scourge of Souls.

Such dramatic names.

Myrddin sighed.

Even now, he could feel the bastard's malevolence radiating from the containment field established above Earth. The true horror came in how quickly people could forget such amorality. In a few generations, the children of Avalon would have no memory of evil as great as *Barung.* They scarcely understood now, even one generation removed from the devastation wrought on Kaerad, Arda, and his own destroyed world of Perth. Their blood would be mingled, and the unique gifts of each race lost — or melded to create something even more wondrous. Such things were not to be known until they happened.

Well, the Kaeradi priest probably knew, at least in the sketchy non-descript colors of future emotion he could see, but he was wise enough not to share his vague predictive visions.

"I know your grief is deep, Brother Myrddin," the *Ord'pa* of Arda allowed. His accent made the name sound more like "Mertin" or "Merlyn," which was how many of Avalon's children hailed him already. "The loss of Perth was tragic, and the ripples will be felt in the fabric of time until the last breath on the last world at the last moment of time. Alas, despite the rightness of our vengeance, even I do not have the power to kill *Barung*. If we blended all of our great skills together, we would still be doomed to failure."

For a time, silence claimed the round table in the round room, in the round tower on the round hill.

Circles, Myrddin thought. *Powerful and yet powerless.*

Kaldor cleared his throat. "We could...banish him, could we not? Bind him in his own squalid energy and send him into other dimensions to find his way back — if he can?"

"And visit his evil on some other peoples? Leave him to return and destroy our children eons hence?" Myrddin snorted even as he saw a dawning agreement on the solemn face of the *Ord'pa*. Perthling blood ran hotter than Ardani blood, without doubt. Arda was about balance — this with that, strength with restraint. Perthling blood ran hotter still than the blood of the Kaeradi, who had more power than any, and an even greater reticence to use it. Perth's greatest wizard wanted death for his people's

11

vengeance. More than that, Myrddin wanted a permanent end to the threat.

"Come, Myrddin." Kaldor's tone took a definitive depth, an absolute command only a Kaeradi could achieve without offending any listeners. "Acknowledge this as our only choice. You cannot deny the truths before us."

"I will not doom the worlds of tomorrow to the fate Perth suffered." Myrddin turned and rapped his fist on the round table. A sound like thunder burst through the room as wild magik skittered over wood, then stones.

Instinctively, the Kaeradi priest and the *Ord'pa* flung up their hands and concentrated their energies on blocking Myrddin's rage-spell before it did harm.

The Tor's tower trembled as the magiks met and intertwined. A few of the stones exploded, leaving menacing, crackling black holes where they once stood. The air took on a sudden smell of burning and melting, and a light smoke curled above the round table in the unmistakable shape of a feather.

Kaldor watched the display without passion, but the *Ord'pa* narrowed his eyes at the smoke-feather, at the flashing streaks of magikal light, in truth, a brief harnessing of the living substance of the universe. Myrddin knew the Ardani was thinking. He could almost hear the man's scientific mind observing, planning. Perhaps "plotting" would be a better word?

Myrddin narrowed his own eyes, studying the executioner. The Ardani *were* a crafty lot. Great thinkers and innovators, much as Perthlings had developed a reputation as naturalists and healers. Kaeradi were deep into emotion, the spiritual arts and the rhythm of the universe. All three races bred virulent warriors, though their weapons were decidedly different. Arda fought with science and the focused energy of the mind, Kaerad with the fire of the heart and resolve of the spirit, and Perth with the force of the body and natural elements.

"What are you contemplating?" Myrddin asked quietly, in deference to the *Ord'pa*'s renewed alertness.

The Ardani clenched his hands before him in the gesture of a supplicant. "Our joined powers cannot defeat *Barung*...now." The silver stripes on his cheeks glittered with sudden manic energy. "We would have to banish the blackheart, yes. For now. But with forethought and cooperation, we could deliberately crossbreed our races and mingle them with the wild energies of this world to build the strength we need. We could also use Perth's destruction to good ends, laying the proper traps in the energy signature of the universe where the planet once orbited..."

"That would take thousands of years," Myrddin said carefully, measuring each word so that Kaldor and the *Ord'pa* might heed him instead of humoring him. "Time carves memory like sand carves stone. How can we be certain tomorrow's children will know that we existed, much less that we planned for a disaster we doomed them to endure?"

"Nothing is ever certain, Myrddin." Kaldor's calm galled Myrddin, but he kept his mouth clamped as the old Kaeradi spoke. "Better we leave our children many healthy years—and some hope—rather than none, yes?"

For that question, Myrddin, despite his powerful passions to the contrary, had no good answer. He closed his eyes.

When he opened them a few seconds later, the *Ord'pa*

was busy drawing pictures, his long graceful fingers borrowing liquid energy from his silver tattoos to create wispy designs on the round table and in the air. A triangle, with three planets—Earth, Kaerad, and Arda—at the corners. In the center, the Ardani sketched a dark hole where Perth should have been, and showed how, with a few alterations in solar winds and the pressures and energies of space, an unsuspecting ship or even an entire world might be sucked into that void and crushed into nothingness. Much the way *Barung* crushed Perth, in fact. With the weight of the universe itself, turned on a single point.

Myrddin watched in silent surrender as Kaldor invested in this far-future design, and began to speak of setting celestial events into play that would produce such a world-crushing void.

Then the talk turned to creating and nurturing bloodlines, and how to establish and maintain channels of energy between the three planets that could one day ensnare *Barung* in Perth's dead space like a fly in an Earth spider's web.

This is fantasy, Myrddin told himself, but as he studied the plan and listened to the *Ord'pa*'s hypnotic bass, a small hope caught fire in his heart. He thought about the relative nature of triumph over an evil as great as *Barung*.

In truth, *Barung* was more creature than person. *Barung* created himself from his own evil intent, from the dark energy he drew from the very pit of the universe. It overwhelmed him, turned him into naught but a twisted, deformed channel, absorbing every negative thought in his purview, every wicked action. Violence, hate, cruelty— *Barung* became a living embodiment of all such bleakness. The Council had joined to bind him with their combined magiks.

With our different commands of the energies of the universe, Myrddin corrected himself automatically, as the *Ord'pa* would have if the wizard had spoken aloud. *Know and name the power you wield, lest your children forget it.*

Myrddin flexed his arms, wishing he could wield those powers to dispel the non-corporeal *Barung* himself.

But he knew he could not. The Kaeradi priest and the Ardani executioner were correct. Destroying the necromancer would release every drop of that formless blackness *Barung* had absorbed, and the wave of dark energy would sweep the universe of hope and joy, light and life.

Unless they could trick the beast into the void.

And the void wasn't created yet, nor the powers that might drive the beast to it without chance of escape.

Banishment was the only option.

But one day, Myrddin thought with increasing vengeance, *Barung will return.* He stared at the shimmering triangle as it turned from silver to gold in the waning daylight. The triangle with the dark center, even now flickering above and across the round table of Earth's tower on the Tor. *If the universe is willing, the Council will rise again then, stronger than ever.*

His mind turned to the writing of scrolls and books and sacred teachings, to the leaving of monuments in stone and iron and every conceivable medium — one hundred ways to pass the needed knowledge through the ages, in case something should happen to him.

It was later that same night, still at the round table in the round tower on the round hill, that he penned the one scroll that the old Kaeradi could have told him would indeed survive, worlds away from its writing.

When Barung returns,
Six shall lead him home,
Blended from the triangle,
Joined by the stone.

Let loose the gentle innocents,
For music soothes the shield.
Feed him on The People's blood,
And drive him to the field.

From the Sacred Scroll of Myrddin
Preserved by The People

Chapter One
Arda
Twenty-Second Century

Krysta Tul'Mar, Captain of the Home Guard of Arda, hovered above whitecaps on the Western Sea in her compact battle speeder. The little vessel's inertial seat held her snug and motionless despite occasional buffets from the air currents rising off the waves. Big sun and little sister, Arda's daystars, had barely crested in the crystalline sky of her home world, and her senses still tingled from performing the *Kon'pa*, the sacred dance to honor the stars, the sails, and *pa* — the silvery living essence that connected all things.

Because of a speeder crash during the Battle of Camford four stellar months ago, her own body bore a wealth of *pa*. It shimmered in her silver hair, which had once been obsidian like that of most Ardani citizens. It glistened white-gray in her eyes, which had also been as black as deep space.

Her *pa* mark, the universe's unique gift to those with Ardani blood, had been small and non-descript before the crash. Now glittering patterns traced her right cheek, trailed across her neck to cover her right breast, and tickled her nipple. From there, her mark plunged down her belly like an arrow sailing straight into her thick bush, turning it silver and giving the lips of her sex an almost continual humming charge. And it didn't stop there. Her left hip and leg sported *pa* as well, all the way to her toes.

Krysta frowned as she adjusted the speeder's flight path.

Elise Ashton Tul'Mar, Krysta's sister-by-marriage, said Krysta's mark looked like beautiful cherry blossoms. Elise's cousin Georgia, no doubt destined to be a sister-by-marriage soon, agreed. *Cherry.* An Earth word. Krysta liked the sound of it, but she wasn't sure her excess of *pa* was beautiful. Absently, she traced its path from her eye to her chest, nudging down the zipper of her black soft-hide jumpsuit to caress her constantly hard nipple. It was damned distracting, always being stimulated. Ki and Fari, her brothers, thought her torture would abate when she found her soul's mate and enjoyed a new depth of sexual bonding—but Krysta had her doubts.

Every priest and warrior on Arda was intimidated by her, especially now that her overdose of *pa* had left her so thoroughly marked. Ardani citizens thought her a Lorelei, one of the legendary supernatural guardians of the Tul'Mar clan, which didn't make her any more approachable in the eyes of potential suitors. Elise and Georgia also held that distinction and bore greater-than-usual *pa* marks, but they didn't mind. They had found their *shas,* their soul's mates in Ki and Fari—and besides, their marks didn't keep them in an endless state of arousal.

Krysta sighed and pinched her nipple harder. The flesh felt rough and hot in her fingers. She eyed the speeder's hard rubber hand control with something like guilty longing. The joystick was perfectly positioned in front of the inertial chair, and she could ride it if she needed relief. She had done so many times in the past stellar weeks.

"I wish I weren't alone," she murmured.

But more often than not, brief sessions of pleasure

with Georgia and invitations to Ki and Elise's marital bed aside, Krysta was just that — alone.

Truth be told, Arda's warriors had always been hesitant with her, even before she achieved Lorelei status. After all, she was a Tul'Mar, daughter of the clan who had ruled Arda for eight thousand years. Her brother Ki was Arda's Sailmaster, their leader, and her brother Fari was Sailkeeper, the bringer of laws and justice. Both were known for their fair-minded benevolence, but Arda's available men seemed intimidated by her royal brothers. Most of them treated her like an unattainable princess. She often initiated sexual contact, and her chosen conquest happily obliged — but in the morning, the warrior would head back to the barracks or his home without a backward glance. All she got from her adventures was a reputation as an insatiable and skilled lover and a few hours' respite from her loneliness. Lately, all she'd gotten was a few moments of relief from the continual stimulation of her enhanced *pa*-mark.

Akad, Arda's enigmatic high priest, kept her supplied with *firemylk*, the brewed elixir used to subdue Ardani males during mating fervor, if necessary. She used it sparingly, though. It had almost killed her brother Fari when he took too much trying to hold off his desires for Georgia.

"Damn Akad, too," Krysta fumed to herself, switching on the speeder's far-ranging sensors with her free hand. "His mind is in the stars."

The priest had always been a willing lover, and in fact one of the few who came close to satisfying Krysta — if any one man could. Lately, though, Akad seemed distracted. Krysta knew he had some attraction to Elise, Ki's half-blood *shanna* — but his odd attitude had to be more than that. Something was troubling the man, and Krysta had wondered about his burdens more than once in the past few stellar weeks.

On Arda, though, there was little time for worry. As Elise often said in her quaint Earth accent, *Arda's a paradise. Men and women equal, complete sexual freedom, no hunger, no poverty, almost no crime...*

"Almost no crime," Krysta muttered, turning loose her nipple and leaning forward as her sensors chirped.

The long-range probes fixed on what looked like a fleet of junk ships slowly entering planetary orbit. Her pulse picked up and her arousal faded to the back of her mind.

Whatever this caravan of space-gypsies intended, it likely wasn't friendly. All space-faring races knew it was tantamount to invasion to breach a planet's outer boundaries without hailing for permission to approach. These beggars weren't yet close enough for her to analyze life signals or make psi-contact, so she didn't know who she was dealing with.

She pushed a red lever to her right, sending a signal that ordered the Home Guard into the skies. In mere moments, five full wings of speeders would be on patrol, shielding Arda's strategic targets.

Krysta banked her own craft back toward Camford, the ancestral home of the Tul'Mars. The small walled city could withstand most attacks, with its strong weathered stone and psi-barriers, but Krysta didn't want to take chances. She was more cautious than her brothers.

Her heart pounded minute after minute, until she saw the greens, reds, yellows, and pinks of the blooms covering Camford's stately towers. Below her, the lush emerald grounds stretched in all directions, ending in the dense blue-green boughs of the nearby forest. Nothing looked amiss on the hunting grounds or the riding fields. Crops of yellowgrain and wheybrown swayed gently as she made a low pass, all the while keeping one eye on the blinking sensor panel.

The ship's hull and her silver tattoo vibrated, but she didn't startle. She knew without looking down that she was passing above one of Camford's Chimera herds. The beautiful beasts always caught her scent and sang to the speeder, creating a resonance in all nearby *pa*.

"Hello to you, too," she sang in a close approximation to their lyrical calls. Below the speeder, a purple Chimera stallion cantered along, moving his long neck and tossing its thick mane until his horn was covered. A yellow female stayed close to him, and behind them, thirty or more thundered along, coloring the ground orange and blue, white and green, pink and golden.

All was well on the ground, it seemed.

Smiling from the peaceful, loving energy of the Chimera, Krysta eased the speeder back toward Arda's expansive azure skies.

The intruders above had taken up a disorganized orbit, reminding her of a clumsy caravan of fergilla beasts on the move.

One by one, her officers checked in, reporting nothing out of the ordinary beyond their rude visitors.

Krysta wondered how concerned she should be. Very few hostiles, especially such a ragtag bunch, would challenge Arda's Royal Fleet. Unfortunately, the diplomatic mission to Bandu-Mother had delayed Ki and his battle frigates, and they were yet hours from planetside. Fari, still in the grip of mating fervor, was next to useless, but he and his officers could get to his first-attack ships quickly, if need be.

She tried hailing the intruders, but they didn't answer.

Starburst formation, she psi-instructed the Guard, and heard their affirmatives as they moved into defensive positions.

Krysta didn't fear attack. She had trained beside her brothers since childhood, learning the fine arts of planetary rule and defense from her parents until their death at the hands of rogue OrTan slavers. She had mastered flight and battle skills even as Ki took on the role of Sailmaster and Fari earned his Sailkeeper's rank.

The three siblings each had charge of different branches of Arda's storied Royal Fleet. Ki headed the impressive array of battle frigates known for lawkeeping in the galaxy and impeding the burgeoning trade of sex slaves. Fari directed the sleek first-assault vessels used to gather intelligence and defend Ki's personal safety. Krysta commanded the heavily armed speeders charged with defending Arda itself. She had always done her job with a fervor almost legendary. Still, in her hundred stellar years of life, she hadn't heard of a group of junk ships wandering into Ardani space before.

The sensor alarms sounded.

More ships drifted in, seemingly from null space.

"Are they cloaked?" Krysta's worry level tripled at the thought.

Full alert, she instructed.

We see them, came the almost universal response from her officers.

Without further hesitation, Krysta tried to reach Fari,

who was on Ammon Island, his private retreat. He didn't answer psi-summons or the hail to his speeder.

"*Knador!*" The curse left Krysta's lips even as she cut her ship sharply south and sped off toward the island.

She hadn't gone far when her sensors indicated incoming text from the cluster of vessels above Arda. She pushed the button to receive and read aloud, "*Tanna Kon'pa* for Ki Tul'Mar."

Her breath left in a rush. Half-relieved, half-annoyed, she conveyed the message to the rest of the Guard.

Stand down. Tanna Kon'pa — The People — *say they've come to talk to the Sailmaster.*

I do not trust those damnable Outlanders, shot back Kolot, her second in command. He clearly held no love for Arda's only rebel faction. Krysta couldn't blame him.

Most people felt uncomfortable with the reclusive group. They had no *pa*-marks, no psi-powers at all, and they stayed to themselves, the gods only knew where, poring over Arda's ancient history and practicing what they called the "old ways." Since before Krysta was born the Outlanders had been predicting the "end of time," which supposedly only they could prevent.

Worse than that, Darkyn Weil, their self-proclaimed chief, had a galaxy-wide foul reputation. Krysta had never seen the bastard, but she had long heard tales of his cruelty to women and his cold, abusive attitude toward The People. Why they tolerated such a barbarian as their leader, she had no idea.

Ki was surprisingly soft on the Outlanders, though. He insisted the *Tanna Kon'pa* had the same rights as all other citizens. Of course, Ki had been away and he didn't know the fools had been stealing Chimeras, burning down barns, blowing up ships under construction, and leaving doomsday messages marked by rare black falcon feathers. Fari was ready to kill them—and that was before they brought an invasion force—joke though it might be—into the outer rings of the Ardani atmosphere.

Superstitious thieves, one of her officers psi-grumbled.

Stand down, Krysta repeated in command tones. *I will handle this.*

She psi-generated a return message to the bizarre Outlander fleet and pressed send.

"Hold your positions. We did not send for you. Why have you come, and why in so many ships?"

A few stellar seconds ticked by. Krysta leaned forward to send her message again, but a sudden sharp pain in her head knocked her back into the inertial chair's waiting fur.

She grabbed her temples, hearing a brutal mind-noise, like an endless, stabbing whistle. Then came a cry, distant and feral, like that of a hunting bird. Her stomach turned over as a strange image seized her thoughts.

A triangle, glowing bright at three points, with an endless, soul-stealing darkness at the center...

A man. Not Fari or Ki. No. Larger and broader. Gods, is that even possible? And something on his shoulder, some sort of raptor, darker... Despite her agony, she made an effort not to broadcast her thoughts. This vision seemed...private, though she didn't know why.

The man had the bearing of a priest or a king, standing tall and still with what appeared to be a black falcon on his left shoulder. Something tugged at Krysta's mind, a bit of recognition trying to make its way to the surface, but she shoved back conscious thought, content to simply exist in the vision with the incredible man.

He was wearing clothes made of tanned animal skins instead of hammered fergilla hide. Unusual for an Ardani, but his build and his sable hair suggested he was indeed of Arda. White-blond streaks highlighted the field of silky black, giving him an alien, dangerous look. His flesh was almost as brown as the skins he wore — and the weapon at his side was most unusual, too. If she wasn't mistaken, he was carrying a double-bladed axe, forged of a strange amber gemstone.

Krysta's *pa*-mark crackled as she stared at his bulging muscles and the squared set of his strong jaw. His visible skin was covered by small scars, suggesting he had seen more battles than she had seen stellar years.

A warrior's warrior. Yes. A man intimidated by nothing. Absolutely nothing at all.

Her *pa*-tortured nipple tightened, followed quickly by her other nipple. The heat between her legs increased faster than she could stand, and the *pa* near her clit almost set her on fire.

"Stop!" she shouted, shaking her head. She was in a battle situation! What was wrong with her?

The vision of the man clung to her mind like a tenacious vine. She couldn't shake it loose. He lifted one powerful arm and placed his hand on his chest, then slowly lifted his eyes, seemingly to look straight into her brain.

By the gods! They're yellow. His eyes are yellow!

With that, Krysta tore her mind free of whatever had possessed her. Her lower lips and core throbbed, and her nipples were in complete agony. All along her flesh, her *pa* hummed and burned. She felt like she had when she'd first emerged from the shuttle crash that had marked her so.

Aching. Blazing.

Such exquisite pleasure, matched with pain almost beyond imagining. Before she could stop herself, she thought about the strange man again.

Orgasm seized her instantly, rocking her body and slamming her head against the inertial chair. Fighting for her sanity, she gripped the chair's arms and steadied herself, vaguely grateful that she had shielded her thoughts from her officers.

What in the name of sky and sea had *that* been? A fantasy about her dream man, a waking vision sexy enough to make her come? Her numbed mind realized it probably had something to do with flying so close to Ammon Island. Being in proximity to a sha and *shanna* in full mating fervor could do that, especially if one or the other was a generational blood relation. Fari and Georgia were no doubt making steamy love on the beach, sending out enough psi-energy to fell a herd of stampeding fergillas.

Fucking, Georgia called it. Krysta liked that word just as she liked *cherry*. She didn't, however, like *pussy*. Both Elise and Georgia called their sex a *pussy*, like they had a cat between their legs. She couldn't get used to that, except to use it to excite them.

Her sensor panel chirped. Krysta glanced down, momentarily unsure what had made such a noise.

A message had come in from the Outlanders in answer to her challenge. A quick look at the stellar clock told her that nearly three minutes had passed since she sent it.

Expecting information that would let her know which actions to take next, she opened the text.

"*Tanna Kon'pa* for Ki Tul'Mar," was all it said. The words seemed to leap at her like a slap, suggesting insolence for daring to ask for more information.

Krysta swore again. She didn't want to tell them Ki and the Fleet were away, though they might already know. Still cursing, she guided her speeder the rest of the way to Fari's island, opened the hatch, and vaulted out to go find the Sailkeeper.

Less than a half a stellar hour later, Krysta was back in the air and more than disgruntled. She was supposed to be taking Georgia back to Camford for safekeeping until they settled this Outlander mess, but the willful bitch had other ideas. Krysta had tried to take her by force and earned an aching jaw and crotch for her trouble.

In position, Fari informed her through a protected psi-link. He had made it aboard his first-assault ship, no doubt unaware of a certain stowaway. *And you?*

Landing the speeder. Krysta made an effort to shield her frustration as she steadied the craft for straight-line touchdown.

What is wrong? Fari asked immediately.

Krysta remained silent as her speeder kicked up dirt and grass on the edge of Camford Forest. As she felt the jolt of rudders meeting solid ground, she tried to select a response.

Fari pressed his thoughts toward hers. *Tell me, Sister! This is no time for games.*

Krysta sighed. *I – uh, when you sent Georgia to the landing pad to gather her belongings, she apparently did not do so. At least, she did not return to me.*

"After she knocked me down as if I were a first year trainer," she added to herself, seething.

For a moment, Fari didn't answer. When he did, his mental signature was terse and frightened. *She…did not leave the island with you?*

No.

Then Georgia is still on the island? Unprotected?

A wave of ill-feeling flowed across their psi-link as Krysta tried not to say what she knew. Sitting on the ground, engines now powered to neutral, the speeder felt too still and too quiet.

I do not think so, Brother, she allowed at last.

Then where is she?

Even as he broadcast the question, he realized the answer. Their link was abruptly severed, leaving Krysta's mind empty but for the distant murmurs of communication between her officers. Her shields were so firmly in place she could barely track their conversations, but a panel chirp or an urgent psi-shout would come through as clear as Chimera song. On her sensor screens, the salvaged Outlander ships reeled in and out of Arda's atmosphere like carrion birds, making slow, watchful circles.

Most clustered directly above where she had landed, over Camford. A few seemed to be patrolling over the ceremonial Tuscan Platform in the center of the forest. Another handful of ships lumbered back and forth in patterns that crisscrossed the sea.

"Makes no sense," Krysta said aloud and in her mind, on a focused psi-sending to her officers. "They are not in position to attack the planet's defenses."

They are not in position or shape for anything, except

tearing up some of Camford's grass, came Kolot's glib retort. *I read almost no firepower in those refits. A few torpedo cannons, a couple of wing turret lasers — what do they hope to accomplish?*

Before Krysta could respond, she felt the warm, powerful pull of her family reaching out to her. Raising her barriers once more and admitting only them, she felt joy from Fari and a deep excitement from Georgia. Elise was present in the link too, as was Ki, though her elder brother's psi-signature was faint due to his distance from Arda.

Hurry, Elise urged. *We don't have much time, and this could be the only time.*

Krysta understood immediately and felt Georgia's shock with a deep, sad sympathy.

Elise wanted the family bond, she wanted to share sex now, despite the odd circumstance, because she thought a battle was approaching. If she was right, anything might happen. The Tul'Mar clan might have no other chance to know the absolute joy of such a joining. Krysta's *pa*-mark flared at the thought, making her quim immediately wet.

"Glad I landed."

She stood and unzipped her jumpsuit, letting the soft-hide slide over her hips like a lover's touch. It pooled around her ankles as she sat down, enjoying the soft bristles of the chair's fur seat against her back and naked ass. The cabin's cool air made her nipples bead all the harder, and she wrapped one of her long legs around the ship's main hand control so she could mount it if she chose. The smooth rubber was cock-length, but not as thick as she'd prefer.

Gods, but her core was flooded.

Through the psi-link, she saw Elise pinch her own nipples and start stroking her clit. Krysta smiled. She had tasted Elise before, and enjoyed every second of her soft flesh and strong woman's musk. The same for Georgia, except the two of them had shared much deeper pleasures, many more times. If Krysta were turned fully to women, she would have picked Georgia as her long-term lover…though Elise would have been a close second. Such was the essence of an Ardani same-generation bond. It was natural to feel attraction to and enjoy the soul's mates of siblings, and sometimes even the soul's mates of cousins.

Each family handled the bonds a little differently, but ultimately they formed a circle of pleasure, protecting and supporting each other, pleasuring each other, caring for each other so that no one ever went wanting for attention, comfort, or love. How many relatives and soul's mates comprised the circle—again, different for different families. Krysta had always figured on a circle of six, and now, there were five. The force of the energy coursing through the link told her she was probably right. A sixth, her sha, wherever he was, would close the circle.

If she ever found him.

Flushing from head to toe with building desire, Krysta ran her long fingers into the heat of the *pa* between her legs, and with her other hand, she pulled the hand control forward and positioned it against her core. All she would have to do was lean forward to take the length inside her quim.

Ki's pleasure joined with hers, and Fari's, and then Georgia's ecstatic energy entered the mix. Krysta felt her sister-to-be's unbridled pleasure as Fari teased her nipples and prepared to enter her. Krysta filtered out her brothers' carnal sensations, instead allowing their happiness, satisfaction, and pleasure to fill her spirit. In return, she freed her own emotions, contributing to their enjoyment.

Yessss... Elise's moans pushed Krysta's tension to the next level. Krysta could see her sister-by-marriage lying in her big bed, stroking her clit fast and hard. Krysta rubbed her own clit until she couldn't ignore the ache in her quim a second longer. Groaning, she rolled herself forward, planting the hand control deep, deep into her throbbing channel.

Shivers coursed up and down her back, and her *pa* burned like slowly streaming oil, over her nipple, down her belly, all along the lips of her slit. She closed her eyes and let herself moan, concentrating on the sensation — and trying hard not to think of her earlier vision above Ammon Island. Her dream man. The force of that orgasm.

What would it be like when she found her own sha, her own soul's mate, and closed the circle of the Tul'Mar family? The pleasure would have no bounds, then. They would soar together, all of them, to heights they couldn't begin to imagine.

Fuck me, Georgia pleaded across the link. Krysta imagined herself saying the same thing to her fantasy man. *I need you inside me.*

Krysta shook from a small orgasm, feeling Elise come at the same time. The sexual energy felt like an all-encompassing sea as Georgia nearly screamed from need.

Release, Krysta sent to her. *Ah, gods. We will wait for you.* Yes. She bit her lip, holding herself back, helping Elise hold herself back, too.

Georgia did scream then, and swore, and threatened Fari. Krysta felt the swell of Elise's warm laughter.

More swearing and threatening from Georgia. More aching need. More pulsing arousal. Krysta's *pa*-coated nipple burned as she twisted it, wishing for her dream man's teeth and tongue to bring her some relief. She raised herself up and down on the hand control, wishing it were a cock, or even one of Arda's expanding toys. To be fully filled, so completely dominated and taken as Georgia was about to be…

Krysta couldn't help another small orgasm, and she took Elise with her. The raw pleasure her brothers felt with their mates suffused Krysta with more and more joy. Georgia's thoughts bordered on madness, and then Fari's.

Oh God! Elise shouted as Fari at last drove himself deep into Georgia's quim.

Yes. Please, fuck me like that! Georgia's psi-signature went ragged. Krysta had a sense of motion and knew Fari's ship had started flying slowly toward Camford. Cunning bastard. He would take her to safety while she was distracted!

It was all Krysta could do not to spill the secret. She kept her eyes clamped tight and rode the hand control, bucking and moaning as Georgia and Elise burned and groaned right along with her. The hand control actually rattled, she worked it so hard.

The pounding clank echoed through the speeder's small cabin as the rhythm of Georgia's psi-gasps caught them all in its swell. Krysta moved up and back, up and back. Her toes curled against the speeder's burnished floor. She fell forward, hands on her instrument panel, and her nipples brushed its cold surface.

Georgia's orgasm was building—and oh gods, Elise. Elise!

Elise came with a rocking, all-encompassing cry, pulling Ki to the summit with her. The force of their explosion made Krysta's quim contract, and as Georgia's powerful orgasm blew through the psi-link, Krysta joined her with deep, wracking screams of her own.

When her body stopped shuddering, Krysta lifted her head, keeping the hand-control in her core. Tears formed in her eyes and slid down her sweat-coated cheeks, hissing as they struck and crossed her *pa*-mark. Now was when she felt that empty loneliness most acutely, as her brothers and their soul's mates gradually dropped out of link with her, when she had nothing but a makeshift toy in her quim instead of a real, warm cock. No arms cradled her in the afterglow. No deep voice whispered love in her ear.

These were the things Krysta wanted most—after a round of wild, hard sex. In that raw unguarded moment, as she leaned back and let the control slide free, she admitted what she wanted most: that warrior's warrior she had dreamed of in that beyond-sizzling fantasy. A man powerful enough to master her, yet respect her. She wanted to feel his strength, his domination. She wanted to be taken to places she hadn't dared to go with her casual lovers.

"When is it my turn?" she whispered, wiping a tear as she reached down to gather her clothes.

And then, almost instantly, the battle was on.

Krysta barely had time to free herself from the hand-control and lift off, much less zip up her jumpsuit.

Almost two stellar hours later, after an unexpected pounding and a brilliantly-executed pincer maneuver, the Guard and Fari's *Lorelei* had the Outlanders on the run. Ki and the Royal Fleet were almost in orbit, and Krysta set her speeder down hard and fast on the edge of the forest surrounding Camford.

She had to get to the castle, because during the battle, she and Fari had thought they heard Georgia give a call of mental distress. All Krysta could think about now was getting to her new sisters.

They had to be safe. They just had to be.

She shut down the speeder's engines. Before the companel lights changed to indicate full energy discharge, she whirled about and hurried to the hatch. Three quick punches of the safety code, and the hatch opened wide — to bring her face to face with two warriors of almost unreal proportion blocking her path out of the portal.

They stepped through fast, forcing her back into the ship. One of them actually had to keep his chin on his chest to fit. The other's head touched the speeder's ceiling. Both had dark hair, shoulder-length, like Ardani fighters. They wore only breeches made of tanned animal skin — and they had no *pa* marks. Krysta made out dull black ovals centered in their chests, and realized they were stones.

Tanna Kon'pa — The People — and these two looked oddly familiar. The one on the left had a bandaged sword hand and healing scratches all across his chest. The one on the right looked like he had been trampled by an angry fergilla — all fading bruises and barely-knit cuts.

These two had tangled with something recently.

Krysta slowly realized where she had seen them. In Georgia's mind, and in Fari's. These two bastards had attacked Georgia only days ago and tried to kidnap her. She had given them a proper fight, and then they had met an angry fergilla — her brother, in full rage, protecting his *shanna.*

"Darkyn Weil's personal guard," Krysta said, shocked at how thin and small her voice sounded.

Both men nodded.

"We do not wish to harm you," said the Outlander with the wounded hand. His speech sounded stilted, and Krysta knew he was trying hard to speak in the modern tongue instead of the old high speech.

"To the deepest pit with you," she answered in flawless ancient Ardani, and felt some small triumph when both intruders looked surprised. Akad had taught her. The priest had insisted at least one of the Tul'Mars be able to speak Arda's first language without difficulty.

Fortunate, perhaps, that she chose to learn it. Ki and Fari knew a passing amount, but they had been lazy in their lessons.

Krysta's fingers itched to wrap around her blasters, which were stowed beneath the chair she had just left in her frenzy to get to Camford.

Knador!

"Why have you come?" she asked, again in the high speech, stalling as she tried to broadcast her distress.

Kolot's mental signature lit up in her mind just as something like a dark, wet curtain settled over her brain. Krysta shook her head, shocked, but the curtain didn't move. Her psi-signal was being blocked! But how was that possible? And how was it possible that the two warriors had penetrated the protective *pa*-coating on her speeder?

"No," said the monster on the right, tapping the side of his head. "Come with us peacefully. Please."

Both smiled, but their eyes were nothing but flat black

ice.

"May your joys have been many, so you miss them in the afterlife." Krysta returned their hollow politeness with an archaic curse she knew they would understand.

They started forward.

She whirled, dove for the inertial chair, thrust her hands beneath it, and pulled out her blasters.

At that moment, Kolot exploded through her speeder's half-open hatch, weapons holstered, arms outstretched in a no-combat gesture.

Krysta jumped to her feet while her attackers were distracted, raised her weapons, and thumbed the primer, ready to fire if needed.

Nothing happened.

The blasters were as dead as her psi-sendings.

Everything happened so fast Krysta's mind could barely comprehend it. Monster the Bruised grabbed her and wrapped an arm around her neck. Then, horribly, oh so horribly, Monster the Bandaged drew a dagger from his belt and felled Kolot before he could even ready for attack.

No! He had his hands raised!

Krysta let out a cry like the black falcon from her visions as her second in command dropped to the speeder's floor. She could tell by the way he landed that his wound was mortal.

"Fergilla!" she shrieked at the bandaged Outlander. "He had his hands raised! He hadn't even drawn his weapons!"

The one holding her tightened his grip and cut off her air.

Black spots danced in front of her eyes as she

screamed in her mind, punching against the blanket over her thoughts. She elbowed her attacker and kicked out at the second one, the murderer, as he grabbed her legs.

"Do not kill her," the murderer cautioned his companion—but Krysta barely heard the bastard's words. A roar started in one ear and spread to the other. She clawed against the arm pinning her throat, heard swearing as she tore into flesh—and then her consciousness switched off like a smashed sensor panel.

Chapter Two

Darkyn Weil clenched his teeth as he positioned his refitted cargo ship in orbit around Arda's most distant moon. Behind him, on her carved wooden perch, his black falcon shifted restlessly. He didn't have Guardian jessed or hooded, relying on her training and loyalty to keep her in place. He wouldn't insult so fine and sharp-eyed a lady by binding her, even with the velvety fabrics and leathers of his homeland.

Modern Ardani citizens called the moon in his viewscreen Arda-yi, but to *Tanna Kon'pa*, The People, it was Uhr, a sensor-shielded and hallowed place of safety, worship, and the work of thousands of busy hands. It was also a place of watching and waiting, and a place where doom hung like a smothering cloud over otherwise unimaginable beauty.

Darkyn's broad orbit brought his ship momentarily closer to Arda's twin suns, one hot and yellow, the other smaller and white. Guardian ruffled her feathers in the sudden flash of light, then settled as they once more wheeled toward home.

Uhr was the stuff of dreams and romantic ballads. From the unforgiving and parched eastern drylands to the jungles of the west, the little moon had so much to offer. Too bad it would be the first to go when the *Barung* reached them.

Whatever, in truth, the *Barung* was. The People had only the sacred scroll to help them interpret as best they could. Darkyn could already see the thing, but it seemed to be made of light or energy. How it could threaten them so totally, he didn't know—but it did. He felt that truth in each muscle and sinew.

Darkyn clenched his teeth again, the pain in his jaws slim comfort as he stopped the ship's forward progress and lowered it toward the ground, rocking it back and forth as swirls of shining indigo dust covered his touch-down on Uhr's main landing strip. Guardian made a popping noise deep in her feathered throat, expressing relief at being under the power of only her own wings once more. She flapped twice, taking herself from her perch to Darkyn's left shoulder, settling with a firm squeeze of talons.

No servants or sycophants ran to meet Darkyn and Guardian as they climbed out of the ship. Such was not the way of The People. Each man, each woman, and every child approaching the age of reason was completely self-sufficient. Uhr itself was also self-sufficient. They traded with no one and asked nothing of any world—except Arda, and what they wanted from Arda had nothing to do with material goods.

The People had settled everywhere on Uhr but the drylands, some living in the western jungles in small primitive groups while many warriors, guild workers, and clans chose to stay in Gese, the Blessed City.

Uhr's only organized village, Gese covered fully half of the moon's surface, extending between the desert and tropical regions. It had been constructed thousands of years ago, after the Great Migration—an event lost to Ardani historians but well-recorded and remembered by The People. The village was arranged in the old way, with a community building large enough to accommodate the moon's population in the center. In concentric outward circles came huts and cabins of craftspeople, healers, and priests, followed by the joined homes of clans. Some joined homes had many wings while others had only a few. To each their own.

On the fringes of Gese lived the sand-scratchers on the east, tenders of orchards in the center, and to the west, the vinemasters—those hearty souls who dared to tame jungles and bring forth such food-plants as the greenwild would yield. These farmers supplied Uhr with nourishment almost as precious as the frothing blue waters of the Steaming River.

As was custom, Darkyn lived among his people and worked side by side with farmers in the sandfields, orchards, and greenwild to feed his people and the sacred Chimera—when his time wasn't claimed by settling conflicts or preparing for the *Barung*.

He and Guardian headed down the night-quiet dirt path leading from the landing strip to the orchards, and Darkyn rubbed a palm across the stock of the two-bladed axe at his waist. Almost unwilling, he glanced at the sky. Far off on the horizon, by the outer stars, his enhanced vision showed him what Arda and most of the universe did not want to see.

A great black space, slowly swallowing stars, slowly moving toward them, emanating the darkest aura Darkyn had ever seen.

It was more than blackness.

More than nothingness and empty space.

Somehow, it was evil. Evil in its simplest, most elemental form.

The past was returning to claim them all, and time

was running out. At any stellar minute, on any stellar day, the blackness would cross the corona and slide into the edge of the known universes like a cancerous rot. Darkyn figured it would enter at the edge of the Ardani system, as it seemed on a direct course for them. On a direct course for Uhr and Arda itself.

And so he had to do what none of his ancestors had succeeded in doing: convince the Tul'Mar clan that The People were right, that time could and would end if they didn't join with him to defeat the steadily approaching *Barung*.

Somehow.

Because the evil was almost upon them. The stress had been eating at him, eroding his typical reserve and single-minded confidence. His hair had even started to streak white-blond, like an older man. The *Barung* was consuming him.

Like his forefathers back through time, Darkyn had studied the ancient scroll to guide him in the upcoming battle with something he didn't understand.

> *When Barung returns,*
> *Six shall lead him home,*
> *Blended from the triangle,*
> *Joined by the stone.*

> *Let loose the gentle innocents,*
> *For music soothes the shield,*
> *Feed him on The People's blood,*
> *And drive him to the field.*

With the wisdom of those who had gone before, he thought The People had worked out some key pieces of the rhyme—the innocents, the music, even the field, if their calculations about space and energy were correct.

Feeding the *Barung* on The People's blood was all too clear, terribly clear. That much, at least, Darkyn didn't have to guess about or calculate.

"The six, though," he said aloud. "'Blended from the triangle, joined by the stone.'"

He touched the smooth black stone in his chest.

Legend had it that in the old days, The People had stones of many different colors. Now, though, they were all black—including his, even though he was *Ta*. The only way it would transform, take on the golden hue of the leaders of old, was if he found his soul's mate. Met her face to face and claimed her. This, of course, could never happen.

Darkyn knew his had to be the stone that would join the six. He knew that at some deeper, more primal level than he knew most things. And yet, who were the other five?

His brother, his two annoying cousins—that would make four of the purest Ardani stock, which his forefathers held to be of utmost importance in this conflict.

But the fifth? The sixth?

It had to be the Tul'Mar brothers, didn't it? On all of Arda, they likely had the strongest blood, the most powerful connection to *pa*.

But to convince the stubborn Ki or the impossible Fari—men he had seen and known only from a distance—of this reality, that would be near impossible. If he showed them the scroll, gave them what he could of the ancient wisdom, used his strength of psi to help them "see" the *Barung*, surely that would make a difference? And so he had taken his forces to Arda in an attempt to bring Fari or Ki back to Uhr.

Instead he found both men missing from their stronghold at Camford, ended up delivering the Tul'Mar heir, saved the life of the Sailmaster's woman, nearly took a sword in the gut from the Sailkeeper's bride-to-be, and fought his own men to leave the two women and the babe in peace.

Darkyn snorted.

At least he had freed a few more Chimera, and given them safe passage to Uhr on the early-leaving cargo ships. They could live out their last days in freedom, and maybe, just maybe, their songs would be of benefit.

Guardian shifted, restless from his frustration. With a short, sharp whistle, he encouraged her to take flight and feed herself, and she obliged him by pushing off his shoulder and sailing into the moody sky of Uhr.

Darkyn watched her go, feeling a true sense of connection and the briefest of fears as he always did—that she would meet with harm, that she wouldn't return. Perhaps it was this connection with Guardian that made him unwilling to take the Tul'Mar women or the newborn child. He felt loathe to leave any man with the gut-tearing reality of finding his nest decimated.

Whatever the reason, Darkyn knew he wouldn't use helpless bait to lure the Tul'Mars to Uhr without their armies, ready to listen. No matter his legendary sharp tongue and sharper justice, he couldn't bring himself to do something so dishonorable. Though both women were surely fighters, they were not warriors. Only warriors would be brought to this battle, unless or until he had no other choice.

Keeping his eyes on the heavily laden fruit trees in front of him, Darkyn stalked forward and refused to look back to search for Guardian, or to gaze at the giant glowing orb that was Arda. The planet bathed Uhr in almost constant reflective light from big sun and little sister, so that it never became truly dark on the moon. Deep gray, yes, but except in the caves of the greenwild, never fully dark.

Sometimes, Darkyn wanted the dark. Sometimes he wanted to shed the responsibility he had shouldered almost since birth—but he had no time and no room for weak will or wavering intentions. Because of the *Barung*, he could not take a wife or have children. He could form no ties past those he had as *Ta'Tanna Kon'pa*, leader of The People. Not that he had any desire to do so. Most intimate contact left him dry or feeling faintly ill. Sometimes, he even felt repulsed or violently sick from the simplest of touches.

The strength of his unusual psi gifts was the culprit, according to his brother. Darkyn wasn't certain. He thought it more likely that he knew his own future, and thus could not bear to involve anyone in his limited destiny. When the time came, if his calculations proved sound, he had to be free to go. To sacrifice himself to save his beloved kin and even the dung-cursed Tul'Mars and all of Arda, and probably the galaxy as he knew it.

For now, though, he had failed his mission so completely he wanted to tear off the first fifty heads he encountered. Unfortunately for him, for The People, for Arda, and for the universe, that would accomplish nothing. He just needed to get to the private rooms in his cabin, sleep, restore himself, and wake on the morn with fresh purpose.

In the distance, a few Chimera hummed in the night. Probably the newcomers, seeking relations and friends long unseen. That sound comforted him. The sight of his personal guard lurking at the mouth of the main orchard — between him and his waiting bed — did not.

Brand, the smaller of the two guards, tugged at the bandage on his hand, still nursing the wound he received when the Sailkeeper's lover had bitten him. Served the bastard right, trying to kidnap the woman against his orders.

Only the men, Darkyn had instructed. *Leave the families alone.*

But Brand was of one thought only: bring back a Tul'Mar at all cost. He was impulsive to boot. Kadmyr, Brand's older brother, wasn't much better, though at least he had an even temperament.

As Darkyn approached them with increasingly long and impatient strides, both men dipped their heads in deference.

"*Ta,*" Kadmyr offered, and Darkyn could see in his eyes that the guard bore news he didn't care to hear.

"What?" he growled, tempted to knock them both aside and keep walking.

"We know you did not find what you sought at Camford, *Ta.*" Brand's voice was rich with emotion. Excitement? Fear? Darkyn couldn't tell. His head began to ache from his sternly clamped jaws.

"But we met with more success," Kadmyr finished, then quickly averted his eyes.

Darkyn felt a sinking in his gut. Anger competed with dread, and he realized he had drawn his eyes so close to shut that he was viewing the world through naught but slits of vision.

"What do you mean?" he asked through his teeth, clenching his fists.

"We could not get a Tul'Mar," Brand admitted, "but we did capture a warrior of high rank."

Before Darkyn could draw his two-headed axe and kill them both, Kadmyr added, "Like us, Arda values each life, each citizen. Perhaps they will bargain for this one, given that high-placed warriors are hard to replace. And because of certain other factors."

Darkyn stood in the partial light of Uhr's night, beneath the heavy branches of a sweetapple tree, and decided not to kill either man. He never killed if he could help it, no matter his thousand thoughts to the contrary. These two tempted him often, however. They were his kin, his cousins, and his banes. They wanted only to help him, to help The People, but he had trouble convincing Brand and Kadmyr that peace, persuasion, and even forceful manipulation brought better and faster results than outright war.

Mother, he thought, fully shutting his eyes then opening them again. *Walk calmly in the afterlife, and feel the sand beneath your feet. Your sister's sons are safe with me. Though if Father yet breathed, I doubt he would spare them.*

"Where did you put this captive?" he asked, at last managing to unlock his jaws. The situation wasn't optimal, but perhaps the wisdom of others, even these others, outmatched the will of the *Ta.* He had been taught all his life to respect and honor this possibility.

"In your cabin." Brand beckoned him to follow and set off through the main orchard.

Kadmyr and Darkyn followed, walking side by side.

Darkyn could tell by the way Kadmyr stared at his brother that some pieces of this tale were yet missing. What those pieces might be—

No. I don't want to know yet, because I can't kill them.

Endless minutes later, they left the orchard and walked down a long row of farmer's cabins. Darkyn's home lay at the very end of the rough-packed road, off to itself beside a pond, in a small field of delicate yellow bayflowers. He had a receiving yard outside his front door, with shade trees and benches in a circle, as would any *Ta*. Other than that, he had the pond and a modest sparring field for exercise and battle training. His cabin had eight rooms, with the front four for the sick or displaced, the grieving or the troubled. The back four rooms were his bedroom, his bath, a small kitchen, and the thinking space used by the village *Ta* across the centuries. This room was kept empty but for a small altar, a meditation post, a single chair with a writing table, a blank scroll, a quill, and an inkwell.

The idea was for the *Ta* to have one place completely uncluttered by the energy of others or the pressures of leading The People. The thinking space was to be used for relaxation, creativity, and quiet conversations with elders gone before.

It was there that Darkyn relaxed.

It was there that he spent endless hours pondering the nature of the *Barung*.

It was there that he found his greatest distress, his greatest peace, and his most private centering.

And it was, of course, to this room that Brand and Kadmyr took Darkyn, even though they well knew its purpose.

Darkyn was about to chastise them when Brand opened the door to reveal a blindfolded woman tied to his meditation post. Her head lolled on her chest, and her hands were secured behind her back, bound by yellow energy bonds. Her legs had been spread to either side of the post, probably to keep her from kicking her captors to death, and they were likewise secured to the post by energy bonds.

Speechless, Darkyn took in what stood before him, even as Guardian fluttered through the open door and took up her perch in the main room.

At least, his stunned brain informed him, *she's a warrior.*

He hadn't called on any psi-abilities to determine that. Using the powerful psi of The People—especially his—on those not initiated was unconscionable and likely to kill. Still, he knew she was a warrior. She looked achingly familiar, though he was certain he had never seen her before. He had never seen anything like this woman in his two hundred years on Uhr.

"A female?" he managed to growl, to which Brand nodded.

In the main room, Guardian tore into whatever small beast she had claimed as her dinner. Darkyn didn't look, but he heard her message and took note. *Females can be fierce, too.*

"The other factors I mentioned," Kadmyr added. "Like us, our Ardani cousins may feel more obligated to retrieve a woman, warrior or no. This one seems to have more *pa* than most. She is likely a weapon in and of herself, with her heightened perceptions."

Indeed.

Darkyn thought of Guardian's keen instincts and cold killing skills, and kept staring.

The woman wore naught but a black jumpsuit, zipper open to the waist, revealing the curve of her ample breasts. Her hair fairly shimmered with *pa*, almost hurting his exquisitely sensitive eyes. And her mark—by the ancients! It seemed to wend from her cheek, down her neck—across her entire body.

No Ardani had *pa* like that!

Except for the mates of the Tul'Mar brothers he had seen on his recent Camford incursion—but he had known them for mixed-bloods. An odd mix, yes. Older Ardani, some type of odd Earther, and something like the main-planet strain of Arda. Darkyn had figured their unusual composition had somehow protected them from whatever accident resulted in such a massive *pa* infusion.

This woman was a mixture as well, but no mixture Darkyn could easily decipher. She also seemed to have an atypical Earther strain within her veins, stronger than he had ever known. Newer Arda, too—and yet, yes, older Arda as well, and powerful, blended seamlessly. It surprised him that she had no stone in her chest.

She was built like The People, much more so than most Ardani females. Beneath the flicker of *pa*, his special vision detected the true color of her hair—black pearl, a shade found almost exclusively on Arda.

To Darkyn, colors were like the print of a finger or the mark of a tooth—no two exactly alike. He often could identify a person's galactic lineage simply by the shade of their flesh, eyes, or hair. He could see so much more, if he kept looking. The shifting air around her contained the rainbow of her energy. Colors of fear, fatigue, defeat…and courage, and anger...and longing and loneliness so deep he could feel them in the pit of his own soul...

Darkyn startled as the stone in the center of his chest hummed against his skin, and something even more unusual happened. His cock swelled and pressed hard against the tanned hide of his breeches. The room went oddly quiet, and a wave of nausea nearly knocked him to the floor. Before he could fully regain himself, a new flood of sensation gripped him, this one hot and maddening and near to setting his brain afire. He literally staggered from the sudden drunken sensation.

Guardian let out a hunting cry from behind him, taking to wing inside the cabin rooms—something the bird had never done before.

"*Ta*?" came Brand's tentative inquiry.

"I'm fine," Darkyn said gruffly, knowing his lie echoed in his tone. He would not—could not—show his unexpected and unfathomable interest in the captive.

Brand nodded.

Darkyn managed a half-smile, then gripped his guards by their shoulders, using them for support under the guise of steering them from the room. "Come, let us leave her to her dreams and discuss arrangements for the soon-coming *pao*. Our guests will no doubt be punctual."

"Or early," Kadmyr agreed as they lurched from the room like a three-headed drylands dragyn. The warrior launched into a briefing on the *pao*, the "big talk," with representatives of planets who sensed and felt concerned about the *Barung*.

Guardian landed with another disgruntled cry, her hard, bright eyes tracking the trio so closely that Darkyn felt the discomfort of her stare.

Be at ease, he urged the bird through the primitive psi-link humans could share with animals close to the heart. *One of us gone mad is plenty.*

They reached the outer room at the moment Darkyn's legs could no longer support him. He let go his guards and dropped heavily to his knees. The butt of his axe handle smacked loudly as it struck the floor, but his sheath didn't give. Nearly helpless, he closed his eyes. Spots, circles, patterns—and the great black nothingness of the ever-approaching *Barung.*

"Get the priest," he told Kadmyr and Brand in a voice so thick and distant he barely recognized it as his own. "Hurry."

As he watched through distorted colors and shapes, Kadmyr and Brand nodded and hurried out of the cabin, leaving the front door wide ajar. Guardian flapped after them, clearly not trusting them to seek aid for her master on their own. And her master knew, even before the falcon left, that he needed aid. He needed more than aid.

Left alone for only a moment, all he wanted to do was gain his feet, stagger back to his thinking space, and ravage the woman tied to his meditation pole.

But that would be madness.

What if she were one of those who made him ill? He couldn't afford being sick now, with the *pao* so close at hand. Still, his cock was a length of molten iron, throbbing miserably. His stone burned as hot as his blood. It took all of his formidable will to stay in his main room, on his knees, refusing the desires raging through every inch and corner of his being.

Darkyn was no virgin. He had known his share of females, warrior and clan alike—but always by plan, with care to check compatibility of touch, and with the express purpose of relieving his physical needs. He couldn't allow entanglements or obligations, and he had rarely felt spontaneous attraction. In fact, he could say with certainty that he hadn't felt such a strong pull toward a female before.

Images of taking the woman fast and rough and hard, taking her where she stood, bound against that pole, shook his mind. He imagined tightening her bonds, leaving her completely at his mercy but gaining her trust, convincing her he could fill the gaping emptiness in her heart. She would tremble as he slowly lowered that zipper, pushed aside the black jumpsuit to free her breasts, and bent to suck her sweet nipples.

What color were they? Pale pink or red like sweetapple wine? Some shade in between? Some shade completely other?

Against his judgment and better sense, he rose slowly and turned back toward the thinking space.

She is in there, growled some ancient part of his mind. *Your woman.*

"She is in there," he repeated aloud in almost the same stiff growl. His eyes flew open of their own accord, and he squinted against the light of Uhr's night. "My woman. *My* woman."

A step, then two, then three—he wasn't falling or crawling. In fact, he felt stronger. In seconds, he stood before her again, teeth clamped, fists clenched, cock straining at his breeches. The *pa* surrounding his stone felt like blue flames as he extended his hand and held it close to the intricate *pa* on the woman's exposed belly.

Not touching, but almost.

And no sign of the telltale sickness or revulsion.

Compatible. Gods, she had to be, or he would die where he stood.

The woman stirred, moaning from the almost-contact.

Words of claiming, as old as time and just as irretrievable, rose to Darkyn's lips. In his wits-drunken state, he almost spoke them, then jerked his hand away as if he'd been scalded. She wasn't of the tribal groups he was allowed to join with, if indeed he ever joined. She wasn't even of The People!

His senses spread out, not just his heightened vision, taking in the scent of her soft-hide jumpsuit, the hot musk of her quim, and something else—light and spicy like the bayflowers in his field. He heard the even rise and fall of her breath, could almost taste the salt of her skin and the fire of her *pa* on his tongue.

She would be infinitely soft if he touched her.

Just the sight of her many hues and colors threatened to blind him.

From somewhere that seemed a million galaxies away, Guardian let out a spine-freezing shriek. Someone stepped into the doorway of the room, casting a shadow across Darkyn's sensitive visual field, and he couldn't hold back a feral snarl.

He whirled, hand on the hilt of his axe, and faced the intruder.

"Get out," he growled. "She's mine!"

The figure in the door, falcon on his right shoulder, didn't move.

This fact and this fact alone penetrated the red-black and wild haze gripping Darkyn Weil.

Not one of The People would dare to stand against him in such a temper.

Not one, except for his brother, the priest.

Darkyn swayed on his feet, fighting his urge to fall on the woman and rut until they both lay filled and sated in the bright, bright dawn of Uhr.

"Akad," he said, his voice like the scrape of sand on rock. "Help me!"

Chapter Three

Krysta drifted, suspended between past and present, real and unreal. For a time she was young and running carefree through the lush fields around Camford. The air smelled unusually fresh, dry enough to sting her nose and make her eyes water. Her parents, always loving and supportive, stroked her shoulder before playing games of hiding and chase amongst the freely grazing Chimera. How the sweet, sweet songs of the beasts filled the air, rippling over her skin and pulling her heart into the melody.

Then she was sailing her speeder low and fast, skimming Arda's fields and coasts, her stomach dipping with each near-miss. A great black nothingness pursued her, but she managed to stay just ahead of it. The Chimera song was gone. All she could hear was a relentless heartbeat. All she could smell was rot, and death, and decay.

Up and down, left and right—if only it would stop gaining on her! The noise it made threatened to crush her ears, even as it crushed all the light and air and earth in its path. Someone was shouting inside the abyss, above the awful blood-thrumming, and the voice was made of rage...

Heart hammering, Krysta woke and opened her eyes to absolute darkness. For a moment, the black void held sway over her, filled with indescribable hunger, a vengeance so wicked and dark it threatened to suck the life straight out of her.

She fought her thoughts into some semblance of order, rejecting the empty, hollow fury she felt all around.

Somewhere off in the distance, a few Chimera joined in song.

Chimera.

Am I still at home, on Arda?

The phantasm of her dream vanished, just like that, dispelled by the sweet notes of the creatures she had loved since birth. Relaxing despite her circumstance, Krysta realized she was sagging back against a pole. Something was covering her eyes—and somebody had tied a gag around her mouth! She started to reach for the pieces of cloth, to pull them off, but her wrists remained locked in place behind her. The smooth, worn wood of the pole pressed into the backs of her wrists. Warm, humming sensations coursed over her fingers and hands—energy bonds?

OrTan technology? Knador!

She started to kick, but her ankles were bound, too.

Kolot…the two big Outlanders…Kolot is dead, and I am, I am…

Anger suffused with dread fueled Krysta's struggle against her tethers. She was prisoner to a group of Outlander miscreants she had badly underestimated. They had attacked with some purpose as yet unknown and slain her second-in-command when he tried to save her.

Worse than that, The People clearly had trade with OrTa. Perhaps they were in league with Lord Gith and his lizard slavers—the same slavers Ki had to battle for Elise when he first claimed her. It was during a second battle with the reptile bastard that Krysta received her overdose of *pa*, which even now tortured her nipple and the lips of her quim with tongue-like flicks of fire and heightened sensation.

"Let me go," she tried to say around her gag, to little gain. "Where am I?"

Her *pa*-mark sizzled with the force of her frustration, nearly igniting her breast and making her juices flow. She took a deep breath, coughed in the dry air, and gave a cloth-blocked scream of rage. Each time she twisted, her unzipped jumpsuit rubbed harder against her nipples. In seconds, both breasts were exposed to the warm, dry air, and her zipper, worked down by her thrashing, snagged painfully in her lower curls.

"*Knador.*"

Her psi-abilities were of no use to her. Her brain felt locked within her skull, like the invisible evil of her dream had severed her connection with the universe. As Krysta fought against the pole, sweating and panting, she tried to use her soldier's instincts.

The wood she could feel had been rubbed smooth, but not by tool or rough-paper. It had a silken, oily feel, and seemingly an energy of its own.

A thousand touches. A hundred thousand, or more. Mayhap as many hands. How old is this pole?

A primitive keepsake, either by design or necessity. She focused on her *pa*, letting it tell her what it could about the room's dimensions with the minimal information it carried about space, light, and motion.

Her accommodations were small and dark, judging by the gray of the light filtering through her makeshift blindfold. It was nighttime, but...oddly bright. The rhythm of movement was almost imperceptible, steady and slow, definitely not a spaceship. Moreover, there was no rotation at all, no deep vibration from an axis.

Tidal lock. So, I am on a planet's satellite, and it must be small in comparison to its world. There are Chimera here, too. The state of her body, still clothed and unsoiled, suggested she hadn't been captive long, less than a day, maybe only a few hours.

Barring use of illegal transport technology or other factors, she was likely still in the Ardani system, or close. Close enough to support Chimera life, and Chimera only survived in and around Arda.

But where, exactly?

Ki and the fleet had searched endlessly for the Outlander base; however, The People only made themselves known when they chose to do so. Fari had deduced that the rebels must live primitively, perhaps in caves thick enough or of proper composition to avoid both mechanical and psi searches.

Krysta shifted against the pole, scrubbed her feet against the ground, and listened to the sounds.

If she was in a cave, it had a packed dirt floor, not rock. With a throw-rug, no less. The general shape of the room as conveyed by her *pa* was square, not rounded. The clincher, though, was the air—arid and warm, with no hint of mold or moss.

So much didn't make sense. So much didn't add up!

A new fear found its way into Krysta's heart.

What if the Outlanders had affiliated with the OrTans or some worse, more violent world? They could be using all manner of illegal technology, and to what end, only the gods would know. Whatever it was, it would be dangerous to Arda—and Ki and Fari had thus far not taken the threat of The People seriously enough.

Thoughts of her family made her soul ache. Her little niece, who might already be born... Fari's children, who would no doubt soon be on the way... Her brothers, her sisters-by-marriage...

These people were her ties to life and happiness, and Krysta realized with a dull throb behind her temples, they meant everything to her.

As did Arda. All of Arda. Her home.

No matter what, I must stay alive long enough to free myself and warn my brothers about how seriously they have underestimated this Outlander threat.

A nearby rustling caught her attention, and her overwrought mind quickly informed her she was hearing moving robes. A thick fabric woven from stout hair not unlike Fergilla wool.

The whispering, sliding sound entered the space where she stood helpless, blind, and unable to scream. Krysta bit her gag and snarled. When she fought her bonds, the zipper of her jumpsuit gave her bush a tear-jerking yank.

"Easy," said a voice so familiar to her she almost cried.

More rustles told her that Akad—it had to be Akad—had come to stand before her. She felt his hand on her head, first stroking her hair, then loosening her blindfold. Instinctively, she closed her eyes as he pulled off the cloth, then opened them slowly, letting her sight adjust to the glowing gray.

Hut...thatch, mud, wood, lit by candlelight and reflective rays. Yet this room seems...deliberately basic and empty. Chair, small table, glowing altar...

Glowing altar?

Yes, the small wooden altar in the corner of the room had an odd, light golden glow that seemed to come from deep inside the hand-smoothed wood. For a moment, Krysta's befuddled brain saw a shimmering dark feather floating in the glow, and then the triangle from her dreams, the one with the darkest of dark centers.

She blinked, and the image—and the glow—vanished.

"I need to speak with you before I remove your gag," said Akad in his typical low, steady tone, distracting her from the altar. "Mind to mind, but it will be painful."

Krysta turned her eyes to the priest in confusion. He stood in front of her like some out-of-place vision, his silken brown locks spilling down his broad shoulders. Intricate, twisted vines of *pa* glittered on his cheeks, highlighting his dark eyes—which seemed unusually narrowed and fearful. He kept glancing over his shoulder like someone else might burst through the door at any moment.

She wanted to ask him why their psi-contact would be painful. They had spoken mind-to-mind since they were children, so what would be different now?

Akad deftly stroked her breasts like the familiar lovers they had been, first bringing brief relief to her *pa*-aggravated flesh, then pulling the folds of her jumpsuit together. Almost as quickly, he disentangled the zipper from her lower curls and slipped it back up carefully.

"There are powerful psi-dampeners here. Only the initiated may communicate freely."

The initiated? Krysta's eyes widened and she made fists against her energy bonds. Akad was talking like an Outlander. Was he a prisoner, too, as she had assumed?

Or a traitor?

No. She wouldn't—couldn't—believe that.

"Are you ready?" he asked quietly, once more glancing over his shoulder. "You must not cry out."

Krysta nodded.

Akad reached both hands toward her temples. "You will...learn things, shocking and uncomfortable. I cannot help that. You may lose consciousness again. In time, I may be able to teach you to withstand such deep contact, given your bloodline, but I don't know."

Grinding her teeth against the cloth in her mouth, Krysta nodded. If she could have spoken, she would have yelled at him to get on with the task.

Still, the priest hesitated, but finally pressed the tips of his fingers to either side of her head, in the hollows beside her eyes.

For a moment, Krysta felt nothing—and then it seemed a sword cleaved her head in half, leaving her shocked and near to dying from the lancing agony. She started to cry out against her gag.

Please, do not make a sound! Akad's leveling energy bathed her thoughts. *He will hear, Darkyn Weil. And he is...not himself. He might kill me.*

Krysta was so overwhelmed she couldn't move. She hurt, gods—so awful—as Akad's mind found hers in a way she hadn't imagined possible. She realized she was touching him more deeply than she had ever touched another human being. Until that moment, she had believed Ardani psi-joinings were total. Now she knew the truth, that they were no more than a psychic hug.

This contact was so total, so completely intimate, that she could barely sustain it. For a moment, she thought she could understand and project every emotion in the universe. That she could send and receive every thought. That she could feel every rock and bird and tide on every planet everywhere, and reach her hand out to turn them to her will.

Just before absolute madness claimed her, the light of Akad's soul took her full attention. His essence blinded her more completely than the cloth that had covered her eyes. She knew he loved her in his cool, measured fashion, as he did many other occasional lovers. She knew he was frightened and angry, and uncertain about how to proceed. More than anything, she knew what he was.

And it wasn't completely Ardani.

He was...*other*. Something more primal? More dangerous?

Within the light of Akad, she saw, somehow, bits and pieces of all he knew. All he had ever known, and all he would ever learn. Stones of many colors, blending to black. Joining with *pa*. Yes, some Outlanders had *pa*. The powerful ones. The ones of the "old blood," carefully preserved and mingled by tribal breeding traditions. The blood of the *Ta*, ancestral leaders of The People.

I am Tanna Kon'pa, Akad admitted in a voice that sounded not unlike Chimera song. *I am one with The People, and one with those who carry that old blood.*

The tears Krysta had been holding spilled from her wide eyes, bathing her dry, tight cheeks. He had been her friend, her lover, the high priest of her people. So many times, he had held their lives in his gentle, steady hands!

And always, I treated you as my own family, because you are. Akad stroked her head as he spoke, chasing back a dark web that threatened to block his contact with her. *The*

People are simply of old Arda, stronger in psi and a sense of the universe, and still able to see what will be as clearly as what is.

No one has reliable future-sight any more, Krysta shot back. Even as she did, she knew he was telling the truth.

More information rushed in, images of Arda of eons past, living in huts, migrating with the seasons and the herds. She saw meteors blazing from the sky, saw the landscape changing, slowly at first, then faster and faster. The pictures slowed long enough for her to see what looked like a round tower on a round hill, with a silver thread drifting from its center. The silver thread grew to connect a vast triangle with three worlds at the points, the space within the figure too large for the mind to comprehend.

A new silver thread danced in her mind, thicker, more tangible, connecting Arda to its most distant moon, Arda-yi. Like a staircase, that one. Strange men stood like shepherds on the staircase, picking and choosing who would ascend.

Earth men? Men with stones in their chests? Men with *pa*? All of them? And beasts, too, so many colorful Chimeras, like a walking, singing rainbow...

Her thoughts blurred. The images sped up again before she could make sense of them.

You are on Arda-yi now, Akad intoned over the rapidly-changing scenes of Ardani evolution. *Only we call it Uhr. You are in Gese, the Blessed City, and you are prisoner to Darkyn Weil. This is his home, his meditation room.*

Krysta stiffened, seeing the bitter images of her kidnapping and Kolot's attack. *Bastard! You set me up, didn't you?*

Akad's denial was instant and completely believable, but she still wanted to kill him. She knew almost as fast that Weil hadn't sent his goons to capture her, that Weil had been in Camford, searching for Ki and Fari. She saw how the leader of The People, the sworn adversary of the Tul'Mar clan, had ministered to Elise and Katryn Tul'Mar, Krysta's new niece. She saw how Darkyn Weil saved Georgia by fighting his own men, *burning* a corridor somehow, to enforce his will that his men leave Georgia, Elise, and Katryn at Camford. Next, and perhaps most strange, she saw him opening corral gates, beckoning Chimera aboard ships readying to leave, with a dark falcon keeping watch in the skies above.

And then she knew three even more startling things.

First, Akad was more than a mere Outlander. He was Darkyn Weil's brother by birth, his *a'mun* twin, called such because he was missing the stone in his flesh with which many of the People were born.

Second, Darkyn Weil didn't know Krysta was a Tul'Mar, or that a woman named Krysta Tul'Mar had ever been born. Like all of The People, he kept himself free of Ardani affairs, relying exclusively on the reports of his brother, who had been left for fostering on Arda long ago. Akad had carefully omitted Krysta's name from the information he provided to The People. In fact, he omitted her very existence, following and respecting a deep instinct about...something...he was shielding from Krysta even now.

Third, and most impossible of all, the Outlanders truly believed Arda and the universe were at risk from something called the *Barung*.

And they were correct.

According to Akad's deepest beliefs, if she, Krysta Tul'Mar, did not remain on Uhr to meet her destiny, the *Barung* would triumph and kill them all.

When Barung returns, six shall lead him home, blended from the triangle, joined by the stone...

Krysta swallowed hard.

From the corner of the room, the altar began its golden glow again. So bright. So hot. It chased away the essence of Akad, taking over her mind completely. The pain in Krysta's head magnified beyond her ability to stand it. She fought not to cry out, but lost the battle even with Akad attempting to help her. He was pulling back from their link, covering her mouth, but she couldn't fight the agony any longer. Screaming with all the force of her lungs, fighting the gag, choking, she started a headlong tumble into darkness as a barely-human roar blotted out all sound.

Someone jerked Akad from the ground and flung him out of the room like a child's toy.

Krysta's dimming mind registered a huge man beside her, dressed in animal skin breeches and bearing a ruffled black falcon on his left shoulder. The bird glared at her with something akin to hatred. The man's presence, however, affected her like a stellar magnet, jerking her sanity inside out and turning her *pa* to liquid fire.

Burning more than she had ever burned, Krysta fought to turn her head, taking in the man's bare, heavily muscled chest. She saw the tanned flesh, the scars—and impossibly, a *pa*-mark in the shape of a two-headed axe with a stone set between the blades.

The stone was glowing the same color as his wild eyes—a brilliant, fiery yellow.

It should be black, but it's yellow. Something about that gave her deep qualms.

And then she saw nothing at all but that yellow-gold, slicing through endless, raging blackness.

A blackness that had a heartbeat and a voice.

Chapter Four

Darkyn Weil fought to remember where he was, who he was. Akad's elixir coursed through his veins, cooling the primal heat. Not fast enough. Not strong enough. His chest was on fire. His stone was changing!

This couldn't happen to him. It wasn't possible. He was *Tanna Kon'pa*, trained in the most ancient of mental disciplines. The People could master mating fervor, unlike their modern Ardani cousins.

"It's a mistake," he growled, holding his head. "I have no mate. I cannot have a mate!"

Yet, the more he shouted, the more his blood and his stone blazed. His cock felt like it would burst through the soft hide of his breeches. Guardian left him in a rustle of wings and muted jealous chortling, sailing directly out the open window of the main room. She gave one last disgruntled shriek before falling silent in the night sky, and Darkyn took the admonishment for her opinion on the matter of their guest.

Before Darkyn, the woman sagged pale and limp against the pole, supported by only her bonds, looking more dead than alive. Her beautiful *pa* patterns seemed drained of energy, and someone had zipped up her black jumpsuit.

The fergilla who had been touching her, causing her pain.

Darkyn growled again and clenched his fists. He

would kill the fool and have done with it. No one would ever touch his woman but him, not without his presence or consent, ever again.

And yet…something bothered him even as he turned to stalk into the hall and pound the man he had torn away from his *shanna*…

No!

He staggered. The prone figure in the hall looked familiar.

"Akad?" Darkyn grabbed the door facing to keep from falling forward on the priest. "Brother?"

Akad stirred, groaned, then swore and brought himself to a sitting position against the wall. He rubbed his shoulder. "Quicker to act than usual, Darkyn."

"I need more elixir," Darkyn managed to say through grinding teeth. "Now."

"More would kill you." Akad pushed himself upward, using the wall to support his weight. "For years, I suspected, and I tried to keep this from happening."

"You know it can't happen!" Darkyn bellowed, then wanted to vomit and fall on his face, maybe knock himself out until morning at least. Anything for relief. "She isn't of an allowed clan. And the *Barung*! You know what I must do. It isn't proper for me to mate at all."

By now, Akad had regained his balance. Darkyn felt relief at the lack of visible bruising. He swore to himself, acknowledging he hadn't even known his own brother when he attacked. He could have killed Akad, his beloved *a'mun* twin, the one man he was honor-bound to protect with his life's blood — miscreant cousins aside.

Still, Akad had touched the woman, and Darkyn had a sense it wasn't for the first time. Heat charged through his muscles, and he thought about killing his brother again.

"You can kill me," Akad said, speaking low and soft, in the eternal way of their people, "but fate is fate nonetheless. This fervor is primitive, and stronger than I have ever tried to manage. Elixir or no, if you do not mate with her soon, you will die."

Darkyn shouted his frustrations and swayed back and forth, clutching at the throbbing stone in his chest with one hand and clinging to the door facing with the other. He gripped the wood so hard his knuckles went white.

"*Mun'halla*, Brother." Akad stretched his arm and rubbed his shoulder again before pointing to the now-glowing yellow stone in Darkyn's chest. No longer black. No longer the same.

Golden, like the spiritually transformed leaders of old.

"The burning stone, straight out of ancient history. It glows because our *Ta* has found his soul's mate."

At this, Darkyn sank slowly to his knees. He felt mad and pursued, as if hounds bayed at his back and greenwild vines bound his arms. A mouthful of dryland sand, a belly full of hot, bubbling water from Uhr's Steaming River.

He could deny much, but the stone in his chest spoke only truth. As *Ta*, and among the purest of preserved blood as dictated by the Council of Worlds at the Tower on the Tor on Old Earth, in the time before time, he knew the stone's truth above all things, save the scroll carefully preserved beneath the altar in his meditation room.

What would become of him now?

And The People — Arda — the Universe — what of them?

Firm, guiding hands rested on his shoulders, and he heard Akad say, "All things in time, Brother. When we plan, the gods laugh, remember?"

"They will laugh as the *Barung* swallows us all," Darkyn murmured, thinking of sex and death at the same moment.

"For now, tend to yourself and your mate. I warn you, keep her bound until you win her heart, her trust. Otherwise, she *will* find a way to kill you."

Darkyn grunted, thinking his brother's words wise. He didn't know his mate's name as yet, but he could tell she was hallas, made of fire.

"At month's end, I will summon you before the *pao*, in case you find yourself too distracted to keep up with the time." Akad massaged his shoulder once more, then flexed his fingers as if satisfied. "After the alliance makes its agreements, and after you have sated yourself, we will convene a *pao* of our own elders and find a new course."

This time, Darkyn nodded, but in his heart, he didn't agree.

He was *Ta*. Feeding the *Barung* was his duty, and in truth, he was likely the only one with strong enough psi-power to blot out the energy of the void long enough to override natural survival instinct. So, yes, he would mate with this female. He would give biology its due. But no matter how she might burn him, his hallas was no match for his energy.

Darkyn Weil was munas, made of stone. He had to be.

In the end, he would do what he had to do to save his world and many others.

"Give me her clothes, Brother." Akad nodded toward

the jumpsuit. "I'll send that suit and one of Guardian's feathers as proof that we have her, along with reassurances that she will not be harmed. For now, that will have to do."

"And later?" Darkyn asked dryly.

Akad shrugged. "Later, I'll get her another jumpsuit. She loves them, you know."

"I didn't mean—"

"Ssshh." Akad put a finger to his lips. "One step at time, and the journey begins. Give me her clothes, and we'll worry about the next steps later."

Chapter Five

She was moving. Floating. A dark feather drifting slowly into the hungry center of a golden triangle, somewhere out over the Western Sea.

No...

Wait...

Krysta tensed.

Darkness was chasing her. That pounding, horrid, roaring darkness. She was flying her speeder faster than ever before, pelting forward in utter desperation and terror.

Three points of light glowed on her companel.

Planets, separated by light years, yet strangely aligned.

To the field, someone said. *Hold us together! Draw him to the center. Dead center. The innocents are loose, they are singing...*

The voice was oddly smooth and flat, both male and female, and backed by the most beautiful music Krysta had ever heard.

Akad?

Was that Chimera song?

No, wait. Georgia and Elise. Her brothers.

And more. Infinitely more.

A chorus, urging her on, to the center of the field, with the blackness rising behind her.

I'm flying to my doom...

Krysta ripped herself from her nightmare and drove herself toward consciousness. Away from the hungry shadows, the all-consuming dark.

And found herself floating again, still hearing soft, distant, soothing Chimera song.

Someone was carrying her. A careful, tender cradling, as if she were no heavier or taller than a child of five stellar years—yet the step was unsteady, almost as if her bearer were intoxicated.

Wake. Krysta felt the voice more than heard it. She reached for it with her mind, but hit a wall of pain so harsh she recoiled.

Careful, Brother, said Akad, who seemed to be speaking from a distance. *You must remember she cannot talk with us mind to mind without risking her health.*

A sense of unfocused chagrin filled Krysta, but it wasn't hers. The first voice said in almost slurred mental tones, *My* hallas. *Forgive my lack of control,* and then faded into nothing.

Hallas. Ancient Ardani for "made of fire," a compliment given to particularly aggressive warriors. Krysta struggled back toward the bright surface of consciousness and at last broke free. As she woke, she realized she was naked, but no longer blindfolded or gagged. Her hands were still bound, but now in front of her, and her ankles were tied together. The energy bonds seemed a little looser, a little warmer.

Someone was indeed carrying her, and it was the man who had swallowed her senses whole before she had fallen into her dark dreams.

Her bare *pa*-coated hip rubbed hard against the

waistband of his breeches and his leather sword belt, and her side was snuggled firmly against a man's—a warrior's hard, scarred trunk. Her shoulder pressed into the rough, corded flesh, and each time she moved, she thrilled at the snap of *pa*, the gentle nudge of the warm stone in his chest, and the criss-crossed marks of many fierce battles.

By the suns, he felt perfect. His strength pleased and frightened her, and set her heart to funny rhythms. It quickly grew hard to think. She could feel his power like an aura, surrounding him and surrounding her, too, so long as she touched him. Oh, yes, she wanted to touch him more, experience him in every way she could.

He smelled of soft-hide and sweat, of bayspice and the invigorating scent of Arda's blue pines. Krysta took a slow, deep breath, drinking in his male aroma like an aged berrywine. Her *pa* pulsed in time with his forceful strides, sparking and jumping in a way she hadn't experienced before. Her neck and chest burned, and her nipple throbbed along with her ever-hot quim. She was so, so wet.

Whoever this barbarian was, she wanted him to stop walking and take her now. He didn't even have to untie her. He just had to fuck her hard and without mercy, right on the dirt floor.

Dirt floor...hut...moon...oh, no that fergilla barbarian is NOT carrying me naked to his lair!

Krysta's eyes flew open. Her heart pounded hard enough to make a painful pulse in her throat. Darkyn Weil was carrying her, but not into a lair. Through a door into a—a bathchamber?

She struggled in his grip. "Put me down," she demanded in the old speech, her voice hoarse from ragged want and prolonged thirst.

The bastard didn't answer her.

Wearing a besotted, distant expression, he carried her straight across the room, small by Camford standards, and placed her on what appeared to be a toilet. His actions were so swift and sudden she sucked in a breath, surprised to find the air heavy and damp. She coughed from the shock, and her bladder nearly ruptured.

"Do as you need," Weil instructed in a thick, deep rumble, gesturing to the toilet before he turned his broad back, strode once more to the door with an uneven gait, and stumbled out.

If Krysta hadn't been so busy relieving herself, she would have leaped up immediately and made a dash for freedom. Even as she considered this course of action, the energy bonds on her ankles and wrists dissipated—only to reappear and multiply to block the doorway and the bathchamber's domed ceiling window, high above her head.

"Fergilla!" she shouted after Weil wherever he had gone, and half-expected an energy bond to break loose from the door, fly over, and cover her mouth.

It didn't, at least for the moment.

Seething, Krysta dispensed with nature's call as she catalogued the layout of the chamber. Four walls, with three-sconce candles flickering a hand's length apart. Throw-rugs in geometric patterns. She occupied a lone toilet opposite the door, and beside that was a bidet for cleaning. On her left was a sink and a mirror that looked to be planted directly into the wall and edged with sandpearl and live vines. On her right she found a natural round pool circled by inlaid stone, uneven and uncut but polished to remove the rough edges. A few jars decorated the stones, along with sea sponges and soap crystals. In the pool, the water bubbled occasionally. Steam rose in plumes, giving the air a splendid dampness that was more what she was used to breathing.

"Like home," Krysta said aloud.

She stood, feeling strangely dizzy, walked under the domed window, and gazed up through the shimmering energy bonds. Stars glittered back, familiar in pattern but not in angle, since she was viewing them from a place utterly foreign to her. When she edged against the natural pool until she touched the wall behind it, she could make out the curve of a brilliant blue-green planet.

Arda. Joy rose even as despair lunged to kill it. *Home.*

When Weil came back, she would need to find some way to overpower him and escape.

"Overpower him." She laughed at herself. "Yes, Krysta. That makes as much sense as trying to swim the Western Sea from shore to shore."

She felt so unsteady and distracted she would do well to battle a besotted three-foot Nostan. Krysta rubbed her eyes, trying to clear her thoughts and calm the heat in her *pa*. Was the steam from the natural pool some sort of intoxicant?

Something was making her drunk, and making her body ache for satisfaction in a way she couldn't ignore. At that moment, she would have given an arm for a good *kala* saddle or three hours with a few randy warriors.

Or ten minutes with that arrogant bastard Weil, on his back, hard and ready for a ride.

"No." She hugged herself and pinched her *pa*-covered nipple, trying to settle her thoughts. She couldn't want

Weil. She needed to wound him, to escape.

Right.

Weil would snap her in half, if he was so inclined. Which he hadn't been, thus far. What little she had seen of him, he was acting not at all like a cunning military chief. In fact, he reminded her of Fari these last months, even drunker than she felt, unbalanced and —

"*Knador!*" Krysta's hand flew from her nipple to her mouth. She nearly fell into the natural pool as reality struck her. How could she have missed all the signs so completely? Her vision of the Outlander leader before she actually met him, her reaction to that vision—and then to him, the way he behaved in their few moments together…

Gods, no.

The man thought she was his soul's mate.

Worse than that, her body and deeper mind agreed.

Krysta pinched her legs together, denying the extra fire and moisture in her quim. Suicide suddenly seemed like a plausible option. Biology be damned, there was no way she would accept this! No way she could. She would not betray the Tul'Mar name or its cause, or her people. *Or poor, poor Kolot, who took a death-wound to save me from this…this…yellow-eyed pirate!*

There had to be a way out of this damnable bathchamber.

Krysta rushed to the mirror and tried to unseat it from the thatch, vine, and brilliant, white sandpearl holding it in place. It wouldn't move. She pounded on it with her fists to break the glass and even tried kicking it, but to no avail. The mirror wouldn't break.

Maybe the pool.

She turned to dive in, intending to swim to the bottom, but at that instant, the energy bonds on the door vanished. Darkyn Weil, naked from the waist up, stalked in, still unsteady but carrying a tray of fruits, sauces, bread, paste, and several carafes and cups.

For a moment, Krysta was dazzled by his utter male beauty and uniqueness. That hair — gods, that alone drew her full attention. Night-black with streaks of shining yellow-white. She wanted to run her fingers across the streaks and see how they felt. As for the rest of him...all scars and hard muscle. He had taken off his amber double-blade and left it elsewhere, and he had loosened the ties on his breeches to make room for an obvious erection.

Against her wishes, her *pa* sizzled, making his sizzle in response. His full, sensual mouth curved upward in a predatory smile, and his eerie, feral eyes narrowed with surprise and obvious desire.

Gods, help me be strong. Krysta fought an urge to plunge her fingers into her quim and stroke her clit. She would not acknowledge this beast as her soul's mate, not while he held her hostage.

Even if he had noble intentions to rescue the universe from some very real threat...

Even if he had saved Georgia, Elise, and Katryn from certain death...

Even if he hadn't meant to kidnap her...

Even if he was, without question, the sexiest man she had ever seen, bar none...

Krysta squared off with Weil, figuring her odds for slamming the tray into his chest or face, dodging past him, and getting through the now-open door. Her mind felt like a falcon on a tether, fighting and flogging against reason and control.

I've seen that falcon, yes. Krysta's thoughts swirled. *She's his, and she doesn't like me.*

Weil set the tray down on the ground, his eyes fixed first on her swollen nipples, then on her wet, aching quim.

Energy bonds reappeared on the door—and on Krysta's wrists, jerking them behind her as if powerful hands had seized her own and snapped them neatly into place. The shock made her thrust her breasts forward for balance, drawing a smile of appreciation from Weil.

Crying out with rage, her first impulse was to kick Weil in the bollocks the minute he approached her. She tried to take a step, but her feet were fastened firmly to the dirt floor. And so, there she stood, naked and furious, facing her enemy in a forced parody of military at-rest.

"You will not strike at me," he said in emphatic though slightly halting modern Ardani. He folded his massive arms over his *pa*-mark and the odd glowing stone at its center.

"Why?" Krysta asked through her teeth. "You can't take a blow from a woman?"

Weil's eyes narrowed another fraction, giving him a definitely dangerous look.

This only fueled Krysta's anger—and her desire.

He walked forward slowly, and Krysta realized the bonds on her wrists were extending down now, fixing her arms in place so she couldn't even lean forward to butt him with her head.

Weil stopped less than an arm's length away.

Krysta felt a sharp, hot pinch on both nipples. She gasped and looked down to see yet another stream of energy sliding back and forth across the hard, nubbed tips.

"Red like sweetapple wine," he said, continuing in modern speech, growing more smooth as he spoke. "And this one..." The energy ribbon flicked against her *pa*-coated breast as he licked his lips. "A dusting of magik."

Krysta choked back a moan, then regained her wits for a brief moment. "Stop this," she demanded.

"Why?" he asked in an infuriatingly calm tone. The speed of the energy assault on her nipples increased. "You can't take pleasing from a man?"

It was all Krysta could do not to moan loud enough to rattle the walls.

Weil closed the small distance between them, coming closer and closer until his sizable erection nudged the top of her quim. "Pity you have such trouble with sensual teasing. I had hoped you had more courage."

The insult, the feel of the tanned skins of his breeches against her *pa*-lined lower lips, the nearness of Weil, of his *pa*, the way he smelled, robbed Krysta of reason.

"You bastard. I can take whatever you have to give. What, you imagine your manhood to be some fearsome weapon?"

Weil shrugged. "Perhaps."

And with that, he stepped back, reached down and further loosened the laces at his waist, and let his breeches fall to the floor. With a grace usually reserved for forest cats and Chimera, he stepped out of them and stood still, gazing at her.

Krysta stared at the length and girth of his cock and actually shuddered with want, with need. Her clit swelled painfully, teased and heated by her desire and her *pa*. She could imagine that fantastic vision in her mouth, sliding toward her throat. In her quim, driving toward her womb. In her ass, making her scream as pleasure joined with pain to push her to releases she had never before achieved. She wanted to touch it, measure it with her tongue and fingers, then test its soundness every way she could imagine.

The energy bonds pinched and twirled her nipples, edging her forward. She bit her tongue to keep from coming in front of Weil, though her defenses were beginning to crumble.

"I won't force you, hallas." He reached down and took his erection in hand, stroking it just as she had imagined doing in his stead. "You will ask for me. Maybe even beg."

Curses rose to Krysta's lips, but she didn't speak them. A new energy bond snaked around her waist. One end dipped into her quim and fastened on her clit, and the other slid between the cheeks of her ass, finding her tightly-closed hole at the same time it seemed to grow another section and reach around, stopping at her wet, waiting core.

"And I won't rest on pride, even if you do." Weil's black hair with those odd white-yellow streaks hung wild and unfettered. His golden eyes blazed as he rubbed his cock from balls to tip. "You are the most incredible woman I have ever seen. What I have touched of your essence, your thoughts and soul—you woke a part of me I thought dead from birth."

Krysta moaned as the energy ribbon teased her clit and both openings, flicking against them, feeling first like tongues and then like fingers. The ribbon across her nipples formed a delicate suction, alternating pinches between left and right in time with Weil's strokes.

"My spirit knows you," he said with a lyrical beat, as if reciting a poem.

Krysta recognized at once the start of the ancient Ardani claiming ritual, even though Weil was using modern speech with more and more fluidity.

Getting it from me, from the forward part of my thoughts. Like soul's mates do.

"No," she gasped, shaking with pleasure as the energy ribbons dipped into her butt and core, spreading to fill her as much as she could stand, then relaxing to nothing and slipping out to leave her empty. "I won't say my part. We can't do this."

"You feel reality." Weil rubbed himself harder, making Krysta want to shout at him to stop, to let her do it. "I, too, would deny it if I could. I can't. Neither can you."

All at once, his energy enveloped her, head to toe, from nipple to clit, all along her burning rivers of *pa*. The energy ribbons delved into her quim and ass again, thrusting with his thrusts, expanding, contracting. Krysta's mind left her completely, surrendering her to the yellow heat at Weil's command. She saw only him, his cock, and the look of determination on his beyond handsome face. Her skin and *pa* melded into molten armor as all of the information Akad had given her came to bear.

She couldn't psi-touch Darkyn Weil, but she knew he was no villain, at least not in the sense she had once thought. A man on the edge, yes. A brooding warrior with temper and secrets—yes.

Her soul's mate. Her *sha*.

She didn't understand him, she hadn't grown up with him nor shared battle with him, she hadn't even spent the time to learn his patterns and dreams—but her spirit did know him.

Time will remedy the rest, went the old saying, from ages when the Ardani population was more scattered and such blind matings were more common.

But he isn't fully Ardani, the last vestige of her better sense insisted. *My brothers believe he is their enemy...*

Time and again, Weil used his energy ribbons to drive her toward the peak only to slow the pace and stimulation before she could explode in orgasm. She thought she would collapse if she didn't achieve release, but his erotic bonds held her in place, stroking, pinching, thrusting until all she could do was moan incoherently.

Eyes half-open, she met Weil's wild yellow gaze.

"My spirit knows you," he repeated. "Speak your name, woman. Say what you know to be true."

"Krysta!" she screamed as the energy fingers pinched her nipples and circled her clit, all the while claiming her in the same rough, ruthless way she wanted this infuriating barbarian to make her his own. "Krysta *shanna* Darkyn Weil!"

And with that, all stimulation stopped instantly.

Krysta cried out with frustration and pain, needing to come so badly she thought she might die.

Her wrists and ankles weren't bound any longer.

And Darkyn Weil—oh gods, her new soul's mate, claimed legally and fully by the ancient rites—stood before her with his hands at his sides. The yellow stone in his chest cast light around her like a halo, and his *pa* coursed along its double-axe design as if blown by stellar winds.

Before she could fall, he caught her in his strong,

encompassing arms, and let her sag in his embrace. Krysta's head drooped backward as he secured his grip around her waist and lifted her, until instinct drove her to fasten her legs around his midsection. She lay back against his arms, her breasts vulnerable to his mouth, her quim pressed against his lower belly, her thighs tight against his waist. Her hair streamed toward the floor, and she barely managed to reach up enough to grab his biceps.

"Look at me, hallas."

Krysta didn't want to comply, but she did, and she shuddered from both excitement and fear. Darkyn Weil's eyes blazed so brightly she thought they might singe her skin. Holding her gaze, he lowered his head captured one jutting nipple in his mouth. The pressure of his teeth on the blazing *pa* made her moan uncontrollably, and he bit her harder then, and harder still until she shouted without knowing whether she wanted him to stop or not. Her clit felt too big for its flesh. The walls of her quim contracted, and she thought she might expire if he didn't ease her suffering.

He released her nipple but kept her gaze hostage. Krysta dug her nails into his arms, gasping, "Now. No more teasing."

"I decide when." Weil—*Darkyn*, she told herself, *Darkyn, my mate*—didn't blink. The heat from his stare stoked the flames of her *pa*, her passion, the juices warming her core. "My pleasure is your pleasure, and yours, mine. Be still or we stop here, now."

A scream of frustration rose in Krysta's throat, but she held it back. No doubt if she argued, he'd put her down and walk away, mating fervor or no. This man was no slave to desire. He was no slave to anything...but she was close, damn close, to losing her own mind from primal mating urges.

With sheer force of will, she forced back all demands, all pleading, all moaning and yelling, and stilled herself in Darkyn's arms. The tip of his cock nudged her quim, only a hair's breadth from filling her in one rough thrust. Krysta's inner walls spasmed at the thought, but still she held herself in check. Unblinking, unmoving, she stared at her sha.

The dark angles of his face were rigid with determination despite the fierce desire burning in his cat-like eyes. His scarred muscles felt like damp steel, containing her in a way she had never allowed herself to be contained.

She felt…suspended. Outside of normal time. Outside of normal space. But definitely not outside of her body. She had never been more fully present in her own skin before, not in her entire adult life.

"Tell me what you want, Krysta. My hallas. Tell me, now."

The command made her heart pound. She opened her mouth to speak, but found her voice hoarse and choked with need.

"You," she whispered. "I want your cock inside me."

"Past that." Darkyn shifted her weight down a fraction, and Krysta felt the head of his cock just inside her aching core.

Her thoughts jumbled together as her madness multiplied. Her nipples felt like fire-rocks, aching for his wet mouth. "I-I want to know you," she stammered.

"And past that?" Darkyn's low rumble made her shiver.

Krysta felt like the man was tearing apart all barriers

between her essence and his. She wanted to fight him, to rage, to demand satisfaction or push him away, but the mating fervor drove her almost as hard as her deepest, unspoken desires.

"I want to be whole," she said in a rush. "I want a worthy match—I want my turn!"

Darkyn's lips parted, half-triumphant grin and half-carnal snarl. Krysta's body drew tighter than a bowstring. He squeezed her hips, shifted her downward, and thrust upward, slamming his cock into her waiting quim with all the power she had imagined—and more.

Krysta moaned and clenched her thighs hard as her slick walls pulsed against his splendid erection. He felt like rigid fire inside her, melting her insides and molding her to fit him and only him forever more. She heard him draw a breath of surprise as the *pa* on the lips of her quim made contact with his shaft. Then, he rumbled with delight.

So did she.

Her clit and *pa*-coated bush rubbed against his lower hair, sending spasms of pleasure up and down her body.

She tried to call his name, or form the syllables to call him her mate, but found both too great an effort. All that came out of her mouth was a single, loud, "*Yes!*"

Wrapped in that one word were a thousand assents and instant compromises. Darkyn's corded muscles rippled, as if accepting every one and offering his own.

"If you want me to beg…" she stammered, holding him tightly, squeezing and releasing his cock as he pumped in and out of her quim.

"As my *shanna*, you beg no one for anything, ever again. Except me." Darkyn's voice sounded harsh, but

Krysta heard his possessiveness, his desire, and it doubled her own. In the mating fervor, suffused by the same emotions that drove ancient berserker warriors to take on whole regiments of invaders, he could and would kill to protect her honor or please her whims.

He rocked her against his heated flesh with each thrust, holding her high above the earth floor as if to show his absolute power. Her own fervor grew by the second, bringing out a cunning and aggression she had heard of but never experienced. She wanted to bite her mate, hard, everywhere, and claw him. She wanted to lay on her back, legs spread, while he pounded into her for hours. She wanted to pull his hair until he roared.

This man was *hers*. No one else's. She would blast anyone who came near to him, who tried to harm him or claim him.

"Hallas," he groaned before ramming himself deeper yet and biting first one nipple and then the other. Krysta shuddered with a small orgasm, and he did it again, this time plunging to the center of her body, all the while biting harder and sucking. She came again, shivering from the fullness of his penetration, the heat of his teeth on her sensitive flesh.

Darkyn lifted her nearly-limp body up and down his shaft, pumping and thrusting his hips with each motion. His strength was amazing. His hot, pulsing cock even more amazing.

Krysta managed to grip his shoulders and pull herself forward as he repeatedly drove into her quim. She fell against him, chest to chest, and their *pa* mingled with a loud crackle and snap.

They both let out sharp cries at the depth of the

sensation. Krysta's whole being shook, and she felt Darkyn bucking against her from the pure electrical energy.

Somehow, he fucked her deeper then, with ever-harder thrusts, lifting her hips and bringing her down exactly where he wanted her. Their mouths joined, tongues mimicking the motions below.

His mouth tasted like paradise and cool water, wetting her dry tongue, soothing her parched lips before he pulled back and whispered, "Come for me."

Krysta's *pa* snapped as he raised her hips and brought them down hard against him, his cock plumbing ever deeper.

"I want to hear you scream. Come for me, Krysta. Now!"

Her body answered him with shudders that seemed to begin in her toes and spread up, up, to her filled, aching quim, sailing along her *pa* to her breasts, her neck, her face. Screaming uncontrollably, she thrashed in his embrace until the molten jets of his answering orgasm shot deeper still into her waiting core.

Her soul's mate, her *sha*, bellowed as her walls contracted on his cock, squeezing until he spent himself completely.

Then he sank to his knees, keeping her impaled upon his indeed fearsome weapon. Her ass resting on his thighs, she lay against his shoulder, glorying in his forceful yet tender embrace.

For that moment, at least, her body had reached complete ease, and Krysta had a sense of homecoming she didn't expect. She had never before had sex without a psi-connection, and yet this man could be no more connected to her if he lived at the center of her soul.

"My spirit knows you," she murmured. "munas, made of stone."

"Darkyn Weil, *sha* Krysta — I don't know your family name." He kissed the top of her head. "My hallas, now and always."

Even in her sated stupor, Krysta had to fight not to tense. She had known the truth before, from what Akad said and showed her, but reality didn't strike until that moment.

Her new and properly bound mate had no idea he had just wed the enemy. Akad hadn't told him, and neither had she.

She opened her mouth to force out the words, but instead buried her face deeper into his neck and sobbed.

Chapter Six

Darkyn Weil knew his mind, his skin, had to be aflame, yet the burning came from within. Already, his cock grew stiff and demanding, still captured in the welcome of his new mate's *pa*-lined quim. Her lower lips felt like slowly working tongues against his erection, maddening his flesh in a way he hadn't before imagined.

And then she was crying, cradled safe in his arms, protected from all that might harm her.

Tears. Darkyn searched his thoughts desperately as he pressed his lips against the brow of his hallas, trying to find the source of her unease. Ancient instincts flared and roared, demanding that he maim and slay whoever caused her pain. As his heartbeat doubled in speed, he ground his teeth and contemplated the fact that he could easier handle an army of miscreant cousins than a flicker of sadness from this woman.

"I wish we could speak mind to mind," Krysta whispered against his ear, her voice heavy with emotions.

With a woman's secrets, a woman's passions.

She sighed. "I wish I could give you what I feel."

"Is that why you cry?" He heard the husk in his own voice as he shifted her hips, positioned his cock in her pleasing depths, and gazed into her glistening eyes.

Krysta didn't answer. Instead, she bit the flesh between his ear and throat with a ferocity he didn't expect.

Darkyn grunted in response, convulsively thrusting deeper into her quim and drawing a satisfying shudder from his *hallas*. The musk of her satiation and redoubling arousal blotted out most rational thought. He barely had time to realize how short-lived had been his relief from the relentless drive of his mating fervor before his lips found hers and the cycle began again.

Krysta caressed the sides of his face, his shoulders, the back of his head as he plied her tongue with his own. It felt so right to be joined with her, mouth to mouth, cock to quim, *pa* to *pa*. The stone in his chest accepted the touch of her flesh as if she were his blood-family.

Taking care to cause her no pain, he eased her backward until she lay on the floor beneath him, then rested between her thighs. The warmth of her eyes drew him closer, but he thought he could see flickers of sadness — maybe even fear. Each tore at his heart in ways he scarcely understood, penetrating the fog of mating desire just enough to allow a single question.

"What troubles you?" He kissed the soft hollow of her cheek.

She kept her fingers in his hair as she drew a slow, quiet breath. "I never expected — so fast — you don't know me, Darkyn Weil."

Darkyn inhaled her bayflower scent and rocked forward, pushing his cock deeper into her channel. "I am learning," he said earnestly as she moaned.

The next time she looked at him, it was with the same blind passion he felt. The sweet wine of her kisses, the wet heat of her walls around his cock, the way her mark joined with his own at every possible point made his blood run as hot as the drylands sun.

He trailed his fingers down her cheek and ear, moving his hand to the earth beside her head. Another kiss, and he placed his other hand in a similar position. Braced above her, holding himself against her skin but supporting his own weight, he began a slower, wordless claiming ritual.

"Mine," he managed in a belly-delving growl. "You...are...mine."

Did the ancients feel like this when they mated?

Each time his cock thrust forward, Krysta groaned and pushed up to meet his stroke. Behind them, the natural pool let out long hisses of steam, mingling fresh water with the salt of their sweat until they moved together like matched currents, flowing, ebbing, breaking, then flowing anew.

Darkyn ceased understanding or caring where he finished and she began. The urge to possess her was total. The drive to please her complete. Rekindled desire scorched him as he picked up speed, burying his cock to his bollocks each time, roaring with each of Krysta's heady moans. She seemed so slight, to take him so easily. A warrior, yes, to welcome a man in fervor without fear, and meet that fervor with her own.

Her nipples rubbed against his chest, the *pa* coating on the right one snapping with every rocking thrust. He shifted her hips closer, and it was that nipple that brushed his stone, and each time, he caught the tip of her thoughts.

Deep...

Ah, gods...

Perfect...

These inner moans drove him harder. He held her head pinned between his forearms and gazed full into her eyes, almost daring her sadness and reserve to return.

It did not.

As he drove his cock home again and again, she offered only ecstatic acceptance, joy, and increasing fervor.

In the old days, Darkyn might have been a wolf, and he would have howled. A bear, and he would have clawed his own chest and bellowed. A greenwild cat, and he would have shrieked his triumph loud enough to rattle the vines and bend the trees. As a man, he simply bared his teeth and rumbled his delight at how she felt, how she smelled, how she looked, at the goodness and truth and passion he sensed each time he touched her thoughts.

She closed her eyes, her body a complete extension of his, or his an extension of hers. "Fuck me," she half-yelled, using an odd word.

Darkyn didn't understand the term, but well grasped its meaning and how it pleasured his mate to use it.

Krysta grasped her ankles, pulling up her legs to take him deeper.

Darkyn obliged with a louder roar of pleasure. The world around him blurred to nothing, leaving only the exotic blend of dark and light that was his new *shanna*, his *hallas*.

She came with a scream then a sigh, clenching his cock in the burning well of her quim. He could do nothing but follow her, spilling himself like a boy-man with no control over his own body. She took his control, this Ardani she-witch, and he gave it over without protest. It belonged to her. He belonged to her, and she to him. He knew truth in that instant, as he barely shifted his weight before collapsing beside her and wrapping her in his arms. He knew the future would be none of what he had planned before seeing her.

He had touched her now, Krysta, his mate, his made-of-fire lover. He had known her pleasures, her wants and needs. He had found emotions he thought he had been born without, and he knew he could never leave her.

Yet, even as he drifted toward sleep, his guilt rose to protest that line of thinking. The part of Darkyn that had been *Ta'Tanna Kon'pa* since he was but a boy called him weak, told him he was surrendering the lives of his people for his own pleasure.

Will you sleep and rut while the universe wails? Will you give over your life's purpose for the weakness of the flesh?

Will you for once be silent and trust the patterns of the universe? Not all things lie within your hands, Darkyn Weil.

That last admonishment came in a genderless, ageless voice not unlike that of his mother, or his father, or the leaders through the centuries, all the way back to the Great Migration. He had heard it before, and always obeyed it. He felt as if he couldn't disrespect it, as if it came from somewhere…beyond.

From the time before time, when all of Arda yet followed the old ways, those who knew, the old ones, the wise ones, sent The People to Uhr to preserve the mix of blood, to accomplish the most important task in history. The time is near at hand. What am I doing here, with this woman, straying from the path so clearly laid before me?

Hush, said the always-obeyed voice, which at times seemed singular, and other times seemed to be the twining of three. Or twice that. Six. Yes, six. *Tend your heart. Mun'halla, Darkyn Weil. The stone that burns cannot be denied.*

Krysta shifted in his embrace and sighed, and the crystalline sound vibrated through Darkyn's fervor-besotted brain. He felt cleaved and caught between the undeniable and the unforgivable.

Ignoring the twist in his gut, he drew his mate closer still and kissed the top of her head. The admonishments of the forceful voice settled in his gut, and he allowed the possibility that there were things he hadn't foreseen. He also allowed the possibility that those things might not be all bad.

Indeed. How could I be anywhere but here? Or with anyone but her?

Darkyn fell asleep, unable to answer those questions.

He woke, still unable to answer them — and after that, quickly lost track of time and space. They moved about the house like a joined beast, on this floor, or that chair, finally wending around to his bed, where they seemed to belong. The yellow-white of day blended with night's subtle gray without changing his focus in the slightest. Other than to eat and bathe, he had one activity, one obsession.

Krysta. *Hallas.*

At some point, his dizzy mind wondered — had it been hours since he first joined with her?

Days?

A week?

There, in the half-dark of his simply-furnished bedroom, standing at the side of his large four-poster with Krysta on her knees before him, he thought it was the latter. Days. They had been together for a handful of days now, and had done nothing but eat, bathe, and explore each other's passions.

A stellar week. Perhaps more. If only he could stop time and the *Barung*, he would keep her to himself for months. Perhaps a year. Or two.

He stroked the top of her head as it moved slowly back and forth. The feel of her warm, wet lips on his cock blotted out all things but the rhythm of her sucking. The single window of his room, located directly in front of him and bound with energy bonds, blurred just like the energy-bound door to his left. Between the door and the room's only closet, a single long mirror reflected their passion when he glanced in that direction. It also reflected the rumpled bed behind him, and beyond that, the room's single long dresser, with five tapers flickering in holders along the top.

They had been through many candles thus far, and they had been at it many times in the bed, tearing the covers, kicking them aside.

And there were many times yet to be.

Krysta ran her tongue along the length of his erection, purring her pleasure as she once more sampled his length, his thickness.

Big. Thick. Just right, she had told him the night before, or was it yesterday? *You fill me,* munas.

And each time they joined—fucked, as she liked to say, an Earth word she had picked up from the mates of her brothers—the sensations seemed fresh and new. His *hallas* never did the same thing twice, in quite the same way.

Today (or was it night?), she was exploring. Teasing as much as fucking.

"So good," she managed to whisper as she slipped his cock free of her soft mouth, only to claim it again and take it slowly, tip to head to shaft, deeper and deeper, until it seemed she swallowed him.

And then once more, she turned him loose completely, lifted his cock, and took his bollocks gently in her mouth.

Darkyn groaned his approval, feeling the electric wash of sensation. The tip of her tongue traced each contour until he thought he couldn't stand another moment. Fighting the urge to come, he willed her to continue.

She did, easing his balls from her lips and returning once more to his cock. The sensation was dizzying. The sight of so willful a woman bending her knees to suck him dizzied him almost as much.

"Take me," he demanded, thrusting forward.

Krysta purred again, sucking him deeper and deeper still. Sublime. Perfect.

She had him by the hips, digging her fingers in, not controlling his cock at all, leaving that to him like a dare.

You bastard. I can take whatever you have to give...

The words she flung at him that first night rushed back, drawing a growl from his depths as he rammed himself into her mouth.

She gripped his hips harder. Sucked harder. The edge of her teeth brushed his flesh, making him gasp with pain, with delight.

Hallas.

As if in response, she flicked her tongue rapidly over the top of his shaft, all the while sliding him in and out of the ring of her lips. One hand slipped from his hip back to his bollocks, cradling, squeezing ever so gently.

Darkyn still fought to hold back. He would let her control some, but never too much. This woman did not like her men out of control. That much he could sense, mind contact or no. As a commander, she would only submit, only trust an even more powerful leader. No matter what, she would never submit in lifestyle. Only in the bedroom, in sex. That much he could easily determine, too.

Fine.

That would be enough, and more than enough.

"Take me," he commanded again, and once more, Krysta obliged by sucking him deep as he drove in at will.

Darkyn knew he was at the very edge, the absolute moment. The next stroke, and he might spill himself. He started to pull out, intent on lifting her up to the bed, but she held tight. Sucked harder. Deeper.

Never underestimate an Ardani female in full mating fervor...

Darkyn roared and grabbed her by the hair, but it was too late. Her fingernails gouged deep into his thigh. She gripped his balls with perfect pressure and sucked so hard Darkyn thought he might come unhinged at his joints. His orgasm ripped at him, tearing his seed from his cock, and still she sucked, draining him. Making him as much hers as she was his.

When she finished, she rocked back on her haunches, staring up at him, mouth swollen, gaze hooded, grinning like some naughty cat.

Another dare.

What will you do with me, Darkyn Weil? Sha. I had my way. I took control. Now what will you do?

The questions were written on every feature of her taut, *pa*-lined body.

Darkyn felt the smarting on his thigh where she had clawed him, and he grinned back at her.

"What do you want, *hallas?*"

Her eyes blazed. "Whatever you have left to give."

Gods, but she was all dare!

He snatched her up as she laughed and held her against him, feeling the sizzle of her *pa* blending with his, coursing over the stone in his chest. When he kissed her, pushing his mouth into hers, she parted her lips and flicked her tongue against his just as she had flicked her tongue against his cock.

Insatiable.

Darkyn bit her lip none to gently, making her moan, then asked, "What if I carry you to the meditation room, tie you to the pole, and fuck you until you faint?"

"Do it," she challenged, "if you think you can."

Darkyn lifted her and turned toward the door, then reconsidered. "No. Because you want that. I'll do what I want instead."

Krysta struggled in his arms, a mock struggle, and gave him a pouting expression that made him laugh. He turned back to the bed, tossed her on the black-hide spread face-down, and swatted her fine ass.

She wriggled and stretched out, leaving her ass vulnerable, and he swatted it again. The imprint of his hand stood out red against the soft silver-white of her skin.

"I can take more than that," she said in a coarse, waiting voice.

Darkyn sat down on the edge of the bed and pulled her roughly across his lap, keeping her face down, pointed toward the door—and the mirror. He positioned her wet quim on top of his cock, let her breasts dangle against his leg, and smacked her ass again.

She moaned loudly, and he felt tingles all along his *pa* from her excitement. She struggled again, this time almost getting free, and Darkyn quickly bound her ankles with energy bonds. Before she could react, he pulled her hands behind her back and bound her wrists, too.

"You're at my mercy," he said, stroking her shoulders and hand-printed ass then, glorying in the burning feel of her *pa* on his thighs and cock.

"You talk big," she murmured, hunching against his shaft, burning him even more with her silvery bush. "Prove it."

Darkyn grabbed her by her *pa*-coated hair and partially lifted her head so that she could see them in the mirror on the wall.

"Watch me," he ordered as he slapped her ass again.

She wriggled on his lap, moaning.

"Be still." He smacked her harder, bringing the red again, and a look of absolute rapture to her face.

His swelling cock rubbed against her quim as he slapped her ass twice more, then left his hand in place and forced his thumb between her cheeks, into her tight hole.

This made her gasp. Her head tried to droop, but he held it up.

"Watch. Keep your eyes open. And be still, or I will stop, I assure you. I'm a man who doesn't fear waiting…and waiting…and waiting…for the right reasons."

He forced his thumb deeper, then slipped his other four fingers beneath to the hot, drenched opening of her quim. Teasing her as she had teased him, he toyed with the opening, pleased to see sweat break across her brow as she strove not to move.

Abruptly, he pulled his thumb and fingers free and smacked her ass, harder than ever. The sound of the pop seemed to fill the room, along with her sharp cry of mingled pain and joy.

"Is that what you want?" he asked, staring at her in the mirror, laying over his lap, breasts with hard nipples slapping against his leg, head raised by his fistful of hair, bound hand and foot, ass brilliant red from his spanking. "Or do you want me to fuck you with my hand?"

"Fuck yourself," she said playfully, and he smacked her ass again. Tears came up in her eyes, but she had a smile on her lips.

Darkyn felt his erection grow painfully hard against her dripping quim. The tender flesh of her ass glowed pink before him, and he smacked it again and again and again until they were both bucking with the rhythm.

Without warning, he forced his thumb into her ass again, and again rammed his other four fingers home in her quim, reaching as deep as he could. He felt her inner walls spasm as she screamed, and it took all this strength to hold her head up.

"Keep watching, *hallas*." He thrust his hand against her, pushing deeper into her ass and channel. "Know who your Ta is. Know that only your *sha* can possess you like this, now and always."

Krysta kept her eyes wide as he fucked her with his fingers and hand, rocking her back and forth. She moaned with each forceful push, struggling to spread her bound legs and give him better access.

He was merciless, holding tight to her hair, keeping her eyes on the mirror as he took her. As he squeezed his thumb and fingers together inside her and rammed into her harder.

She cried out, eyes rolling back as she came, shuddering against his hard cock. Her ass and quim clenched on his fingers, and still he kept at her. Thrusting, pushing into the trembling moisture, loving the hot *pa* on his erection.

"Who am I, Krysta?"

She groaned and trembled, close to another orgasm.

Darkyn teased her, slowing the strokes and pressure, making his strokes gentle until she squirmed.

"Be still!" he commanded forcefully, and met her wide eyes in the mirror. "Who am I?"

"My *sha*," she said, trailing into a groan as he once more plunged his fingers as deep as they could go. "My munas."

"Yes," he said, rocking her hard on his hand, rubbing quim to cock, pressing, pushing inside her until she exploded again.

And then he abruptly pulled out his hand.

Krysta looked shocked and disappointed, and barely conscious, then wide awake and excited as he stood holding her carefully in his arms, turning her around to the bed so she lay face down, ass up, knees on the floor.

He released the bonds on her ankles and spread her legs, but left her arms bound behind her back. Her ass still glowed red from his slaps.

Darkyn thought his cock might burst as he reached down and gently turned her head toward the mirror again.

"Watch," he commanded. "If you close your eyes, I stop."

She trembled as he positioned his cock at the opening of her quim and teased, sliding in, then slipping back. Sliding in, then slipping back.

Bending over her, still not fully inside her, he reached around her bound arms, lifted her slightly, and grabbed her nipples.

As he pinched them, she screamed.

"Noisy, noisy," he muttered. "Shame. Can't have that."

Concentrating hard, he sent an energy bond around her mouth, gagging her but leaving her plenty of room to breathe.

She bit against it, wriggling, and groaning.

Damn you, her eyes said. *Fuck me. Fuck me!*

He used her nipples to pull her back down to the bed, then pull her against him as he rammed his cock deep into her quim. Again and again he slammed into her wet channel as she screamed against the energy-gag. Her face was a study in pleasure. Her eyes stayed wide, though defiant and misty.

"Harder," she managed around the gag. "Harder!"

Darkyn roared and fucked her as she demanded, planting his cock to the bollocks and drawing it back, then planting it again. His own orgasm was so close, he didn't know how he could hold it, but he did.

He pinched her nipples as he pulled them, dragging her toward him for each penetrating push.

She came sweating, howling, convulsing against his shaft, and he couldn't hold himself another second. With his own wild howl, he emptied himself in her in three shuddering, impossibly deep thrusts.

Then he lay atop her, chest to back, cock in quim, staring into the mirror with her as he released her energy bonds.

He wasn't sure he could move, or that he wanted to.

Krysta smiled at him, stretching her arms and glancing at him through the reflection.

"I didn't faint yet," was all she said.

Chapter Seven

Krysta slept fitfully, dreaming of an oddly growing darkness and the glare of Darkyn's falcon. The damnable bird had come and gone since that first mating, always with cries of jealous disapproval. Of all things, a little feathered raptor was driving Krysta to her first possessive moments as woman of Darkyn Weil's house and heart.

Guardian had best learn to respect me, she decided in her groggy half-waking state. *I'm not above jessing her until she finds her manners.*

And yet part of her appreciated the bird's wary loyalty to Darkyn. Krysta had no doubt the falcon would die to defend him. There was honor in that.

Morning's brighter light drew her into full awareness, and she found herself alone in her mating bed. Her *sha* had taken his leave, but Krysta sensed she wasn't alone. Her flesh crawled with the sense of someone studying her, someone despising her.

Battle-wary, she lay still as the dead and cut her eyes left, then right.

Nothing.

When she glanced toward the foot of the bed, she saw the source of malevolent energy. Guardian, thumper mouse in beak, glared at her like a disgusting interloper.

"Will you hate me, then?" Krysta kept her voice even and kind as she addressed the raptor. "We have the same aims, you and I. And we both care for him."

Guardian shivered, ruffling feathers, as if to say, *We shall see.* Then she was gone, leaving a single black plume at Krysta's feet. Unable to resist the allure of the unusual feather, she sat up and reached for it. A shock hit her the moment she gripped it. A force driving her backward and down, down into unknown depths of cold, starless space. Everything vanished, even her body, and yet she could feel it, and feel its pain.

He is coming, a voice informed her. *Out of all time, from a distance that did naught but fuel his hatred and power. He will kill you if he can.*

Krysta struggled against suffocation. She felt cut loose from life, from sanity as a weight drove down on her chest. No air. No air!

The dispassionate voice seemed to sigh. *Your allies are coming. Your allies are here. Still, only you can hold the six to their purpose. Fail, and it ends here, now. Fail, and everything ends.*

Knowing she would die before she escaped this bizarre trap, Krysta sought to crush the feather in the grip of her phantom-body. She hadn't the strength to move.

Had the falcon murdered her, then? Did it carry some poison in its pinions?

"*Hallas.*" Darkyn's voice sluiced across her crushed flesh, washing away the darkness as if it never existed. Bright light blinded her even through her closed lids.

Krysta realized she could open her eyes now, and did so slowly. Her *sha* stood beside her bed, dressed in a tanned animal skin shirt and breeches, with his unique streaked hair pulled into a neat ponytail. His pupils were large, and his glazed look suggested he had taken *firemylk.*

Shaking inside, Krysta sat up. Nothing seemed amiss. The bedclothes were not even disturbed.

Did I dream it all? But…no, the feather is still in my hand. Crushed.

"I have brought some of Akad's best elixir." Darkyn held out a small vial, clearly unaware of her inner distress. "I want you to take it. It is time my people see you, if only for a short while."

"I'm not sure I'm ready for that," she whispered as she took the vial, hearing the tremble in her response. She drank the tangy liquid in one gulp, hoping it would soothe her nerves.

Darkyn knelt by the bed as she sat up, swinging her legs over the side. He positioned himself between her knees, so that they were chest to chest. The soft feel of his shirt against her nipples made her shiver from warmth instead of the fear of her night-terror. It seemed far away now, that dream, as she gazed into the hot yellow depths of her *sha's* eyes.

"Do not fear The People." Darkyn pressed his cheek to hers. "They will welcome you without question."

"Like Guardian?" Krysta stifled a laugh. "She has been less than accommodating."

Darkyn's mirth rumbled against her ear, sending chills of pleasure along her neck and spine. "She's been my woman so long she forgets her place. Give her time, *hallas*. I think you can wait out a jealous falcon."

"I-I had a terrible dream just now," Krysta said, deciding honesty was best, since there was already enough deception between them. "Of an evil thing coming to kill us. I thought I had been poisoned."

"*Barung*." Darkyn pulled back and studied her with gentle affection in his gaze. "You sense it, just as The People, only filtered by your lesser psi gifts. It comes, true enough. We plan to stop it. We must stop it."

Krysta blinked. *In my dream, the voice called it* he, *not* it. *Perhaps that was just my mind's understanding.* "Such nightmares are common, then?"

"And growing more so." Darkyn nodded. "Which is another reason we must make an appearance. My people need the comfort. My presence reassures them."

A distant part of Krysta thought to make a wisecrack at that statement, but she heard the earnest truth in her mate's tone. He was Ta, after all. No different than Ki Tul'Mar was to the people of Arda. Darkyn was right. He was the leader of his people, and if they had nightmares like hers, they would need to see him.

He helped her up, pulled her into the protective steel of his embrace, and kissed her. Even with the *firemylk* working through her blood, Krysta's senses opened wide to the rough sweetness of his tongue, the rhythm of his breath, his smell of leather and man's musk. Her body thrummed as he stroked her back and cupped her bare ass, and she moved her hips automatically against his growing erection.

"Not now," he whispered hoarsely. "The elixir will only help us for so long."

"What shall I wear?" she whispered back. "You took my jumpsuit. Do The People have some sexy garment for their women?"

Darkyn pulled away from her, and Krysta saw the reluctance on his face. His clear desire made her smile.

"I'd rather not see you dressed," he admitted, "but your jumpsuit is your taste and preference, *hallas*. Akad had another smuggled from Arda, a new one. I'll get it for you, and you can wear that. Let my people see you for you." He rubbed a hand over his chin. "That garment will be sexy enough, I assure you."

And so it was that dressed in her shiny new leathers, complete with a new pair of flying boots, Krysta took the hand of her *sha* and strode out his cabin at his side.

The day seemed unbearably bright, and her *pa*-lined body already ached for Darkyn's touches.

First things before second things, she told herself. She had been daughter and sister to leaders, Captain of the Home Guard, and now she was wife to a *Ta*. The demands of leadership she well understood.

At first, Krysta saw only Arda and the twin suns above her, and flowers, grass, and dirt path around them as they walked. Presently, Darkyn began to point out subtle differences to her left. The trees grew more thickly there, and the spaces between them grew less.

"The orchards," he said. "I have spent many hours there, harvesting fruits of the limb for our people. Beyond the orchards, the greenwild waits. It's naught but a tangle of vines, trees, and stones, with lakes and caves in abundance. I have worked there, too, but the greenwild yields best for our vinemasters."

Before he could speak again, harmonic singing rose to fill the air.

"Chimera!" Krysta stopped. "And many of them. I had forgotten—you have stolen so many from Arda. Why?"

Darkyn's hand stiffened in hers. "We haven't stolen them. We've liberated them. They are a race in their own right, the sacred innocents. By our figuring, they will raise the alarm when the *Barung* makes its move toward us, and they may have a role in driving it back."

Krysta kept pace beside Darkyn. "I didn't mean to offend."

"You did not, *hallas*. I simply forgot your main-planet thinking for a moment. You have blended so well into our ways and beliefs thus far."

At this, Krysta stopped walking. They were still alone but for the yellow flowers, blue-green grass, and thickening trees. A number of Chimera emerged from nearby thickets, heading toward them. Red and gold and lavender, these, singing a bright, soothing morning song.

"Main-planet thinking," Krysta said slowly. "Why does that feel like an insult?"

Darkyn let go her hand and lifted both palms in greeting to the Chimera. "And I meant no offense to you either, *shanna*. The People simply believe differently than main-planet dwellers, that's all."

"But I am to be of The People now, am I not?" Krysta couldn't hold back a smile as the first Chimera reached them. A golden stallion with brilliant purple eyes. It swung wide of Darkyn and came straight to her, nuzzling her neck with its petal-soft nose. She kissed the Chimera without thought, and stroked the silk of its fur and mane as it purred.

It took a moment for her to realize Darkyn was gaping at her.

"What? Have I again broken some law or custom in my ignorance?"

"No." His tone carried more respect, if she wasn't mistaken. "It's just that Chimera living in their natural state avoid most humans. They approach us, but touch is usually reserved to those especially attuned to their ways of being and thinking."

More Chimera crowded around Krysta, nuzzling and humming. She thought she recognized a few of them, perhaps from the villages around Camford. Quietly, she sang back to them, and stroked each offered nose.

Let her new mate figure what to make of it. Perhaps she was attuned to more than he credited.

In the distance, men and women dressed in the garb of farmers and workers of the land began to fill the path. Some went into the orchards. Some, dressed in netted hoods, took a different path, presumably headed into the greenwild. Still others with sun-wraps covering their heads headed away from the orchards.

They rake the drylands, Krysta remembered from earlier talks with Darkyn. *Hearty beings, those.*

She noted how the workers saw their *Ta* and seemed to relax. Many waved. Most stared at her, first with shock, then with growing approval, noting her harmony with the Chimera. No doubt they would speak of it amongst themselves, and the story would spread. The Chimeras approved of the *Ta*'s new mate.

The sacred innocents, she said to herself, trying to memorize the ways of her *sha's* world.

"Thank you," she whispered to the Chimera herd.

They seemed to understand, offering her a few more affectionate nuzzles before moving away to feed off the nearby sweetgrass and tender morning blossoms.

From overhead came the shriek of a falcon, and Krysta startled. Darkyn glanced up into the bright light of big sun and little sister.

"Guardian," he muttered. "She remains unsettled. Come. We'll eat near the orchards this morn."

Krysta sighed.

The falcon wasn't going to give her a smooth path. That much was certain.

Darkyn watched his *hallas* absorb the nuances of her new home, from the curve of the grains to the applefruit of the orchard trees. They feasted on fruits and berries that morning. In the afternoon, he led her to the edge of the drylands, where they lunched with some of the weathered women who raked plantroot from the grit and dust. Soothsayers, most of those old ones, and they took to Krysta like the Chimera had. Touched her. Even touched the unusual leathers of her new jumpsuit. He saw Krysta grit her teeth when a few brushed fingertips across her *pa*—felt the shock of the contact in his own *pa*—but his *shanna*, his made-of-fire bride never flinched nor stepped away. This was good. The women would tell The People of her acceptance, her strength.

She was born to be a leader's mate, or a leader herself. The thought gave him both pleasure and pause.

Could Krysta lead the People, perhaps with Akad, after the *Barung* came and Darkyn did what he was fated to do? He frowned as they crossed the orchards, headed for a closer look at the greenwild. Perhaps that was why fate had brought him a mate at this final hour.

His frown deepened. He knew he should tell her everything, about the *Barung*, about his plans. As his mate, it was her right to know. On the other hand, it was their new-mating time, a splash of joy in a rain of despair. He didn't want to ruin it for her. In truth, he didn't want to ruin it for himself either.

Following an early dinner of vine stew and tubers at the edge of the greenwild, Krysta walked a few steps before Darkyn, brushing long fingers against colored tree barks and leaves strange to her senses.

"*Hallas*," he began, then found his words failing as she turned to face him. So fluid and graceful, and how she sparkled beneath the blaze of big sun and little sister! The white-golden light played off the vines of her *pa*, and Darkyn realized the *firemylk* controlling his desires was waning. His cock strained against his breeches.

"Come," he said hoarsely. "I would show you something."

Krysta remained silent but took his hand, going with him willingly where he led. It might have been madness, but he intended to show her some keys to his plan. Not even his *pao* allies had laid eyes on these secrets, and this woman he had claimed only days ago—he would show her willingly.

"She's a pilot," he murmured to no one, where only he could hear. "It makes sense."

Following the wending trails, they went deeper into the greenwild barrier, where none but the vinemasters usually traveled. Darkyn remained alert for the slither of dragyn lizards or the hunting howl of vinecats. It was early in the day for such creatures to be about, but it was wise to be cautious.

Above him, Guardian circled, an extra pair of wary eyes on Uhr's most dangerous ground.

Krysta never asked him their destination, nor protested the walk. She appeared content at his side, trusting and open—which increased his guilt over what he had and hadn't revealed about the *Barung*.

At last, they reached the massive wooden battlements marking his hidden compound. Krysta might have walked directly into the gate-wall, so well was it hidden amongst the trees and hanging greenery.

"Hold," he said, pulling her back.

Guardian wheeled and gave her lengthy alert call, part of the entry code for the guards on the gate-wall's inner recess. Darkyn supplied the rest, pounding a quick rhythm on the nearest hollowed tree trunk.

The sound of ropes on pulleys creaked through the afternoon breezes, and a door opened near Krysta's elbow—just wide enough to admit them. Darkyn stepped within the secret enclosure and motioned for his new mate.

Krysta didn't hesitate. She entered, eyes wide with the thrill of discovery.

A leader. A warrior. Darkyn felt a surge of pride. *Hallas. My mate.*

At that moment, his mate saw one of The People's greatest secrets.

"By the gods." Her voice held a note of rapture Darkyn preferred to be his and his alone, but he supposed he understood. "Those are the most beautiful ships I've ever seen!"

And then she was off, running toward the sleek two-seater crafts The People had constructed using the combined technologies of all the worlds concerned about the *Barung*. The ships took up most of the room in the circular enclosure, with just enough space left over to allow technologists to work. Along the wall were quarters for guards and observation outposts. The guards had already withdrawn, giving their *Ta* and his mate their privacy. Darkyn knew he could call them with a whistle, or that Guardian could summon them with a warning. He also knew such an alert would be unnecessary.

Showing her good tastes, Krysta went straight to the lead vessel. *Arcus*, The Bow. The others beside it, triangular in shape, slightly smaller but no less impressive and deadly, were *Calamus* and *Telum*, The Arrows. *Arcus* was honed to a fine triangular point, boasting an arc-shaped shield generator in the front, designed to throw a field wide enough to protect all three ships.

"They're… They're *made* of *pa*," Krysta breathed. She shielded her eyes against the glittering silver. The hulls of the ships pulsed and shimmered in response to her voice.

"Yes." Darkyn nodded. "Stable, held in check by a net of ions."

"Long have we spoken of such technology, but I never thought I would live to see it." Krysta reached out and brushed her knuckles against the hull of *Arcus*. "Gods and goddess. My entire body hums when I touch it!"

Darkyn joined her, his excitement mounting in the face of Krysta's thrill. "Would you like to go inside?"

She gave him no answer, only the visible tensing of muscles and widening of eyes, waiting for him to show her how to board.

In the old language, Darkyn asked the ship to open.

Immediately, a portal appeared beside Krysta, and a set of *pa* steps for them to climb.

"Is it—?" she began, whispering as if fearful of speaking the thought aloud.

"Sentient?" Weil nodded. "We believe so, yes. In her own limited way, at least. *Arcus* will admit none but those who have business aboard, and *Telum* follow her lead. I didn't know if she would allow you or not, but it seems everything on Uhr favors you, *hallas*."

Krysta grinned, and in one fluid motion, climbed into the ship's cabin. Darkyn followed, and the breach in the hull sealed itself as if they had never boarded. Darkyn noted a soft hum almost immediately, a sound he had never before heard the ship produce. It sounded…almost like a purr.

"It has more room than I imagined," she said, running her fingertips over the seats and walls. "And I can still see outside as if the ship were made of glass! Can we be seen?"

"No." Weil could not hold back a grin at her look of astonishment. "The hull is like a special mirror, allowing us to look out, but none to look in. There is always room enough for those on board, but for flight, she takes only two. Her speed is ten times that of any known vessel."

"You've flown her?" Krysta sounded awed. "But there are no instruments!"

Darkyn drew a slow breath, then tapped the side of his head. "The controls are here, *shanna*."

Krysta sat down heavily in one of the two fluid seats. Her expression was one of mingled rapture and shock. "The People could have taken Arda at any time with such a weapon as this ship. Do our enemies have them?"

Stiffening without intention, Darkyn said, "These ships are not for petty wars, *hallas*. They have a single purpose — to stop the *Barung*, the Eater of Worlds. Or try to stop it."

"Are you telling me that Or*Ta*, that Bandu, Nosta, Kaerad — all the Council worlds and other worlds, too — have cooperated in the making of these vessels with no intent to use them for their own gain?"

Darkyn sat in the chair opposite his mate and gazed into her narrowed eyes. "You may believe me or not, but good sense will supply the answer. None but the most skilled in telepathy could wield such a weapon. Who but one of The People could fly these creations? The Kaeradi, perhaps, but they have no interest in ship-traveling unless they're dealing with outworld passengers."

"But why?" Krysta leaned forward. Their knees touched. "What do you think you can do against this — this whatever it is?"

Darkyn found himself devoid of words again. The time had come to tell her, but how to make her understand?

He cleared his throat, reminding himself that this woman was a leader in her own right. Perhaps she would understand.

And perhaps I am mad.

"We know the *Barung* is some type of energy source," he said quietly. "We know the ancients encountered it and turned it back once before — apparently through energy then, as well. They could not destroy it."

Krysta leaned back and toyed with the zipper of her jumpsuit. Even with the weight of the moment, Darkyn found this simple gesture highly distracting. Outside, big sun and little sister moved toward rest, filling the cabin with remarkable shades of pink, purple, and red.

"From what we have been able to interpret from artifacts and old writings, the ancients left us a course of action we must follow, with the key points wrapped in the simplest of rhymes."

"When *Barung* returns, six shall lead him home," Krysta intoned. "Blended from the triangle, joined by the stone. Yes. I know the rhyme from Akad. I think I've heard it in my dreams."

Darkyn reined his surprise and managed a nod. "The triangle, we believe, is three planets—Earth, Kaerad, and Arda. In the center was Perth, a world the *Barung* destroyed the first time it came."

He paused, letting this information sink into Krysta's mind. He saw the weight of her thoughts etched into her frown, but left her with her emotion.

"The survivors of Perth settled on Earth, and deliberately bred with the wild telepaths of that planet. Since then, bloodlines have been carefully mingled and cultivated amongst our three telepathic cultures—the Ardani, the Kaeradi, and the descendents of old Perth. We hope that now we have a strength of mind, of psi, that the ancients had not developed. We hope we can attack and contain the dark energy the *Barung* possesses."

Krysta kept her silence for a moment before whispering, "And then?"

"And then we hope that six of us will be able to fly these ships, lead the *Barung* to the site of Perth's destruction. We have reason to believe we can destroy it there."

"That explains the first part of the rhyme, if we assume the stone is the stones borne by many of The People." Krysta nodded toward the tawny gem in

Darkyn's chest. "'When *Barung* returns, six shall lead him home, blended from the triangle, joined by the stone.' And I've gathered that the Chimera and their song play some role, which explains the next few lines. 'Let loose the gentle innocents, for music soothes the shield.'"

Darkyn felt the dryness in his throat as she approached the point of the matter.

"'Feed him on The People's blood and drive him to the field.' So the field is the place where Perth once turned in space. What of the feeding, then? 'Feed him on The People's blood?' What does that mean, Darkyn?"

He found he couldn't answer her, and then he realized his silence was answer enough.

"You believe death will be necessary. Some sort of blood sacrifice from The People." She stood slowly, hovering above him like a silvery vision against a silvery background. Her voice dropped to a whisper. "You plan for the blood to be yours."

"I am *Ta*," he said with what little conviction he could muster. It seemed the only answer, inadequate though it was.

Krysta sat back down and put her face in her hands. Darkyn reached toward her, but felt her wish to be left in her solitude for a moment. He had the strangest sense that *Arcus* would have changed her hull's fundamental shape to block his hand had he persisted.

Big sun and little sister faded completely, and the ship immediately supplied a soft amber hue, like candlelight. It even flickered. Did *Arcus* think of that, or was the ship drawing from Krysta's mind?

Darkyn felt more unease. He sensed he had lost control of the ship somehow, that he was outnumbered.

Two powerful females were set against him now—and not to forget Guardian, either, who no doubt perched on a branch nearby.

At long last, Krysta raised her eyes to meet his. "I've realized we both have our secrets, my new *sha*. Very well. I'll tell you mine in my own time, and soon—but hear me. You will not sacrifice yourself to kill this *Barung*. I'll find an alternative."

"No one can speak the future with confidence." He reached to brush her cheek, but she eluded his touch.

When she clenched her fists, eyes blazing, Darkyn heard a low growl from the ship's hull. He decided not to press the issue. Best to let his made-of-fire *shanna* adjust to facts in her own time. She would see reason when the time came. Of that, he had no doubt.

"The elixir wears thin," Krysta whispered, her voice heavy with frustration and perhaps tears.

Her words loosed the laces on the last of Darkyn's control. He moved forward, kneeling before Krysta's chair. She opened her knees to permit him to hold her, then permitted his kiss as well.

Her lips felt like water on parched skin, soothing and cooling, then heating all at once. Nevertheless, when she locked eyes with him, her expression held no hint of forgiveness. Only flinty resolve.

Before he could speak or master the situation, her hands plunged into his pants. He felt her fingers grip his cock, squeezing gently but firmly as he kissed her again. His erection, already prominent, swelled to unmanageable proportions. Her hold on him was maddeningly perfect. She started at the base, cupping his bollocks, then sliding from stem to tip and back again in a fluid pumping motion.

Mating fervor in a pureblooded Ardani female. Is there anything sweeter?

"You taste like honeyfruit," he murmured, biting her ear and neck, struggling to unzip her jumpsuit despite his brain's centered focus on the action of her hands.

Her breasts sprang free, tempting his mouth. *pa* glittered on her skin like the wild vines all around the secret enclosure, now only shadows barely visible through the walls of *Arcus*. Krysta's *pa* pulsed with each pump on his cock—and the ship's hull seemed to pulse at the same interval.

"What are you doing, *hallas*?"

"Making sure you understand something. You will not tear me from my home and family, give me what I've forever desired, and take it away." Her stroking of his shaft became merciless, fast and gut-flaming. His bollocks felt like engines, swelling with power and purpose. "I am starting to love you, Darkyn Weil, and I don't surrender what I love."

Darkyn was vaguely aware of heat on his thighs and calves. When he glanced down, his breeches were gone. Burned to ash without so much as a blister on his flesh or the slightest smoke. The remnants vanished, absorbed into *Arcus*.

Krysta pumped him again, bringing his seed with a violent explosion. He watched as the white liquid landed on her vines of *pa*, watched as it vanished into the silver rivers, consumed just as his breeches had been.

Something about *Arcus* was giving his mate power beyond reckoning. As he sat on his knees, spent, almost gasping, Darkyn thought to be relieved that his *hallas* had said she loved him. The many gods forbid she felt otherwise, for certain.

Krysta kept her gaze on him, steady and smoldering, as she stood before him and unzipped her jumpsuit the rest of the way. He reached up and pulled the leather down past her hips, to her ankles, gazing hungrily at her breasts, belly, and mound as she stepped out of the garment.

Her power excited him, challenged him. Her resolve gave his heart a balm he had never known.

I am starting to love you, Darkyn Weil…

Fervor or no, he knew he would die for her, kill for her. And yet, the needs of The People, his people…

"Think of heavy burdens later," she murmured as she sat back down and spread her legs. "Think of me now."

Krysta gasped as Darkyn seized her legs, almost roaring his desire as he buried his face in her *pa*-coated quim. She ached for his tongue, his mouth, and he gave them to her fiercely, flicking hard against her clit as he sucked and nibbled the wet, tender flesh all around. His grip on her thighs ached and gave her thrills all at once. She leaned back against the chair *Arcus* allowed her to occupy, aware she was in tune with the truly living vessel, feeling the ship's will and power possess her even as her mate did.

Arcus charged her *pa* with new power. She saw and felt the world in ways she couldn't describe — the sound of colors, the rhythm of smells.

Darkyn thrust three fingers deep in her channel, and she cried out as her sensitive walls clenched around them. Orgasm flooded her quickly, too quickly. She wanted more—*needed* more. He slid his hand back and forth, pressing upward as he sucked her clit. With the other hand, he kneaded her *pa*-gloved nipple until she came again, bucking against the force of his thrusts.

Acting more on primal instinct than conscious thought, Krysta shoved her mate backward then, stood and turned, and bent down holding the seat. Her breasts rubbed against the strange *pa*-infused fabric, burning and crackling with each touch.

Darkyn needed no instruction or invitation. He claimed her hard and fast, grabbing her hips and driving into her quim from behind like an untamed beast. She braced against the chair with all her strength to keep her feet. His powerful movements lifted her feet from the ship's floor with each thrust.

Outside *Arcus*, vines swayed in the eerie night gray of Uhr. Guards moved about, unaware of the action in the ship. Krysta sensed Guardian's ever-watchful eyes, staring from some unknown location. The bird could see into the ship, she was certain. If *Arcus* permitted this, Guardian must be safe, all other factors aside.

See me, then, she thought to the falcon, and to any human or alien woman who might have known Darkyn, or even wanted to know him. *He is mine now, evermore. Don't think to interfere. I share only what I wish of him. See me!*

"Deeper," Krysta gasped, pleading more than demanding. Her skin pulsed and ached. Her nipples throbbed against the ship's chair as her vision shimmered. She wanted to feel her mate enter the depths of her body. She wanted to swallow him, to be sure she could never lose him.

"*Shanna*," he growled, finding the sweet recesses she wanted him to share. "*Hallas*. Mine. My woman. I am beginning to love you, too."

He let go her hips and seized her burning nipples.

Krysta came with instant screaming shudders. Wave after hot wave of pleasure crashed on her consciousness. Darkyn's seed shot into her, filling her, marking her most intimate regions as his.

She raised her head to howl, but in that one perfect instant, she could see the distant reaches of Ardani space. See the malevolent, oddly shining blackness that was the *Barung*.

This must be how Darkyn sees it with his special eyes, she thought in that split-second, and knew it to be true.

The past rushed at her with the speed and force of another orgasm, consuming her. She saw bits and pieces of a puzzle too great to understand—old Arda and old Ardani. The Kaeradi with their stones, and so many without. Strange, supple beings that could only be the Perth survivors Darkyn mentioned. Reeling through time, all of the people and places and pictures she could scarcely understand. Everything moved so slow and yet unbearably fast, all coming to a point here, now, on Uhr, with Darkyn in the center and her beside him.

I won't lose him, she thought, desperation equal to determination as she collapsed forward on the chair, only to feel her mate gather her into his infinitely powerful arms.

"You will not die," she whispered aloud.

From outside *Arcus,* and seemingly within the ship as well, came the feral cry of a falcon.

At last, Krysta sensed an accord with Guardian. In this purpose, they could unite.

Chapter Eight

Almost two full stellar weeks after her first encounter with *Arcus*, Krysta woke naked and alone on the dirt floor of Darkyn's bathchamber. The morning was filled with Chimera song, lightening her heart and mind even as she ticked off yet another set of plans to force her brothers to see and to believe what was happening in the universe around them.

They trusted her, yes—but now she had joined with a man they believed to be their lifelong enemy. Would they still have enough faith in her opinions to accept something as fantastic as the *Barung*? As *Barung*, her mind informed her. She couldn't stop thinking of the entity as human, as male.

They hadn't even believed Akad on that accord. Superstition and doom-saying, they had told him the many times he had broached the subject. Finally, they had asked him not to bring it up again. The Royal Fleet had investigated the area Akad described, but found nothing—sensed nothing.

Krysta understood why now. The *Barung* was, as yet, beyond the psi-senses of a normal Ardani. Ki and Fari and all of Arda with their wisdom and arrogance, had come to believe that their senses were so powerful as to know all, to see all. Therefore, if they couldn't sense it, it must not exist.

Sighing, Krysta brought herself fully awake, then smiled despite her heavy thoughts.

The night before had been spent as every night since she arrived, feasting and touching and making love with her *sha* until neither of them had the ability to move. Their fervor was at last easing, but in its stead a new sort of fervor was growing—that born of deep affection and blistering desire. They had at least used different rooms in the house—Darkyn's tidy bedchamber, atop his spread of hides and fur—and the main room on floor cushions so soft they felt like clouds.

Her favorite, though, had to be the bathchamber where she now lay. Krysta loved the heat, the steam, and it gave her relief from Uhr's drier-than-dry air. She could shout and moan with much greater force.

Grinning anew, Krysta felt the heat of big sun and little sister. The light filtering in through high-placed windows and the dome was bright, turning everything a startling, warm yellow-white.

Her *sha's* powerful, elemental scent still filled her nose, and the salt and sweat of their lovemaking lingered on her lips. Her body ached in the sweetest way as she ran her fingers over her skin and realized yet again that her *pa*-coated nipple wasn't bothering her as much as usual. The lips of her quim also seemed calm. Like she'd had a large dose of elixir, but with none of the side effects.

In quiet moments such as these, she had a sense of detachment, of unreality, that her life had taken such sharp turns. Her roles on Arda, as Captain, as sister, as sister-by-marriage, seemed so distant.

Will you let a few weeks with a kidnapping Outlander change your destiny?

That was Ki's voice as she imagined it. Fari's would have been naught but a growl with interspersed swearing.

And what would she say?

"Yes," she answered aloud to her imagined brothers, both of them, scowls and all. Krysta had never been a fainting-female sort, or giggly, or blushing. More than that, she had never been indecisive. Her time as Captain of the Home Guard sharpened her wit and instinct, as well as her belief in her own ability to choose.

Another woman might have been full of doubts, or torn by angst. Krysta was simply torn by desire, and by a growing need to communicate with the rest of her family first to let them know where she was, and second to convince them of the danger coming in the days ahead.

She needed to show them that Darkyn Weil was no threat to Arda or her family. He was her family, too. For now, for always. He had claimed her, but she had claimed him, too. Without doubt, he would be surprised to learn her identity, when she could bring herself to tell him. He would cope, yes, just as she coped with being his hostage, and then discovering the possibility that he might shed his own life's blood to stop the approaching evil.

But Krysta Tul'Mar no longer thought of herself as a hostage, or her mate as a potential sacrifice. She also didn't think of herself as a Tul'Mar, not in the complete, absorbed sense she once had.

"It's my turn," she murmured as she dove into the pool to cleanse herself before dancing the *Kon'pa*. The fragrant streams closed over her, cleansed her and soothed her sore muscles. Even as the pains eased, she wanted nothing more than to make them ache again. With her *sha*.

And she would be having a say to him about leaving her alone during their new-mating time, even at this late point, and even if only for a while.

Warm water caressed her shoulders and neck, her nipples and belly. She surfaced and breathed in the sweet, moist scent of Uhr's flowers and trees.

"Uhr," she said aloud before once more diving down, deep, deep into the pool, stretching her body to its fullest length. The water below grew darker and darker, and warmer still, swirling up in jets and eddies. Some part of Krysta realized she might be able to follow its feeder streams as she had sought to do the night she first arrived — but that desire was fully gone.

Instead, she enjoyed the feel of the water on her skin, the hotter bursts especially. She halted her dive and floated in the near darkness, gazing back up at the surface. Her quim pulsed as more bubbling jets moved through her legs.

Kicking, she stared upward again, fingering her swelling clit. It took only seconds to drive her arousal to a level only her *sha* could fill.

Where was he, damn it?

Had Akad come into the bath this morning to get him?

Her sex-drunken brain could barely remember.

Though she did have a smile at the thought of sucking Akad's cock while her mate thrust inside from behind her. And another wild thought of Elise and Georgia, one on each nipple as Akad and Darkyn Weil had their way with her.

Soon, when this madness has ended and life can find its normal rhythm again, it will be time to close the circle. To be a whole and complete family.

She was back to thinking only of her *sha* and his many, many talents. Her mind filled with images of their lovemaking, of his cock plunging deep inside her core, driving upward toward her center as he rocked her with his muscled arms.

She quickened the strokes on her clit, rubbing hard and fast. She wanted him. Needed him at that basic, total level. In her mind's eye, she took him in her mouth and drank him dry. Then she took him in her quim, lying back as he held her down and pounded into her. Rougher. Harder.

Krysta felt ravenous. She wanted all of him, over and over. As she rubbed her clit faster and faster, she drifted toward the water's surface—and for the briefest of moments, she thought she sensed Georgia and Elise. Both reaching for their nether lips and clits in a mimic of what she was doing.

Krysta? Elise's sharp, strong psi-voice shot through her consciousness like an arrow as she shuddered from her orgasm.

Yes! There was a connection, however slight. Images flew back and forth, wordless. Her niece, born! Her brothers, beside themselves with distress. Fari doing something to ruin his relationship with Georgia before they could be joined, then making amends at the Festival.

Krysta felt a rush of joy and allowed a cautious stream of her own emotions to flow through the breach. Desire, satisfaction, joining. Then by accident, Akad's image. She moved toward the surface of the pool, lungs burning, halting her thoughts before she showed Elise the true face of her new *sha*.

I'm not ready, she thought. *This is still mine and only mine, for now.*

From Elise came a single muffled question, as if a wet towel had been laid over the thought. *Are you safe and happy?*

"Yes," Krysta answered in her mind and aloud. "Have no worries. We'll all be together soon."

And then a roaring, gnashing darkness burst into her mind so painful that she gave an airless, chest-crushing scream. All motion toward the top of the pool ceased. Krysta felt like she'd been shot with an energy weapon that severed her head from her body.

Like something — *someone* — was trying to kill her.

Limp, lungs filling with water, consciousness draining away, she drifted back down, and down in the water. Fighting seemed pointless. She wasn't strong enough. She was already drowning.

Rough hands grabbed her, yanked her from the pool, and dragged her harshly over the lip and back to the dirt floor. Sunslight slapped her eyes, sobering her mind and beginning to dispel the pool's murderous darkness. She coughed and spit water, tried to stand, but the same hands that saved her cruelly forced her to stay on her knees.

Darkness still clawed at her, but it seemed put at bay by the brightness of big sun and little sister. Soon it faded, leaving only lingering pain in her head.

"Who were you in contact with?" demanded a male voice she instantly recognized and just as instantly despised. All fog cleared from her mind.

The bastard who'd murdered Kolot!

Krysta looked up, still spitting out water and clutching her sides — but glaring and ready to kill the murderer if she could. The big hulk was standing right in front of her. His companion, the one who had helped kidnap her from Arda, was holding her down. An Outlander female stood beside the murderer, hand over mouth. She looked young, more girl than woman, and horrified.

"Beg pardon, Lady," she said in a mouse's voice. "The *Ta* sent me to see to your needs in his absence, but when I found the chamber empty, I thought you had met with harm! I would not have called the guards if I had known—"

"Guards?" Krysta couldn't help a derisive snort. She managed to turn her head to look at Fergilla Number Two who had her pinned. "These men are not fit to guard a herd of besotted Chimera. Take your hands off me, or I swear I will make you regret it."

She didn't care that she was naked, with no weapons but her wits and fists. She'd find a way.

Krysta heard soldier-force in her voice, as well as the confidence of a woman who trusted her *sha* not to leave her in another man's hands too long. She made a rudimentary effort to touch her mate's mind and indeed brushed something like it—Akad, perhaps? Or her *sha*. Was he drugged? Did he still need elixir to manage a few hours of sanity?

An eerie keening filled the bathchamber, and Fergilla Number Two released her suddenly and stepped away.

"What are you doing?" Fergilla Number One, the murdering bastard, asked his companion as a black falcon sailed into the room. He moved to grab Krysta himself, but the bird landed on the back of his neck, talons first. Powerful wings instantly pounded him about the ears and face as he swore and reached back, trying to grab his feathered attacker.

Krysta didn't hesitate.

Springing to her feet, she delivered a thundering, crushing kick to Fergilla Number One's bollocks. He doubled over and tumbled unceremoniously into the pool they had dragged her out of only moments before.

The falcon, preternaturally fast, swooped upward over the water, circled the room, and landed neatly on the edge of the sink. Feeling joy at their growing kinship, Krysta raised a fist of unity toward the predatory bird before wheeling on Fergilla Number Two.

He threw up his hands in the age-old Ardani gesture of no-combat.

"Kolot had his hands raised," Krysta said, her words low and deadly. "It didn't save him, did it?"

A new keening noise rose in the bathchamber, and Krysta realized the girl was crying out. She was hearing the sound almost in slow time, her battle senses were so focused.

On the sink, the falcon took up the call. It sounded like an accusation, a shaming condemnation.

Fergilla Number Two actually trembled.

Commotion at the door caught her attention, the girl running out as people came in, but Krysta noted the newcomers only to be certain they weren't charging in her direction. She didn't take her gaze off the kidnapping bastard with his hands raised. Behind her, in the pool, Fergilla Number One groaned and sputtered, still no threat as yet, since he hadn't managed to reach the pool's edge.

"Stay back from her!" Darkyn Weil's command silenced the falcon instantly and brought complete stillness to the room. His voice was slurred, but no less forceful. "If you touch my *hallas*, I will cut off your hands!"

"Be at ease," came Akad's calm voice, seemingly from great distance. "They mean her no harm."

"She was deep in the pool," said Fergilla Number One as he struggled to swim. His voice had a satisfyingly thin, reedy quality. Soon he would have no voice at all, Krysta thought, since she would kill him when he managed to get out and find his feet.

"Communicating," said Fergilla Number Two. He tapped his thick head on the side.

"Psi-dampeners do not reach to deep water." Akad sighed. "Krysta, did you speak to your family?"

She spared the priest a glance and wished she could wither him with her fury. Darkyn stood beside him, supported on his arm, clearly medicated to manage his remaining mating fervor. He was dressed well in hides and belts, almost ceremonially formal, and he was wearing his double-bladed amber axe. His expression was feral and murderous as he glanced from brute to brute, sizing up the situation. Krysta knew that if Akad had not been with him, if he had not been drugged, he might have dismembered the men who had bothered her.

Somehow, this only angered Krysta more.

A man armed during new-mating. What in the name of nine hells was going on in this mad place? Who would let a fervor-bound male have access to his weapons?

Fools.

"If I spoke to my loved ones," she growled to Akad, careful to omit names even in her rage, "it is my business, is it not? Do they not have a right to know I am alive and well, and that I have chosen to stay here with my soul's mate?"

Akad murmured an assent and seemed surprised, or relieved. With his damned stoic countenance, who could tell?

Her *sha* stirred at Akad's side, and looked at her more directly. Almost wide-eyed. Suspicious, yes, healthily so. Also pleased and aroused. He had an erection despite treatment with elixir.

Good.

Krysta scowled at him, hoping her nakedness tortured him beyond measure. She had half a mind to touch herself right there, before all the male onlookers. It would serve him right.

But there were other matters at hand.

"I want life for life," she demanded in the formal, high speech of the People. "I claim the ancient rights of vengeance, to honor the memory of Kolot, my second in command, who fell with his hands raised. You do follow the ancient rites, yes? A commander may claim rights to execution for unjust deaths, even in battle?"

Fergilla Number Two flinched, and Number One sputtered in the pool. Akad stiffened, as did Darkyn, as much as a man could stiffen on a hefty dose of *firemylk*.

"Yes," Akad answered without hesitating, and Krysta figured it was because the priest had known her for so long. She was close to killing both of Darkyn's men with her bare hands if she could, fueled by indignation, fury, and the remnants of fervor. He probably hoped to forestall her actions, at least for a time.

"Get out," Krysta ordered the fool in the pool, who was, in point of fact, trying his best to do just that. "Would you let a single kick drown you? What a weak, useless piece of dung you are, cowering in the water. It is no wonder you killed a man with his hands raised."

Akad and Darkyn were approaching. Krysta expected them to begin to argue with her, or for the brutes to begin to plead their case. Instead, the big hulk standing near her simply lowered his head while the one in the pool stopped struggling to hoist himself to the rim.

The priest paused at the pool and helped the murderer out. The murderer crawled over to his companion, pulled him up to stand. When he reached his full height, though, the man stooped. He stood in that posture, like a chastised child, before Krysta, Darkyn, and Akad.

"Brand? Kadmyr? Speak the truth to me, cousins. What have you done?" Darkyn questioned them in slurred, over-controlled tones. The big men hung their heads further, chins on chest. "Did you kill a soldier with his hands raised?"

Krysta found herself relaxing. She had expected many things in the split-second she attacked, but such complete support wasn't among them. Nor such complete surrender from the murdering brutes.

She let her arms drop.

Cousins.

These two were her *sha's* family.

How painful for him!

Krysta could see weary horror and deep, abiding anger etched in every line of the stern face she had come to know in tenderness and passion. She could also see that Darkyn intended to do the right thing, whatever it might be — and whoever the wrong-doers might be.

He was a fair man, her *sha*. On top of being sexy and powerful and wonderfully dominant in all the right ways—he was also honorable. She had known this from the things Akad had shown her the night she came to Uhr, but now, she saw it for herself. She felt it. She had joined with an honorable outlaw. *Outlander.*

Ta. Ta'Tanna Kon'pa.

A new awareness stirred inside her, giving her an older translation for the phrase than "Chief of The People." She heard it as keeper. Keeper of the living substance of the universe.

Yes, said a voice that seemed neither male nor female, but older than time. Beyond time. Krysta startled, for a moment forgetting her present and her purpose as phrases from the ancient rhyme drummed in her brain. '*Six shall lead him home, blended from the triangle, joined by the stone, let loose the gentle innocents…*'

It played out in the lyrical ancient Ardani language until the falcon keened, driving it back. Krysta almost sagged from relief and forcefully closed her mind from further intrusion.

Steam from the pool filled the bathchamber.

She tensed.

Had she missed anything?

Quick glances at the faces of her *sha* and Akad, and even the bastard guards, told her she had not.

Brand, the murderer, was the first to speak. "Yes, *Ta.*"

He hesitated, then coughed. Hesitated again. With a heavy whisper, he admitted. "Her soldier surprised me. Without thought. I killed him even though his hands were raised."

"Without control," Akad said sadly.

"I had no time to stop my brother," Kadmyr confessed, shame evident in his dark eyes.

"Neither of you should have been there," Darkyn said. "I had called you back. The mission failed."

"We thought—" Kadmyr began, then stopped himself.

This is an old battle, Krysta realized, seeing her brother Ki dressing down her brother Fari for taking idiot's chances. and vice-versa.

"On your knees," Darkyn commanded in a voice ragged with pain and disappointment.

Kadmyr and Brand knelt without hesitation.

Each raised their head, looked directly at Krysta, and murmured, "We are sorry for wrongs against you and yours."

She gazed back at them, studying their eyes for any sign of dissimulation or manipulation. There was none. Then, they turned around, still on their knees, showing their vulnerable backs to her in gestures of absolute surrender.

Darkyn faced her then, clearly as *Ta* as much as her soul's mate. He unstrapped his axe and handed it to her without comment.

She took it, almost overbalanced by its weight.

"A wrong has been done," Akad intoned. "You may claim payment. A life for a life. The choice is yours."

Krysta couldn't help gaping at Akad and Darkyn for a moment. Both turned their backs on her and knelt, as was true to the ancient rite. The *Ta* and the high priest, also accepting responsibility for the conduct of their own.

Her part now was to select a life to claim in payment for Kolot's.

The axe felt overly heavy as she walked a small circle, amazed — and pleased — by how seriously the men took their traditions of honor and justice. There was no hypocrisy here. Only a genuine mistake, and genuine regret.

Kill the Ta.

The thought came like a strike of black lightning. It was so overwhelming that Krysta actually turned toward her *sha* and hefted the axe as best she could, all the while crying out inside with horror and resistance.

Kill the Ta.

The sexless voice returned, murmuring, but she couldn't hear it.

What she did hear was her own will telling her to *fight. Fight it. It's not true. It's not you.*

Kill the Ta.

Kill the Ta!

Swaying, arms trembling, Krysta fought with the black cloud around her brain. It was trying to confuse her, blanket her choice and take it from her. If she had full control of herself, she would have screamed with rage or called out to Darkyn or Akad or anyone who might help her.

As it was, Krysta forced her eyes away from her mate's vulnerable neck.

The black cloud in her mind bellowed in protest, equaled only by the sexless voice roaring back at it.

Get out of my head, Krysta told the two forces, slowly, carefully, with as much psi-strength as she could muster.

They continued to yell back and forth across her consciousness.

Krysta steeled herself, bracing her knees and elbows. With every ounce of psi-energy she possessed, she focused on the two forces and emitted a single mental order.

GET OUT OF MY HEAD!

A sound like thunder startled her as the dual presence departed. She stumbled, letting the axe down to the chamber floor to steady her. All around, the four men still sat, heads down. Obviously, they hadn't heard the argument inside her, or the thunder. She shivered, then tried to regroup.

Whatever was happening, whatever was attacking her mind, she would need to discuss it with Akad just as soon as she settled the issue of Kolot's honor. Breathing hard, she studied Brand and Kadmyr from behind. Even through her rattled distress, she sensed they were much like Fari, indeed, before tragedy taught Fari to always take his time, to never allow himself to lose control.

Would Kolot want one of them killed to avenge him? True enough, he had no love for Outlanders. But blood for blood would do little to restore anyone's honor, or honor anyone's memory.

Krysta let go the axe and let it clatter to the chamber floor.

"Get up," she instructed. "All of you."

The four men rose and faced her, still expressionless.

"My choice is this," she said with a spurt of her usual confidence. "Kadmyr will go to Arda and offer himself to the family of Kolot in service. He had many children. His soul's mate will require much assistance. Do you agree to these terms to spare your brother's life?"

Kadmyr nodded.

Brand looked miserable. "I should do this. The crime was mine."

"No." Krysta shook her head. "His *shanna* would never accept your presence. She would kill you, perhaps feel some closure, but still be without the support she needs."

"*Ta'shanna* is as wise as the *Ta*," Brand acquiesced, paying her an ancient compliment along with a slight bow. Then he turned to his *Ta* and lowered his head again.

"Go to your cabin," Darkyn instructed. "Remain there until I tell you otherwise. I have much to consider and accomplish these next days. After that, I will decide what to do with you."

To Kadmyr, he said, "The Tul'Mars may kill you when you arrive."

Kadmyr stood stoic and nodded.

"They will not," said Akad quickly, before Krysta could reveal her identity as she fully intended to do. The priest cut her a warning glance, holding back her confession.

Why? she wondered, but too many years of trusting him held her silent.

"I will send a scroll with you, giving explanation. The most the widow will do is reject you, or perhaps deal you some bruises. The Tul'Mars will not intervene."

Kadmyr nodded, remaining silent, eyes straight forward.

Akad took him by the elbow. "Come. I will help you ready for the journey, and then come back to assist my brother in readying for the *pao*."

Another pointed glance from Akad told Krysta to make use of the time they would have in the interim, to relieve the mating urges swelling yet again.

When the priest had gone, Krysta faced her *sha* feeling a mix of respect and awe, coupled with renewed fury...and yes, desire. And a little bit of fear and dread, remembering her murderous impulses earlier.

No. Not me. That wasn't me, I would never do that.

"Why did you leave me with no word of where you were going?" she demanded, shoving her fears aside with the help of renewed Chimera song drifting in the distance, somewhere outside the cabin. Seemingly all around it. "Why did you take elixir instead of relieving your desires with me before you left—as you should have?"

"I want you." Darkyn's husky words touched her as surely as his fingers. "Later for explanations."

Clearly reading her furious gaze, he added, "Please?"

Chapter Nine

Darkyn struggled out of his clothing and held his breath as his *hallas* approached, virtually shooting fire from her eyes. The elixir he had taken—useless. Already run its course. Rehearsing for the *pao* be damned. The fate of the known universe be damned. He had to spend some time with Krysta.

If she didn't try to kill him for leaving her alone at so inopportune a time. He pointedly tossed his garments over his axe, as if to hide it.

Krysta's unabashed nakedness thrilled him, though he knew it was custom for modern Ardani women to take no shame in an unclothed state, even around strangers. The People had a few more reservations—but at the moment, modern felt finer than fine to Darkyn. Though if Brand and Kadmyr had seemed to enjoy her overmuch, he might have beheaded them.

"I don't take well to being abandoned at such a sacred time without giving you leave," Krysta said in a low, sultry voice that doubled the pain in his cock. "Explain yourself, *sha.*"

This last word she said with a definitive bite.

Darkyn reflexively covered his painful erection with both hands as she approached. Two parts of his nature went to war: dominating *Ta* and simple man in love.

In love and in heat, he corrected himself. He studied the fiery creature before him, her petal-soft skin alight with silver from her striking cheek-to-toe *pa* marking. His own *pa* burned, as did the stone in his chest.

"You were a commander of men and women, my *hallas*," he said huskily. "You well know some responsibilities cannot wait, even for natural—and intense—passions. Akad was putting me through my paces, making certain I am fit for duties later this week, when our many interstellar guests arrive."

Krysta halted an arm's length from him. She seemed to consider his words, discard them, then consider them again. Two parts of her at war as well? The commander and the woman?

That thought only fueled Darkyn's passion. If his made-of-fire bride felt division in her nature, surely he could help her meld her energies into one undeniable force.

"Enough of this," he growled, feeling the ancient madness of the fervor creeping once more through his blood. "You should trust me to see to your best interests. To ours. You should know I would not leave you now, during new-mating, unless I could not avoid it."

"And you trust me for nothing," Krysta growled back.

Darkyn saw the gleam of fervor in her eyes just before she sprang at him. He caught her, half-surprised, half-enraged at the challenge. Old biology. Feral biology. An Ardani female in full fervor, yes, gods. Nothing sweeter.

The two of them hit the ground hard, taking Darkyn's breath. Krysta landed on top of him, her hands at his throat.

"You still keep me prisoner here, though I have given myself and my heart fully to you." She bit his shoulder, his ear. Her *pa* joined with his, her lips joined with his, her hands moving from his neck up into his hair. Fighting for breath, Darkyn felt fire melt into fire as their bodies became one from head to toe.

"You leave me with guards and attendants like some helpless, flighty female without her own brain, her own will." She bit him again. "I've had enough. I'm your *shanna*. I've accepted you. Now accept me!"

His cock was a misery, needing relief and sanctuary. Without a second thought, he upset Krysta's balance and flipped her over, bracing his arms beside her head as he tried to settle between her clamped thighs.

"Spread your legs," he commanded, rubbing his chest against the hard nubs of her nipples. *pa* crackled between them.

She pushed against his tooth-marked shoulders with her fists. "Make me."

Darkyn kissed her, consumed her mouth in his as she gripped his shoulders and bit his lip, fueling the fire in chest and cock. Using just his strength and no energy bonds, he grabbed her wrists and forced her arms over her head. In the same movement, he used his knee to push her legs apart.

"Why do you challenge me?" he asked, rubbing his cock on the wet lips of her quim. "Do you enjoy a fight?"

"I'm a warrior," she answered simply, and bucked against his positioned cock, sucking it in so fast and deep that it was his turn to gasp.

"You're a woman, here, now, with me." He pulled back out, grabbing her hip with his free hand to control her.

"I don't know what I am anymore," she grumbled. "Don't leave me again without telling me you're going. No more confinement. No more secrets."

Darkyn studied the silvery-black eyes of his *hallas*, weighing the merit of her words. As his stone made contact with the *pa* on her chest, he caught visions of them coupling outdoors, beside rivers, in rivers, in jungles, on mountain plateaus. Images of others joining their pleasure bombarded him. The two women he had seen at Camford—Elise and Georgia, those names came to him easily. His brother Akad.

With the fervor easing, Darkyn took no offense at these fantasies like an off-worlder might. To each family, their own freedom. Though he could scarcely see himself mating with the women of the Tul'Mar Clan, even to please Krysta...

The thought trailed off into stunned nothingness, taking his arousal with it.

Krysta realized the wrongness in his lack of motion. The fire in her expression dimmed, and she gave him a look of pure concern.

"What is it?" And then absurdly, "Did I hurt you?"

Darkyn felt like his world had narrowed to the few stellar inches surrounding the two of them. He let her go and stood over her, and still she gazed up at him innocently, seeming confused.

"Get up," he said darkly, no play in the words. No play in his heart, not anywhere.

She complied, getting slowly to her feet.

"What is it?" Her tone reflected nervousness now, perhaps some fear.

Of what? Him? Of those secrets she mentioned once before, then accidentally shared?

"How could you not tell me?" he asked quietly, using his psi abilities to switch off the dampers and summon his brother. He took a step back from her with a sense like wheels turning in his head. "I could understand at first, the way you were brought here against your will, but have we not shared enough for me to earn your honesty?"

Awareness was breaking across her lovely face as Akad entered the room.

Darkyn turned on his brother. "You knew, didn't you? You knew she was a Tul'Mar, and you let me join with her without warning?"

"I wanted to tell you," Krysta said dryly. Darkyn wouldn't look at her, but he figured her for chagrined, or still afraid. "Akad advised against it—"

She cut herself off.

A wave of fervor-enhanced rage blazed through Darkyn as he studied his brother. "Why?"

Akad's expression flickered for a moment, to uncertainty, to a dark sort of frustration. After the longest moments Darkyn could remember, his brother said, "The ancients forbade it. It wasn't yet part of the pattern. But what is, is. There's no putting milk back in the teat."

"What?" Krysta's irritated question came out at the same moment Darkyn's did.

"Though you have little reason to, you will both have to trust me in this." Akad's shoulders sagged. "I have long been hearing and respecting the voices of the ancients."

He looked up sharply, as if daring either of them to scoff. "I think you've heard them, too. A strong voice that sometimes comes as one, and sometimes comes as many, sexless and ageless. It fights the darkness, and it fights our doubts."

At that description, Darkyn felt his rage deflate. He wanted to argue with his brother, tell him he was stupid and wrong, but the stone in his chest was burning in a familiar, cold, and painful way. Telling him he had to listen.

To the truth.

Krysta was not arguing either, which meant she likely had heard the voice of the ancients, too, or something similar.

Darkyn opened his mouth to speak, but his brother cut him off with resonant, eerie words. "Will you for once be silent and trust the will of others? Not all things lie within your hands, Darkyn Weil."

As Akad spoke that startlingly familiar admonishment, a golden glow surrounded him in the shape of a triangle. Darkyn had a sense of *presence*, of otherworldly occupation, and the feeling that all that had happened concerning the *Barung*—and all that would happen—was now on an exact time-table not of their making. It would be their task to do the work, to rise to the almost unimaginable challenge, but the field and the players, the nature of the game and its ticking clock, was not of their making or under their control. It was theirs only in the sense that they could fail their parts in the grand scheme, and thus fail the universe.

Gods, what an awful thing to know, though I think I've known it at some level all along. Darkyn grimaced, feeling the pressures of the universe settle along every nerve ending and sector of flesh.

The sense of otherworldly presence departed, leaving only his brother in its wake.

For the first time Darkyn could remember, Akad looked tired, and frightened, and in need of comfort. He literally sagged where he stood, looking bowed at the shoulder from the pressures mounted on his mind.

Darkyn moved to him without thinking, taking his *a'mun* twin into a firm clasp. "How long have you borne this alone?" he whispered, feeling Krysta join the embrace and welcoming her presence. She felt suddenly close to him again, all guise and discord vanished at the shocking sight of Akad's weariness and his…his…aloneness.

As the three of them stood there, it occurred to Darkyn that his *shanna*'s other family ties truly did not matter to him. It was clear that she had surrendered much of that old identity, that she was struggling to find her new way, her new role.

Her new self.

She was just as much a part of his family now as any. No matter, really, for he would have loved her and claimed her all the same, just with more self-doubt and angst and difficulty. As it was, the way to the truth had been smoothed. By his brother, as usual. Akad the priest. Akad the healer. Akad the *a'mun*, who was supposed to be the weaker of the two of them.

"How long?" he repeated, feeling a dread of knowing all the same. "Tell me."

"I have heard the voice—the voices—since I was a child." Akad's forehead rested against Darkyn's and Krysta's. He was the only one of them still clothed, but Krysta was remedying that with one deft hand, pulling off the brown robes to expose Akad's *pa*-patterned skin. Great ropes of silver glittered beneath her touch, and she traced them as if she knew them well.

Darkyn felt the greatest relief that his *shanna* knew his brother in such a way, that she was already comfortable with him, and he with her. What had enraged him weeks before gave him peace now, and hope that they might bring Akad some pleasure to distract him from his many burdens.

I have been a selfish man, Darkyn psi-spoke to his twin. *Focused only on my own worries. All the while, you have carried the weight of the ancients within you. Forgive me, a'mun. Share what is mine, and take from us what strength we might give you.*

There is nothing to forgive, Akad said, and then Krysta slipped between them like an adhesive, binding them even closer to each other through her very flesh. Darkyn experienced his brother's relaxing as Krysta kissed him, and then his attention turned to Krysta's pleasure and Krysta's pleasure alone. Darkyn lifted her hair and bit her neck, and she moaned into her kiss with Akad.

The sound of her excitement roused Darkyn's cock quicker than he could form a thought. He pressed his growing erection into her soft ass, rubbing up and down on the cheeks as he nipped her neck. She smelled of sex and fresh water and oh, so lightly of bayflowers. Subtle. Intoxicating.

And so giving as she turned slowly, joining her mouth and *pa* to his. For a moment, Darkyn knew only her, only her touch on his face, his shoulders, only the taste of her tongue joining with his. Her breasts rubbed against his chest, and then she stepped back a little so Akad could cup them.

Darkyn kept up his kisses and rubbed his swollen cock against her *pa*-coated bush.

She moaned softly, "Yes, yes," as Akad pinched her nipples and Darkyn slipped his fingers into her nether lips.

She was wet and ready.

They had only to tease her a little further, and she'd be back in full fervor. Dangerous, perhaps, but deeply satisfying.

Time suddenly seems so short. If we had forever, Akad, we could find many ways to please her.

Akad's answer was swift and forceful. *We may have forever, and we may have only a few tomorrows. Let us be certain she never forgets this* first *sharing of our family, Brother.*

Chapter Ten

Krysta gasped as Darkyn found her clit and pinched. She was facing him, loving the bright streaks in his dark hair, the rough rub of his scars on her flesh, the feel of their mingled *pa* and Akad's skillful tweaking of her nipples. She felt like liquid between them, their growing heat and sweat like kisses all along her flesh.

It felt so *right*, being with both of them, giving some of their joy to Akad for all he had given them.

For all he had given everyone.

Krysta knew she couldn't please the priest like a soul's mate, but sharing the pleasure of her marital bed was as close as she could come.

As he held her from behind, his erection pressing against her ass, her mate held her from the front. His cock thrust against her quim, awaiting entry.

She could take them both. She had taken two men before, and even three. Yet they held back.

Akad maddened her by squeezing her nipples harder and harder. He rolled the stiff flesh between his fingers until it ached, then held them both forward for Darkyn to flick with his tongue. The wet heat of Darkyn's mouth, the sharp nip of his teeth on the already tender points made her cry out and squirm. Her clit throbbed now, pulsing as Darkyn flicked and teased it with his fingers just as he teased her nipples with his mouth.

"Be still," he said in his deep, rumbling command-tone.

"Do you want her still, Brother?" Akad rumbled from behind her, just as deep. She felt his hold on her tighten. He pulled her against him, using her nipples for leverage.

Darkyn grinned and bent down, suckling first one and then the other as he let her clit suffer. Akad's erection parted her ass cheeks and nudged, but went no further.

Krysta fought them both, to arouse them and make them fight her harder in return. Her blood pumped and pounded, and her quim felt like a molten river as Darkyn once more rubbed her clit with his thumb.

A little shock traveled through her, and Akad clucked softly in her ear. "No control. What a shame. Now we'll have to start over, won't we, Brother?"

"Mmmm," Darkyn agreed, returning his lips to Krysta's mouth as she screamed in pleasure and frustration.

His mouth tasted of salt, of metal, of man, and he smelled the same. All man. Akad's scent was spicier, more exotic. It whispered of incense and temples and long-buried secrets. Damn the priest's strong, wiry arms, for holding her so firmly!

Darkyn broke away from their kiss, gave her another grin, then lowered his attentions to her neck, biting her softly, then briskly, and moving to her nipples. Shivers of pleasure threatened at his every move, but Krysta held them back, determined there would be no more "start-overs."

"That's it," Akad whispered in her ear, keeping her arms pinned as Darkyn ran his tongue between her breasts and down across the crackling *pa* on her belly. "Steady. No coming without our granting."

She nodded, plotting revenge for later. Oh, yes. For this, there would be a later...

Lower and lower went Darkyn's mouth, until he was tasting the top of her wet bush. Her *pa*-coated lower lips pulsed with each light touch, but she managed not to scream or thrash.

"Open your legs," Akad commanded. "Just a little."

Krysta complied, giving Darkyn more room to tease her with the relentless strokes of his tongue. He took his sweet time, circling in the silvery hair, slowly licking the sides of either lip. Occasionally, he would flick across her swollen clit, making her jump.

"Ah-ah," Akad said each time, holding her tighter.

Her arms almost felt numb.

She would get the priest for this, in some sensual, torture-some way.

Just see if I won't get you, she thought, making the sort of rudimentary psi-contact she had always made with him.

His laughter filled her mind even as Darkyn's tongue once more touched her clit and nearly made her explode.

"Are you ready?" Akad whispered, nudging her ass with his rigid cock again. "Which way should we take you first?"

Krysta thought about answering, then decided they would only torture her more.

"No finishing," the priest cautioned, and Darkyn fastened his mouth on her quim and began to suck and lick her clit at the same time.

Despite her best efforts, Krysta moaned and had to fight to keep her knees from buckling.

Darkyn pressed harder, brushing his tongue in circles over the ever-hardening button, drawing it through his lips and letting it pop free again and again. Krysta arched into his mouth.

"I'm going to come," she said, barely able to speak.

Instantly, Darkyn pulled back, lightly kissing her clit, her lower lips.

If he says anything about starting over, I swear I will maim them both.

But Darkyn said nothing. He simply stood, gazed deep into her being with those wild yellow eyes of his, wrapped his arms around her waist, and lifted her into his embrace as he had the first time they joined.

In turn, she wrapped her legs around him, feeling him grasp her ass to better support her. From behind, Akad let go of her arms but moved in close, holding her with his hands on both breasts. He slid her nipples between his fingers and kept up constant pressure. She felt the priest's lips moving along her shoulders, and she moaned as Darkyn eased forward to kiss her.

His *pa* snapped as they touched, giving them both a deep charge of fire that transferred to Akad. Krysta felt the priest quake against her, and she felt the delicious heat of his *pa* on her bare back and ass.

She also felt their cocks, poised and ready. One pushed at her quim. The other at her ass. They seemed to be taking turns, keeping her uncertain of which entry to expect first. She was only vaguely aware of Akad lubricating himself with a bath oil. The fragrance teased her nose, doubling her anticipation.

Her mind drifted into fervor again, and time seemed to stop as they drove her arousal higher and higher. She was getting wetter and wetter, and crazier and crazier.

"Fuck me," she whispered, making a bet with herself that neither of them would be willing to start over now.

With hedonistic growls, both men plunged into her at the same time, tearing a scream of pleasure from her depths.

She had never felt so full, so whole or complete. There was some pain, yes, but it was perfect pain. The kind that made her crazier still. Moaning without reserve, Krysta grabbed Darkyn's hair in one hand and Akad's in the other, then rested her head on Akad's shoulder and went limp, letting them support her as they thrust in and out of her ass and quim, building speed and force with each movement.

"Beautiful," Darkyn murmured, kissing her lips, her chin, her neck.

"So tight," Akad said, pounding into her ass until his bollocks bounced and slapped against her thighs. Every few seconds, he gave her nipples a fierce pinch, starting a new round of groans.

This time, as Krysta felt orgasm threatening, she knew she couldn't turn back. "Let me come," she said, more a demand than a request. "You have to. I can't stand it!"

"Yes, you may." Darkyn kept his strokes even and refused to gain any more speed. Akad followed suit, and the devils held her there, right over the edge, suspended, just as she was suspended between the two of them.

Her body seemed like nothing but sensation, a raw nerve stroked along its entire length. Her quim and ass clenched and pulsed around their cocks with each movement, keeping her on the precipice. She thought her nipples might explode. She thought she might explode.

Are you ready now? Akad asked in her mind.

Yes! she screamed, aloud and through the psi-link she had with the priest.

"Then come," Darkyn ordered, moving her up and down along their shafts as they both plunged in and out with new frenzy.

Krysta had a sensation like melting, and then like catching fire. It started in her legs and arms, then drew to her center with lightning speed as she relaxed into the pure pleasure of fucking her soul's mate and his brother at the same time. Every corner of her body burned with excited satiation. She shook and cried out, convulsing like one who might be dying. Her *pa* blazed into Darkyn's, and in turn into Akad's, and both men emptied their seed into her waiting depths.

Their come felt like the hot jets of the natural pool, shooting and swirling through her, joining her to both men in new and deeper ways.

Darkyn and Akad pressed against her, groaning from their own releases. As Darkyn's stone pressed into the *pa* on Krysta's chest, she felt the shock of unguarded and blissfully full mind-to-mind contact with both men.

She saw what her *sha* really thought of her, felt how he really felt, and rejoiced in the truth and beauty of it. In his absolute love and devotion, still newborn but growing stronger by each stellar minute.

For the briefest moment, the contact lifted her to new heights. It didn't hurt. For the briefest moment.

The pain came with no warning, so terrible and complete she thought her head might blow off her shoulders.

"Pull out!" she heard Akad yell to Darkyn, but even then it was too late. The psi-energy had overwhelmed her ability to absorb it.

How stupid, she told herself as she tumbled toward oblivion. *Akad yelled at Ki and Fari when they nearly killed Elise this way with too much psi-force...*

Just before her mind was attacked and absorbed by the awful, screaming, darkness approaching Uhr faster than she thought possible, she thought she heard Elise shouting at Georgia over a baby's plaintive wail.

No, don't even tell them! The idiots. Damn it, what is it with men and enemies and wars? Just get us a fucking speeder now. Now!

Annie Windsor

Chapter Eleven

Time had stopped for Darkyn Weil. Minutes, stellar hours—he had no understanding of the passage, nor did he care. He had never known such complete misery. As he sat on a rug by the side of his *hallas* in the sick room of his home, without his weapon, without the force and fury and sureness he had used to lead The People, he felt furiously helpless. This was the same room his people had come to for comfort across the many centuries, but there was no *Ta* to advise him. His brother Akad was bound by his own guilt. Not to mention absorbed by the task of preparing for early-arriving participants in the *pao* and explaining to the citizens of Gese what had happened to their *Ta* and his new mate.

Every telepath within range—and then some—must have sensed Krysta's psi-cry of distress, dampeners or no.

Overload. Overwhelmed. The formidable mental powers of The People flowing unchecked through an uninitiated mind. How Krysta withstood the shock, he couldn't imagine.

Damn me eternally for my stupidity. Darkyn gazed at his mate, who lay limp and seemingly lifeless before him on a mat made of greenwild vine and grass. He longed to scoop her up and hold her to him, to pour out his regret and beg her forgiveness.

Akad had administered medicines that might help, but advised against touching her. The emotional response to her *sha's* touch might worsen her condition or kill her outright.

We just don't know, Brother. I'm so terribly sorry. I didn't think.

"We didn't think," Darkyn said aloud, studying Krysta's sleeping form. She was naked, covered by the softest sheet he could find. It was golden in honor of harvests and light and Uhr's native Chimera strain, which tended to be yellow or golden. Gold was the new color of Darkyn's stone, and of *Ta'Tonna Kon'pa*.

The room around them was of modest size, but carpeted with hand-woven rugs. The walls were covered by tapestries showing the tending of herds, the culling of the greenwild, harvesting the orchards, navigating the Steaming River, and claw-farming the sand of the drylands. Darkyn's attention was captured by the bull dragyn in the drylands scene, rising from behind a dune like judgment itself as some of the farmers raised claw-hoes to drive it back.

"Attack and defeat always come from situations unseen or unexpected." He shook his head and inched his fingers toward Krysta's exposed shoulder. Leaving a space no broader than a falcon's feather between them, Darkyn forced his eyes to the window of the sick room.

Low sunslight glinted off the clean glass as Guardian sat quietly on the sill. She stared at him with what seemed like empathy and caring as Chimera song drifted through the open space around her.

"I've made a mess of things," he told the raptor. "I've harmed the woman of my heart. I've involved my brother and worsened his lot. The *pao* will begin in a day, and what use will I be?"

A debilitating blackness crept into his heart as he gazed first at Krysta, then at the falcon. It came first as a natural feeling, but doubled and trebled until it filled his senses. His keen vision dulled, and his hearing. Even his sense of smell.

You are worthless.

You have no power.

"Worthless," he echoed. His muscles became leaden, as if turned to stone and cemented to the floor.

From a great distance, and too slowly, a falcon shrilled.

"Guardian?" he tried to say, but the words came out slurred.

Was the falcon still in the window?

Was the window still in the house?

The house still on Uhr?

He was…drifting…

Sitting cross-legged in space, it seemed.

A presence surrounded him, at first suffocating and then less so.

"Die," said a voice so bleak and harsh Darkyn recoiled — and yet he felt gripped by a power unlike any he had battled in the past.

The warrior in him rose like the cry of a raptor, shrieking through the bonds of his unnatural stupor. "Release me," he demanded. His tone matched the harsh coldness of his captor's icy command. With every scrap of strength in his mental arsenal, he pushed back against the force possessing him.

His stone hummed and burned in his chest, and for a moment, his attacker seemed surprised. Perhaps stunned.

The hold on Darkyn's mind eased just enough for him to blast free, rushing back toward sunlight and familiar sensations.

"Die here or die there," the voice said, feigning dispassion. "Makes no difference to me."

At that, Weil forced himself back to consciousness.

His eyelids felt like rock slabs, but he lifted them. A reddish glare seared his vision instantly—a glare he had seen before, but where?

Ruby, like blood captured in stone…

Ruby, like the twin swords wielded by the Sailkeeper's bride, on Arda, the day Georgia Tul'Mar almost killed him.

Darkyn felt the bite of sharpened blades against his throat, and didn't dare even to swallow, to breathe. He knew without seeing that Krysta's female kin had come without guise or preparation, slipping through Uhr's defenses as if they didn't exist. They had come without political motive or the slightest care over the workings of men and the intrigues of the universe. They had come like she-cats in fierce answer to Krysta's cry of pain, and they might slay him before he had a chance to explain.

Guardian yet perched on the windowsill, but the falcon made no move to intervene. Her raptor's eyes bored into him as if to accuse, as if to tell him he deserved whatever tortures these women might offer.

The old Earth poet Kipling was correct. Darkyn stared straight ahead at his turncoat falcon, making himself a mimic of marble and stone. *The Female of Her Species is more deadly than the Male. Why is it that men of every star system persist in deluding ourselves about this fact?*

"Tell us what you did to Krysta and why," came a warrior-woman's icy command. "Then tell us why an OrTan skull ship is orbiting your moon without being intercepted."

"Along with twenty more vessels," another female voice added. "Our companel didn't even recognize six of the ship designs. Arda's sensors haven't picked them up at all. How is that possible?"

"Don't fuck around," the first voice instructed. This was the holder of swords, the Sailkeeper's bride, no doubt. Darkyn felt a small trickle of warmth on his neck, proof of Georgia Tul'Mar's serious intent. "The only reason I haven't killed you is I owe you for saving Elise and Katryn. Kidnapping my sister-in-law, hiding her away from us, hurting her, and letting our enemies orbit without detection—I'd say we're even now."

"I deserve whatever judgment you pass," Darkyn said quietly, careful to move as little as possible. "Krysta, my heart and my *shanna*, might die because of my foolish error."

"Do not take this all on yourself," said Akad, entering the room with his usual quiet, yet confident stride. "It was our mistake, together. The three of us."

Georgia's swords grazed Darkyn's throat again. He knew she was surprised.

Elise Tul'Mar confirmed this with a gasp, followed by a shocked, "We thought you were dead!"

"Not dead." Akad's even tone betrayed no concern or surprise, but Darkyn felt his *a'mun* twin's concern over whether he could persuade Georgia to put down her blades. "I had to come home. It was time."

The sound of a thudding kick, followed by a wheezing groan from Akad filled the room.

"You traitorous bastard!" Elise's voice pealed like a summoning bell. Guardian shrieked at the sound of it and took to the wing, quickly flying out of Darkyn's sight. "My *sha* trusted you with his family's life—with his own, and our daughter's safety!"

A scuffle followed. Darkyn wished he could see what was happening, but the next he knew, the ruby swords left his neck and someone kicked him sideways. He landed heavily beside Krysta, using all of his strength to avoid touching her flesh and possibly worsening her condition. When he righted himself and turned, his brother was standing against the far wall.

Pinned against the far wall might have been a more apt descriptor. The Sailkeeper's bride had thrust her blades beneath both of his arms, turning the priest into a wall hanging with a tense and still pained expression. She had her back to Darkyn, but there was no mistaking the fire of her hair or the virtual sizzle of air around her presence. He remembered the odd pattern of her *pa*, like a creeping vine in bloom.

"We will not fight you." Darkyn felt a surge of weariness so deep he didn't know if he could keep standing. "Your anger for the betrayal is just, but I am *Ta*, and I bear responsibility for the actions of my people. Slay me and take my *shanna* back to her home—whatever you believe is proper repayment for my wrongs—but please, do not harm my brother. He did but report on the Tul'Mar clan. Otherwise, he served you honestly, as he always would and will, as your High Priest. The office and the man were true to you in all other ways."

Georgia remained motionless, facing her captive. Elise stood to the side, a fearsome-looking emerald sword raised and drawn back to skewer Akad.

Once more, Darkyn was near to overwhelmed by his brother's exhaustion, by the pain and fragility in Akad's dark, unblinking eyes.

"Please do not harm him," Darkyn repeated. His voice cracked, and he fought a tremble in his hands. He would not fight these women any more than Akad would, but his brother's helplessness felt like a dagger in his own gut.

Elise gave Darkyn a drylands-withering glare, but she stood down. With a grace befitting the Sailmaster's woman, she slipped her curved sword into a sheath hanging from her silken belt and folded her arms. She wore only a knee-length tunic with that belt at center. No shoes, no breeches, no other weapons. Her golden hair hung loose about her shoulders, highlighting the smoothed ridges of her cheeks and the curve of her chin. Flames of *pa* marked her neck and cheeks, and Darkyn remembered them on her belly and hips as well, from when he delivered her daughter Katryn Tul'Mar.

Her build and those crystalline blue eyes. The way the pa chose to mark her. The fact she survived accidental over-contact with pa at all… Darkyn's mind worked feverishly, aligning pieces of a puzzle as yet beyond his reach. Now that he had joined with Krysta, he felt newly aware of these two women she loved. *Elise is part Ardani, yes. A mixed-blood — but mixed with what?*

When the *pao* attendees gathered, he might gain more clues about the truth of Elise Tul'Mar's lineage. It suddenly felt right for her to be on Uhr, for her to attend the gathering. New discomfort suffused Darkyn. *Too many unknowns. Akad worn so thin, my hallas drifting in the shadow worlds…ill omens, all.*

The Sailkeeper's bride at last extracted her ruby blades from the wall, releasing Darkyn's *a'mun* twin. The priest sagged against the dirt and thatch, his expression pale and distant.

Darkyn let out a sigh of relief.

Georgia Tul'Mar wheeled on him. Her redder-than-red hair matched the raging flush in her cheeks. Her vine-and-blossom *pa* markings wound down her face, popping and snapping with the force of her emotion.

Gods. This one too! The power, it goes so much deeper than they know. A mix of Ardani and…what? What does it mean?

The first possible meaning absorbed him, blotting out all other emotion or responsibilities.

"I believe you might help us revive Krysta." His pulse quickened as he turned back to the pallet where his *shanna* lay. "If you joined with Akad and with me, the four of us might reach her in the dark places—"

"No." Akad's refusal came forcefully, despite the man's pallor. "It's too dangerous. We could lose all three of them."

"These two have power I didn't realize," Darkyn countered. "Perhaps you've underestimated them as well?"

"They aren't initiated!" Akad pushed away from the wall and strode to Darkyn, standing only a hand's reach away. "We have risks enough ahead, brother. We cannot chance such a linking, for their sakes and our own."

"Excuse me?" It was Elise who spoke. "Do we get a say in this?"

"Forgive me, Grace, but no." Akad gave her a swift, shallow bow. "You do not understand the force of The People's ancient psi talents. They have been preserved in the pure form, and can break an unprepared mind."

Georgia Tul'Mar moved to Krysta's side, then knelt. Darkyn noted her instinctive avoidance of touch, and the way Krysta's *pa* lightened in her presence.

"So *prepare* us," Georgia said, more a command than a request.

"There isn't time." Akad sounded like a man speaking to eager toddlers. "To train a mind to join with one of The People would take stellar months. Perhaps years."

The Sailkeeper's bride stood and turned so quickly that Darkyn stepped back. Tears shone in her green eyes. "Why are men so infinitely stupid?"

Before anyone could react, Georgia lunged forward and grabbed Akad by the shoulders.

The priest shouted, tried to detach—but then jerked and flinched, as if he had taken a blade between the ribs. Darkyn actually looked at Elise's hands to be certain she hadn't pulled her dagger.

She was standing beside Akad and Georgia, her mouth open and her expression growing more slack by the second. Darkyn realized with dread and elation that Georgia had used her formidable will and hidden strengths to force psi-contact with Akad. Elise's mental ties to Georgia were pulling her into the joining as well.

Darkyn had no time for second thoughts, doubts, or recriminations. The process had begun. If the two women died, the shock would likely kill Krysta, and possibly Darkyn and his brother as well.

He could do nothing but offer a quick prayer to the gods and goddesses of all worlds, then add his strength and skill to the link.

Krysta strode down the corridors of the flagship in Arda's Royal Fleet. Her heartbeat kept jerky time with her footsteps because Akad had impressed upon her the graveness of the situation.

The psi-joining overwhelmed her mind. I've done what I can, but the rest is up to her...

Poor Ki. *Krysta worked to keep her expression even, to find words to ease her eldest brother's suffering. Fari, the brother closest to her in age, had already passed her on deck, wordless and inconsolable.*

"Well, well," Krysta said as she walked into the infirmary where Ki sat watch over his new and unconscious mate. "It is about time a woman humbled you."

Through his fog of fear and concern, Ki's relief shimmered like silver sunslight. "Krysta."

He stood and turned, greeting her with a fierce embrace. Krysta felt dwarfed by him even though she was as tall as Fari, and almost as strong. Still, she knew her presence steadied and comforted Ki.

"Take heart, Brother." Krysta pushed back from him and gazed at Elise. "Akad says your feral mate has strength beyond our understanding."

"From his lips to the stars." Ki let out a rattling breath. "I curse myself for this misjudgment."

Krysta continued to study Elise, taking in the lighter-haired woman's lanky yet petite frame. "Is it true that she is with child?"

Ki's cheeks colored. "Yes."

"Good." Krysta grinned. "Cheers to both of you! To the

dreg pools with Lord Gith and his foolish pursuits."

A smile tugged at Ki's mouth. "Thank you, Sister."

Krysta met his eyes, then hugged him again. "I need to bear her home now. Can you let her go?"

"I-I-" Ki's words failed him. He had never seemed so clumsy and helpless in all of his stellar years. "Yes. I will carry her."

"Let me take her." Krysta's heart ached for her brother as she squeezed his shoulders. "Wait until you hear the departure horn. It will be easier than watching me spirit her away."

"As you wish," he muttered, clearly struggling.

"I will care for her like my own firstborn." Krysta did her best to reassure him with every smile, every touch. "In a stellar week, she will be hale again. Trust me."

"Without question or doubt." Ki's positive words were forced, but Krysta knew he believed in her caretaking and healing abilities. "The stars speed you home."

Krysta stooped and swept Elise into her arms as if Elise were indeed a child. She felt so small and fragile in her arms, a wisp of a woman, yet with incredible inner strength. Krysta could sense that even though the woman's mind slept so deeply.

Before Ki could object or change his mind, she turned and carried her new sister-in-law away from the chamber.

Krysta felt no labor from the weight of her sister-in-law. And yet, something plagued her mind. The ship around her felt less than real, and Elise—almost a phantom instead of a woman.

A woman she had known, in every sense of the word.

But I only just met her...

Slowing her step, Krysta examined her surroundings.

Where ship's walls had been, shadow now played. Elise vanished from her arms like so much smoke, and Krysta's consciousness gradually cleared until she found herself standing on an odd tropical beach draped in moonless darkness, yet oddly luminescent. A soft yellow glow seemed to arise from the sand itself.

Krysta's head spun. Where was up? Down? Then and now? She wrapped her arms around herself and shook, feeling past crest over present, sensing present retreat off the sands of the future, emptying into a great black nothingness that seemed to be laughing…at her.

Just then, a man-shape appeared on the beach, just out of her ability to make out his features. As he approached, the darkness seemed to follow him, to flow into him and through him.

"Why do you play here?" he asked in a sweet-poison voice that turned Krysta near to ice. "Perth was destroyed long ago. A woman of your strength would have no use for such weaklings. Come to me. I'll teach you strength, give you wisdom you could scarcely imagine."

The horrible magnetism of his offer pulled at Krysta despite her instinct to resist. Something niggled in the back of Krysta's mind.

A warrior with the eyes of a lion and the heart of a dragon…

A picture of this warrior worked its way into her being, giving her the strength to hold her place on the eerie yellow sand.

"Come to me," ordered the shadow-man again.

Krysta blinked. He was so much closer now. She could see the depth of darkness comprising his limbs, his chest—and lights and swirls within that blackness. What were those?

"Do not move," the hypnotic, awful voice instructed. She felt it crawl across her skin like predatory insects, stinging her, draining her of will and memory.

This thing will kill me, she realized with dull certainty. *It will eat my flesh, my soul, the essence that made me who and what I am. And it — he — will laugh as he does so.*

She thought of fleeing—but how? And to where?

He flowed forward like an unstoppable tide, and Krysta realized that everything behind him was gone. No sand, no water, no rocks, no sky. He had consumed everything he passed.

And now he was losing his human shape, pulsing and throbbing, opening a maw filled with dead stars and devastated planets. Screams swirled through the holes where his eyes and nose should have been. So loud. So many!

Krysta trembled against the power surging around her, but she could do nothing. Pain unlike any she had known gripped her at the head and joints. Piercing, tearing like the teeth of a prehistoric beast.

He is…eating me…

Her desperate gaze caught a glimmer to her left. Another shape, fast approaching from an unknown vector. This shape drew the glow to it like a great magnet, swirling through the light like some old Earth charger bearing his knight into battle.

Krysta felt rather than saw the shadowed man hesitate, and she also felt his distinct sense of surprise. Perhaps a bit of incredulous fear.

"How can this be?" he whispered, low and harsh, a death-rattle. "Who are you? Show yourself!"

In that instant, Krysta managed to glare full into the light—and saw an image of her sister-in-law Elise riding a golden Chimera stallion, with a falcon pumping wings above her and Ki's diamond sword drawn and pulled back as if to slice the head right off the shadow-man's formless shoulders. Her *pa* shone like suns and stars as she screamed like a primitive, calling up images of centuries upon centuries of battle.

Another Chimera appeared, this one red and bearing Georgia and her ruby swords. Like flames rolling down a dry mountain break, she came, hissing and shouting.

Another golden Chimera, and another. Two men. Akad with his silvery blade drawn. The lion-eyed champion, bellowing his own war-cry and wielding a two-headed golden axe.

The present settled back on Krysta with the force of a storm surge. She staggered. "S*ha!* Darkyn!"

And they were on her, hands lifting her, weapons swinging forward, striking at the shadow-beast, holding her as they thundered across the sand and into the cool, gray-blue ocean waters beyond. She felt her mind link with theirs, felt the welcome heat of their presence and the complete tingling-singing response of her body.

Home came the single thought between them, and Krysta gave her assent, momentarily seeing the halls of Camford—and her brothers.

All motion stopped, though Krysta still felt the four pairs of hands holding her, caressing her, still sensed the Chimera bearing them and the black falcon in the air above her. They had gone to Camford, but not completely.

Like spirits, they hovered just off the ground, watching Fari read a note aloud to Ki, who was scowling despite holding Katryn to his chest.

"'Do not be male idiots and insist on following us. This is women's business'" Fari *lifted his head to gaze at Ki and the crying babe. "What do they mean, Brother? Where have they gone? I have ill-feelings. Something is wrong. My shanna faces some great danger."*

"Yes. Elise as well." Ki turned then, directly toward Krysta, Elise, Georgia, Akad, and Darkyn. As he pressed his lips to his daughter's head, he stiffened. Narrowed his eyes.

Krysta felt herself stiffen in response.

Katryn pointed to the spot where Krysta knew their phantom images hovered.

"Yi," said the baby, already precocious in her babbling sounds like most Ardani infants. "Uhr. Mommie. Uhr. Yi."

Oh, gods. Krysta ground her teeth—and that fast, she was gone from Camford, and waking to the feel of a pallet beneath her, tight muscles, a pounding headache—and four pairs of hands resting on her—shoulders, belly, and legs.

They were in complete rapport, a state of total understanding. Emotional and sexual feelings rushed back and forth too quickly to name or understand, or even manage. Krysta sensed the continued presence of Ki and Fari as well, though they were not present. Their awareness had followed their *shannas* without fail, and the energy of the circle could not be denied.

Lips brushed Krysta's, and she looked up to see Georgia, tears shining on her freckled and *pa*-flecked cheeks.

"Sister," Georgia whispered.

More lips brushed Krysta's forehead, and she saw Elise, who was also crying. Akad stirred beside her, caressing her stomach tenderly. "Welcome back."

Time still seemed to skip and jump, because in seconds, the three of them were gone and the force at her feet had moved upward, over her, and then down beside her to cradle her tightly.

She took a deep, drinking smell of Darkyn at his most elemental, heard the rumble of his voice as his whispered his love and rocked her safely in his muscled arms.

Krysta wanted to lose herself in his caress, in his kiss. She wanted to spread her legs and arms and welcome Akad and Elise and Georgia to their lovemaking and know the joy of connecting at such profound levels.

The psi-presence of Ki and Fari broke off abruptly, and Guardian, who had reclaimed her perch on the windowsill, gave a call of distress.

"We have trouble," Krysta whispered, pushing back from Darkyn. "My brothers are furious, and they're coming. Now. With the Guard, the Fleet, and anyone who will answer their call."

It was Elise who summed the feelings of the group with a single, emphatic, "Damn!"

Chapter Twelve

It took some time to talk the Tul'Mar women out of their blades, but at last they understood the conventions of *pao*. Akad stored their weapons with Darkyn's formidable double-axe, showing them where the weapons would be after the *pao* disbanded.

"Weapons of the hand will do us no good henceforth," Akad said as Darkyn gazed at his axe.

Darkyn hated being without the familiar weight about his waist. He felt more than disarmed. More than naked.

Incomplete.

Who am I, if not a warrior?

His deepening relationship with Krysta, the *pao*, the uselessness of all his battle training against an ancient, virtually formless evil—these things gave him doubt. He understood the struggles of his *hallas* in finding her new roles, her new paths in the face of love-wrought changes and new types of menace.

Darkyn led Akad to the door of his cabin, leaving the thank-the-gods swordless Elise and Georgia to help Krysta dress. He felt clear-minded for the first time in weeks. The mating fervor had, at last, eased to a bearable level, and not a moment too soon. The gathering-space outside had begun to fill with The People, from vinemasters to sandscratchers. They stood in their robes, also seeming partially naked without their blades and clawhoes. In the outer reaches, weaving through the trees, Chimeras grazed and drifted and watched, occasionally humming. Many were golden Uhr natives, while others were multi-colored rescues from Arda.

Shuttle engines and ship thrusters roared in the distance, from the edge of the orchards, as the *pao* participants landed in rapid succession. Bands of different races and species marched down the path toward the fields where *Ta'Tonna Kon'pa* had decreed they would meet. Darkyn could make out the tall, swaying purple forms of the fierce women of Bandu, followed by the tiny Nostans who ever-persisted in their foolish attempts to court the wild female warriors. Behind them came the unarmed but heavily armored OrTan delegation.

"The slavers have arrived," Akad said in low, disgusted tones. He stood on Darkyn's right side in the cabin's doorway, glowering down the path.

A wide circle of distance had opened around the reviled lizards of OrTa, the galaxy's infamous sex-slavers. Obviously, no one wanted to be too near them. In other circumstances, most of the participants would have attacked the OrTans on sight. But this was a *pao*, a meeting of native peoples under the sacred peace of all gods and goddesses. Should any participant commit violence during a *pao*, all attendees would be bound to avenge it.

Darkyn believed serious violence unlikely, as most of the species present could sense or see the *Barung*, and had an interest in stopping it. The OrTans, however despicable, had excellent technology despite recent war losses, and a healthy interest in saving their own skins. That combination made them formidable allies, though Darkyn doubted that even he could bring himself to shake their slimy scaled paws.

Excuse me, Ta. The psi-communication tapped through Darkyn's low-level mind-shielding, temporarily pushing aside his awareness of his nearby *shanna* and her family. The voice belonged to a technician, one who worked the landing strip. *There is great activity on Arda. The Fleet appears to be taking off, as well as the Home Guard. I do not much like their direction, as it seems to be the heart of Uhr. Our shielding will hide the pao ships, but...*

Akad tensed beside him, obviously picking up bits of the communication. Guardian, who had been in one of the cabin's windowsills, took off in a rush of feathers and screeching.

Darkyn sighed. *Do not allow the Fleet to land a ship. Block human transport for all but the Sailmaster and the Sailkeeper, and warriors from the Home Guard to serve as their entourage. Make certain to transport no weapons. Use as many psi-technicians as necessary to block any action by the remaining vessels.*

There was a hesitant pause. Clearly, the technician would have preferred remaining invisible to Arda's otherwise all-seeing eyes. Further, he would have preferred the Tul'Mars to stay clear of Uhr's surface. Once The People's haven was revealed, it could never be fully reclaimed, only defended.

If they survived long enough to make defense necessary.

Understood, the technician replied, and despite his reticence, Darkyn knew the man would obey. Darkyn's consciousness detected his call for psi reinforcements to head for the landing strip. Almost immediately afterward came a question from his cousin Brand, who remained confined to his cabin by order of the *Ta.* There had been no time to pass judgment on Brand's fate for killing Kolot on

Arda when the opposing soldier had his hands raised for no-combat.

Darkyn sighed again. *You may go to the landing strip, Brand. When your duties are finished, return to your cabin.*

Yes, Ta. The answer held no rancor, nor hint of deception. Brand simply wanted to contribute in whatever limited fashion he might.

There would be time enough to decide his punishment later.

"What will you do with the Tul'Mar men when they arrive?" Akad asked quietly.

Darkyn shrugged. "What can I do, Brother? Treat them as any other *pao* participant and give them voice when it's their turn to speak. Mayhap this gathering will convince them of what my communications, documents, and finally my raids could not."

Akad gave a rumble of unease. "Those two will not willingly or lightly accept your authority."

"Their psi isn't strong enough to override the wishes of The People. I think it's time they understood that." Darkyn glanced at his brother. "Besides, their women may help persuade them to the truth."

"I will not be used to coerce or humiliate my husband," came the icy retort of the Sailkeeper's bride behind him.

At this, Darkyn's temper flared. He turned to face Georgia. "You will be used to save his life, and yours, and your family's. If that isn't acceptable, then I have greatly underestimated you."

Feeling the burn in his gut, not wishing to alienate his mate's kin, Darkyn turned back to the crowd and stalked down the path to greet more arriving delegates. From behind him, he heard Elise Tul'Mar say, "Well. I guess we know where he stands."

Just as he reached the middle of the outdoor greeting area, the OrTans filed into place amongst the delegates. Simultaneously, Krysta, Elise, and Georgia left the cabin to stand by Akad at the head of the path.

Three female gasps rose over the murmur of the crowd, followed by lizard growling and leg-slapping as the OrTans grabbed for weapons they had surrendered upon landing.

"She-witches," bellowed Lord Gith, the leader of the OrTan delegation just before the sounds of melee ensued.

Darkyn didn't want to look, but he knew he had to. The rigid posture of the Bandu, the worried expressions of the Nostans, and nearby members of his tribe…his temper roiled even as his spirits sank.

Please, goddess, let Akad have blocked the path back to those women's weapons…

Slowly, he made himself turn back toward the cabin.

Akad and Krysta had Georgia forcibly pinned inside the cabin door. A group of The People had sealed off the OrTan delegation. Standing dead center were Lord Gith and Elise Tul'Mar, virtually nose to nose.

"My property," Gith hissed. "How convenient to have you return yourself to me."

"If you touch me, I'll kill you with my bare hands." The woman's voice was level and confident, and Darkyn had the passing thought that Elise could back up her threat.

No wonder the Sailmaster accepted her as mate Your Grace and strength, and strength of will. A good match for a Ta, just like my Krysta.

Darkyn shook himself from his distraction and strode over to stand before them. "This is a *pao*," he said coldly. "If you cannot put aside your differences for the good of your respective peoples, you will be detained until the *pao* is finished, then dismissed from Uhr without further welcome."

For a moment, neither potential combatant looked away from their battle-stare. Darkyn felt a stab of fear from his *shanna* at the thought of one of her family being forever banished from her new home, but it could not be helped. He could not lose control of this situation, no matter the grievances between these two combatants.

"Choose," he demanded.

And to the well-broadcast surprise of Elise Tul'Mar and Georgia as well, Lord Gith responded to Darkyn's demand as if the OrTan emperor had issued a command backed by a dozen swordsmen with poison-tipped blades. The lizard leader yielded two steps, offered a small bow to Darkyn, and said, "Your pardon. This dispute can wait."

To Elise, Lord Gith said, "I nor any of my people will offer you further affront while you enjoy the protection of Uhr."

Elise seemed baffled about what to say in response. Finally she gave a small shrug. "Okay. Whatever. Georgia and I won't hurt you either — for now. You should know my husband and his brother are coming, though. It might not be good for you to be here when they arrive."

Lord Gith cut his slitted eyes toward Darkyn, who suppressed another sigh of weary frustration before reassuring the lizard slaver with, "It will be no issue for you."

As Lord Gith retreated to his contained entourage and Elise returned to her shocked kin at the doorway of the cabin, a murmur of excitement traveled through the crowd. Darkyn turned his attention back to the path to behold a delegation finishing the rare and difficult process of matter transfer. They seemed to materialize, to appear from thin air in gracefully flowing rivers, then coalesce into whole forms. Some twenty sapphire-robed figures led by a stately man in white robes and a fierce-looking warrior in crimson robes. The group began to move toward the gathering, and Darkyn noticed five more red-robed figures walking behind the first group. These men had a rougher and more predatory appearance.

The newcomers matched him in height and build. Most had the black-black shade of hair usually associated with descendants of Arda, though some were yellow-blonde, a shade similar to his own increasing streaks. All wore capes and protective gloves the same shade as their robes. To a one, the regal men wore expressions of detachment, and they fairly radiated dignity as they walked.

Darkyn felt a new ripple of surprise and wonder, even though he knew they would answer the summons. They moved as one body, matching steps without any visible sign of practice or coordination, until they reached him. The white robed man stepped forward then, and dipped his head to Darkyn.

"I am Hoth, First Priest of the People of Kaerad. We answer your call in this time of need."

Darkyn returned his nod and surveyed his entourage. The First Priest, the peace chief of his world, had also brought his war chief, the crimson-robed man. Attending the war chief were five of Kaerad's renowned *Legio*, the protectorate rumored to be able to take the shapes of wolves if needed. The men in sapphire robes were the under-priests.

The legendary Kaeradi, the galaxy's foremost telempaths and future-seers, had no quarrel with any known world or species. Unshielded touch by an incompatible person or species could kill them, or kill the one who touched them—and any within empathic range. Thus, they typically entertained audience only on Kaerad, and even then only in times of great strife. To see them off-planet was...stunning...and sobering.

More than that, the Kaeradi had brought their entire government, their strongest men, so great was their respect for this and their understanding of the need to defeat the *Barung*.

"Your presence is most gratifying." Darkyn gestured to his cabin. "My home is your home, should you require respite or haven."

"Thank you. Our gloves and robes should be shield enough." Hoth held up a gloved fist. "They are blessed and strong, and should block the effects of most physical contact."

The Kaeradi's gaze shifted to Elise Tul'Mar, who stood beside Akad near the cabin door. Hoth broke away from Darkyn then, giving a hand-signal to the *Legio*, who followed him soundlessly. Their feral eyes darted left and right, taking in any possible menace. In that, they reminded Darkyn of Guardian, who was circling high above, keeping watch.

Hoth of Kaerad came to a halt before Elise. Then, to Darkyn's great shock, he knelt before her. The part of his delegation that remained in front of Darkyn turned as one and knelt with him, even the war chief. The *Legio* dropped to one knee, wary eyes continuing to survey the crowd, which had fallen into a freakish, still silence.

Elise seemed flabbergasted by such attention, but Darkyn felt more fitting of pieces of the great and timeless puzzle created by his ancestors.

"Long have I waited to gaze upon you, and hoped that it would be within my lifetime." Hoth's forceful timbre suffused with awe as he lifted his head to look at Elise. "Daughter of Kaerad, Daughter of Arda, raised by our long-displaced allies from Perth. *Ban'ania*. Mother and savior. We honor you for the sacrifices you've made, and the sacrifices you will make."

Elise's mouth came unhinged. When she at last gathered her wits, she managed a graceful, "Thank you, though I don't understand."

"In time you will, *Ban'ania*." Hoth rose slowly, keeping his head lowered slightly in deference. "We will have more discussion when the *Barung* is defeated."

With that, he turned back to his entourage, but gestured for the *Legio* to remain with Elise. The five red-robed warriors took up positions around her without question or change in expression.

Elise's expression, however, changed several times, from confusion, to fear, to a touch of amusement as Georgia inspected the *Legio*, shaking her head. Akad kept a warning hand on Georgia's wrist, as did Krysta. Darkyn knew they were in psi-link, and that his *shanna* was giving Georgia a history on the Kaeradi and their fearsome telempathic power.

One by one, the different races and peoples took up positions in the welcoming yard. Darkyn watched them all, occasionally looking skyward, to the stars where the *Barung* pulsed malevolently.

Was it closer?

Did the formless evil understand what they were doing here on Uhr, conspiring to bring the might of the galaxy against it, using a plan conceived thousands of stellar years before?

Once more the crowd gave a murmur of surprise and interest.

Bringing up the rear of the procession from the air strip were a group of beings that could only be described as ethereal. Most had deep black or stunning white hair, while a few had shining auburn tresses that spilled to their hips and thighs. They were tall even by Ardani standards, but not slight—well-built and well-proportioned—and physically perfect. Their clothing, of all basic colors and hues, had a loose, flowing style. The men wore tunics and breeches, while the women were scarcely clad at all, but seemingly more of pride and comfort with their bodies than a statement of sexuality or sexual servitude. The fabrics they wore sparkled like their flesh and eyes, like the very air around them. Their chests, mostly visible through the threads of loose-fitting garments or body girdles, bore tattoos of a sun, a moon, and a star.

Darkyn felt a lift in his *pa*. Such energy! Could these be the telekinets of old Perth, who had so long sheltered on Earth? No one knew for certain how many were left, or the power they yet wielded. Judging by his instincts, Darkyn thought that power remained intense, indeed.

A woman with red-streaked raven hair and deeply slanted green eyes broke to the front of the group. Air shimmered about her, and Darkyn felt a rush of surprise as wings emerged from her back and unfurled behind her.

This was the proof his teachings told him to look for, the sure truth that these were Perth's descendents.

When the woman saw his nod of acceptance, her wings folded, then retracted until they disappeared entirely.

"I am Arygain," the woman said with an air both regal like the Kaeradi but infinitely haughty. "We heard your summons, and we come as representatives of Perth, the destroyed world. Though we respect your leadership, none but the child of Myrddin, raised far forward from her time, may command our loyalty. Is she here?"

"Gods," Akad muttered from behind Darkyn.

For his own part, Darkyn felt only muted surprise. Once the bloodline of Elise had been revealed, he had suspected this possibility about Elise's "cousin."

"Georgia Tul'Mar," he called in his Ta's voice, hoping she would respond to the form of his authority, irrespective of its substance. "Will you come forward to stand with your blood-family?"

For once without comment, Georgia did as she was asked. When she reached Darkyn's side, she murmured, "Did she say Merlyn? Like, Merlyn the magician, from King Arthur's time?"

"Daughter of Myrddin," Arygain intoned, ignoring Georgia's confusion. "Child of Perth, Child of Avalon, Child of Arda. How would you have us?"

Darkyn sensed the one hundred inappropriate retorts that flew through Georgia's consciousness and elbowed her discreetly.

"I—uh." Georgia coughed, then pointed to an opening in the crowd, next to Elise and her surrounding *Legio*. "I would have you, er, there. Beside me."

Akad released a breath of relief as the survivors of Perth followed their surprised leader to the designated spot.

The crowd had composed itself, and at last seemed complete but for the Ardani leaders, who would arrive unwillingly and all too soon.

Darkyn's throat tightened. Typically, he had no doubt in his own skill and ability, but the fate of his People, the peoples of all the galaxy, rode on his decisions and persuasiveness. He felt suddenly small in the face of so much import, and wondered at his own sanity to take on such a task.

I did not take it on. It was appointed to me eons ago. I was born to this, just as Elise and Georgia Tul'Mar, beyond my consent or knowledge.

The bone-grating tiredness of the past few days threatened to weaken the force of his presentation, and he felt shame that Elise and Georgia were accepting their roles with aplomb while he, *Ta'Tonna Kon'pa*, wavered.

A surge of strength startled him, and he felt the deep physical and mental contact of his brother—and then his *shanna*. Krysta moved to stand beside him, taking his hand in hers. She bared her psi-self to him then, offering her love and poise so openly that it made him want to take her into the cabin and plant his cock deep in her sweet, fertile essence.

For a moment, Darkyn closed his eyes, using years of training to master the sudden rush of blood from his head to his swelling staff. Elise and Georgia joined in the psi-contact, momentarily embarrassed, then interested in his arousal.

Would that there were time to explore this more completely, Krysta psi-spoke in a teasing, knowing tone.

Darkyn thought he might explode. It took all he possessed to rein himself in and return to his role as leader of The People and this most important *pao*.

"Greetings, all," he said with the most forceful voice he could muster. "Welcome to Uhr, to the Blessed City. We are at *pao*, under the eyes of all the gods and all the goddesses. Henceforth, we will make no violence toward anyone but our true enemy, the *Barung*."

Krysta waited for the murmurs of the crowd to die down before she sent a piece of her consciousness in search of her headstrong brothers. With her newly tapped psi-strength, this fraction of her awareness sailed easily above the heads of the *pao* attendants, and higher, to ride with Guardian in her endless patrol, then higher still. Off of Uhr. Into orbit around the moon.

She found them shortly, cursing and raging, trapped on their ships by psi-power they could not comprehend. On the landing strip back on Uhr, a group of The People had joined hands. Using their combined mental strengths, they rendered the instruments and devices of Arda's Royal Fleet completely useless. One by one, ships other than Fari's *Lorelei* and Ki's *Astoria* went dormant. Their crews fell into a harmless but profound sleep, and The People protected their orbits and safety.

My sha's tribe could have crushed Arda's storied forces any time, Krysta told herself with final certainty, feeling a new depth of respect for her mate and the peaceful methods he had thus far chosen to make his point to her brothers. She also wondered at a people so powerful who kept themselves so completely removed from the daily politics of the universe. Like the Kaeradi and the survivors of Perth's destruction, The People could have assumed domination of the Galactic Council and any or all of its worlds, on psi-talent alone.

It isn't their way, she realized. *If I'm to be joined to my mate and to my sisters-by-marriage with their newly discovered blood allegiances, it can't be mine any longer.*

She turned her attention to Ki, who had ceased to rail against the binding psi-forces he clearly could not fight. Fari, of course, continued to rage. She could see things so clearly now, the beauty and paradise of Arda, and yet the dangerous, growing arrogance that had led them to this juncture. For all their natural ways, and despite the blessing of *pa*, they had started to become disconnected from the basic heartbeat of the universe.

Oh, my brothers. The three of us have so much to learn. Will you be willing, or will I lose you?

Sadness washed over her, and the force of her emotion flowed outward, touching Ki and Fari. She saw the emotion speak to them like no words could have done. Their faces softened. Almost as one mind, they reached back for her, pouring a ragged, grateful joy into their connection.

My sister, came Fari's plaintive call. *I feared you were lost.*

I have missed you, Ki's psi-voice rumbled.

Krysta let loose her love for them then, watching it wrap around them and soothe them. She understood now that as the only female of equal status in their lives before they so recently found their mates, she was priestess to them as much as Akad had been priest. She had become both sister and mother, and they looked to her to light paths when all other options eluded them.

Another fact crystallized in her mind, then. That leaders, even such powerful and competent leaders as Fari and Ki and even her own *sha*, should never be treated as gods or even near-gods. They were in fact human and human only, and the people they led shared their blind spots. Akad's role, that of gently showing such blind spots of spirit and self-discipline, had never been more obvious to her.

I know you will be confused and uncertain, Krysta psi-spoke, careful to keep her new and powerful mind-voice at a whisper to spare *their* sanity. *You must trust me now as you've never trusted anyone, with your lives, with the lives of your mates, and all of Arda in the balance. Will you do this?*

Oddly, it was Fari who didn't hesitate. *Yes, Sister. I would give all of my breath and blood at your asking.*

Ki took longer, and his psi-voice was colder and more removed. *I will trust you. Do not make me regret it.*

Krysta withdrew from her link with them slowly, carefully. "They are ready," she told Akad. "As ready as they can be."

The priest nodded, careful not to interfere with Darkyn's ongoing address to the crowd as he sent the psi-instruction to transport the Tul'Mar brothers and their entourage to the surface of Uhr.

Chapter Thirteen

With the *pao* formally invoked and greetings exchanged, Darkyn granted a brief respite for rest, freshening, and morning nourishment. This break occurred as the landing strip guards, Brand included, escorted Ki and Fari Tul'Mar and about thirty of Krysta's Home Guard down the path, through the milling participants.

Darkyn received his two former foes along with four of their select guards in the large front room of his hut. He felt tense, standing between Akad and Krysta, possible traitors in the esteem of the Tul'Mar brothers. Elise waited along the far wall with her Legio, who shadowed her movements like wolves shadow prey.

Georgia was beside her, accompanied by her own guard of three of the eerie telekinets. Darkyn thought that he wouldn't much like to tangle with the three towering red-haired men. They had Georgia's fighting temper and the feral, hungry smile of the legendary Perth's greatest leader, Myrddin. These were a desperation-tempered people, who had nothing to lose and centuries of reinforced vengeance as their only motive. They wouldn't hesitate to maim or murder on Georgia's command, Darkyn had no doubt. He only hoped Georgia Tul'Mar realized this and didn't speak rashly. Judging from the anxious edge to her typically confident countenance, he thought she had some idea.

As Ki and Fari entered with two members of the Home Guard flanking each of them, their expressions flattened and their eyes glinted with wariness. Almost immediately, Darkyn felt the warm, welcome psi-connection of his *shanna*.

Be gentle, my love. For me. They are stripped bare of all they know, and all they treasure.

Truth, Akad agreed.

Darkyn gave no response as Elise and Georgia's thoughts turned toward the danger of attempting to initiate the brothers into their link. Surely, with the newfound unified strength they had discovered in reviving Krysta, they could do this. They *had* to do it.

The brothers halted, glaring first at Darkyn, Krysta, and Akad, then turning wounded gazes to their *shannas*.

"What is this?" Ki asked Elise in a quiet, deadly voice. "We had a bond of trust. After the fiasco of your cousin's rescue and the speeder crash that almost took your life, you told me you would never leave me again."

"Do I look like I've left you?" Elise's impatience lashed like a whip, and Darkyn saw Ki's shoulders slump momentarily. He felt a sudden, new, and deep kinship to the man, having recently learned what it felt like when a woman held such power over heart, mind, and soul. "I'm on Arda's moon, for God's sake, not off in some distant star system risking my life. I came here because I thought Krysta needed me. You wouldn't have done less."

Ki's expression softened. He started for his *shanna*, only to be blocked by the five *Legio*, who seemed to disappear and materialize in new positions, so quickly did they move.

"Be still," Elise commanded, and Darkyn heard the force of Kaerad's dignity and the strength of an Ardani *Lorelei*, a wild tribal leader of old, in her instruction.

So did the *Legio*. They froze in place, not so much as blinking.

"This man is my mate and husband," Elise said forcefully. "Whatever you think you're supposed to do, you will never again stand between my *sha* and me. If he chooses to march straight over here and snap my neck in two, you won't lift a finger to stop him, or a fist in vengeance. Are we clear?"

The *Legio* nodded as one, but Darkyn saw the look in their eyes. If Ki ever did choose to harm his *shanna*, this strange, mystical fighting force would never stop hunting him until they tore him apart with bare hands and teeth.

"Leave us now," Elise instructed. "Wait outside. I don't need to be guarded from my own family."

The slightest of hesitations showed the doubt of the *Legio*, but they flowed out the door like a red river, leaving a layer of wolfen growls in the air behind them. Simultaneously, Ki dismissed the four Home Guard protectors, who kept a respectful distance from the Kaeradi as they left the hut. In moments, he had his woman in his arms, kissing her, joining with her in the psi-ways he understood.

I don't grasp who they are, really, no, Elise was saying to her mate. *Or why they think they have to protect me…*

Fari eyed the intimidating protectors around Georgia, but they seemed less suspicious than the *Legio*. Probably because they were less attuned to the thousand emotions surging in the air between *sha* and *shanna*. Or perhaps because they were more carnal beings, accustomed to the freewheeling bonds of the flesh.

Whatever the reason, they simply stepped back as he claimed his bride with a fierce, deep kiss. As her protectors departed the cabin, Georgia welcomed her mate with a steamy groan, and there seemed to be no mistrust or confusion between them at all.

Darkyn ground his teeth against the rush of sensuality and arousal flowing out of the two reunions. Akad let out a soft groan, and Darkyn sensed his *a'mun* twin's frustrated arousal, yet felt slightly separate from it.

For his own part, he turned to Krysta and kissed her to relieve some of the unbearable tension. Her lips felt like wet, welcoming heaven as his cock became a throbbing misery against her belly. The exposed *pa* on their chests crackled as it touched and blended.

In olden times, a family rutting would have commenced immediately, with sex and food and music, blissful satisfaction and release extending for hours, perhaps days. This was their proper circle of pleasure, yes. The six of them. Elise, Georgia, Krysta, the Tul'Mar brothers, and him. Akad was related to the circle, but not a part of it. Darkyn could sense all of this as surely as he could sense the *Barung*.

But these men will never accept me. They will never welcome me as a brother, or willingly share with me what they hold dear.

"Be wary." Akad's firm grip on Darkyn's shoulders brought him back to the immediacy of the present. "The mating fervor is yet fresh, and could easily be rekindled. We have no time or space for that now."

Indeed, the mind-boggling arousal was surging, surging, surging, pushing upward and threatening Darkyn's stability. He pulled back from his *hallas* though his fondest wish was to strip her from her jumpsuit and take her deep and hard and fast, here, now, irrespective of who accepted him as family and who did not. Releasing her and stepping away, he said, "I want it clear that I don't hold Krysta against her will. My *shanna*, my *hallas*, stays by her own choice, and she has since the first days of her time on Uhr."

Fari let go of Georgia, and before anyone could speak, he grabbed his sister and held her tight against him, kissing her head. "Krysta. Ah, gods. You look wonderful to my eyes."

The more reserved Ki approached and took his turn at embracing her. "Are you truly mated to this—?"

Elise cleared her throat.

Ki frowned. "This man?" he finished lamely.

"Darkyn Weil is my *sha*," Krysta replied with a note of pride that made Darkyn stand straighter. "Stone to my fire, and my match and mate in every sense of the word. He is the man I've waited for, and the man you've misunderstood and underestimated."

Ki's frown deepened. "As dear as you are to me, that's for me to judge, Sister."

Krysta took a deep breath and seized her brother's hand. "Then judge, Ki. Reach into my mind and judge."

Her brother's trepidation tried to push her out of his thoughts, but Krysta forced her way into his mental patterns, beliefs, and perceptions.

Darkyn ground his teeth as his consciousness followed hers. This sort of intimacy—especially with any man beyond his brother—would never be his choice. Yet, if instinct saw true, this was their only shot at a successful *pao*. At survival.

In the dim reaches of Darkyn's awareness, he saw Georgia reach for her mate both physically and mentally, and saw Fari's unquestioning acceptance.

Gods, thank you. Darkyn closed his eyes. *Some little piece of this might be easier than I thought.*

Krysta shrank away from what she was doing. She had never in her existence deliberately risked the health and well-being of her brothers. There was no choosing in her actions, she knew. If she didn't do this thing, didn't force open Ki's inner eyes and help him through the transition to the deeper awareness shared by The People, he would never see, would never believe.

At least she didn't have to do it alone.

Elise's thoughts and strengths flowed with her own, wrapping Ki Tul'Mar in a blanket of love and affection.

There is no trick here, Elise assured him. *We just don't have the time for the usual training and willing release of barriers. We wouldn't do this if we knew another way, my always-love. I hope you understand that.*

Ki's response was a mental howl of betrayal and blended physical and mental pain.

Krysta felt herself stagger, felt Akad catch her.

Her brother was fighting so hard he might kill them all!

I don't have the strength and heart for this, she said desperately, only to feel the even, steady support of Akad's arms, of her *sha's* thoughts mingling with Elise's, of Georgia—and then of Fari, who, amazingly, was already in rapport with the four of them. He gave a mental shrug at her questioning amazement, and an answer in images that had to do with his complete trust of Georgia and Krysta, and the fact that he had always respected Darkyn as an adversary.

There is at times a thin line between enemy and soul-deep friend, Darkyn agreed. *Strong passions, for good or for ill, make for strong bonds.*

The five blended minds melded into a new whole, with Akad's consciousness hovering at the fringe where it seemed to belong, monitoring and assisting. All reached in to open the closed, agonized mind of Ki Tul'Mar.

Krysta, or the part of her she yet recognized as a distinct entity, felt a surge of guilt over the fact that she had never known the depths of her eldest brother's pain. The loss of their parents, the burdens of his leadership and many battles, all of his perceived failures, stacked up like Fari had once stacked his own. Only Fari turned his feelings outward for all to see and debate. Ki's pains were his own private, inward struggle. How had Elise not killed him for being so reserved, even with her?

Elise's loving laughter drifted through the link, lightening the mood of the group, even Ki. *He's been as open with me as he can be with anyone. Whatever he gives me is enough, always. I love the handsome, stubborn ass, in case you've failed to notice.*

Krysta found herself laughing then, too, thinking of Darkyn, and Georgia, thinking of Fari. The three men gave surly mental grumbles as men tend to do at such moments of inexplicable and maddening feminine unity.

And in that moment, the six connected completely for the barest of moments.

Ki's struggles against their invasion lessened, and in turn, they lessened the invasion.

Don't force us to come in, Brother, Krysta urged, aware more than ever of her many roles in Ki's awareness — sister, priestess, surviving piece of his lost and much beloved mother — balm of his past and doorway to a new and as-yet barely imagined future of love and closeness. *Come out to meet us.*

Ki gave no response, and Krysta realized with a sinking sensation that she had done what she could to reach him. Any more would injure him beyond repair, and yet the job remained incomplete.

Sensing her distress, Darkyn joined with her more closely. She felt his touch in the physical world, stroking her shoulder.

Elise's consciousness ebbed forward then, a warm river through the banks and rocks of their connection.

She didn't speak at first, only stood soul-naked before Ki.

I've always only offered myself, sha. This step is smaller than it seems. Take it, I beg you. For me, for Katryn. For everyone you love and might love.

Once more, they stood on the gentle, glowing sands of a world long destroyed. All six of them, naked as the day they were made, joined hand to hand and mind to mind.

Where are we? Ki's previous suspicion seemed much lessened.

Krysta thought to answer, but before she could, a trio of voices drifted out of the sea.

"You have come to the place of the ancients," the chorus said, and three men came strolling out of the waves that seemed to part for their passing. "In spirit, though not in body, as such would not be possible."

One of the men was clearly Ardani, with sharp, striking stripes of *pa* on his cheeks. The other Krysta recognized from her day's experience as Kaeradi, and as old a man as she had ever seen. The third—well, there could be no mistaking his relation to the Perth survivors who had arrived to give their allegiance to Georgia.

Oh my, but he's handsome, Krysta and Elise thought at once, staring at the man's carved muscles and white-yellow hair. A deity, this one, from some other place, some other time.

Would you shut up? Georgia's words were emphatic. *I think he's my father, for God's sake.*

All of this information was instantly shared in the link of the six. Each knew what the other saw, felt, and knew. Ki and Fari instantly came to speed on the true problem facing the peoples of many worlds, perhaps all worlds. They kept their regrets and shames at bay for now, but Krysta knew that later, her brothers would have to deal with their grievous miscalculations.

The yellow-haired god-man approached Georgia and cupped her cheek in his hand. "My exquisite second-born, heir to Avalon's blessing and the heritage of Perth. I knew you had the strength for this task. I wish I could have been with you in your youth, but all was as it had to be."

The six shared a moment of mesmerizing relaxation at the sound of the man's voice.

"I've heard you before," Krysta said quietly.

"As have I," Darkyn agreed.

"Yes." Myrddin of Perth turned his green-blue eyes on her. "Both of you, and the priest called Akad. I have tried to help you, to protect you. Mind-speaking over time and distance…it is a talent of mine, one I have been forced to use more often than I would choose."

And then he gazed at Elise. "How fair you are, second daughter of Ysbet and Eduard, heir to all that was Camelot. It is right that you are joined with my daughter in this. The line of Arthur and the line of Myrddin should never be separated."

"Oh." Elise rubbed her forehead. "This is entirely more than I can manage."

"You can manage much," said the ancient Ardani with the stripes on his cheeks. "And you have much left to manage."

In his words rang the force of duty, the same dark dedication to purpose that had haunted the Tul'Mar clan since time before memory. This gave the group quite a chill. They knew instantly that this was a man of death, a man who killed with the force of law and the fervor of righteousness. They also knew him for the distant ancestor of the Tul'Mars. Such thoughts did not bring them comfort.

The ancient Kaeradi made his way forward, hand on the golden stone in his chest. His movements were slow, labored, but pointed.

Krysta felt her shock as the old man reached out and placed his palm over Darkyn's stone. "Far back in time, the peoples of Kaerad, Perth, and Arda were of one blood, though many different talents and minds. Join them anew, my grandson many times over. Keep them joined by the stone most of our people no longer have the strength to bear."

The feel of Darkyn's startled understanding rippled through the six.

"Go now," said the old Kaeradi with a softness Krysta hadn't expected. "*Barung* knows a circle has been joined against him. He is coming for you. We will do what we can, remnants that we are, to assist you."

"So he is a man, then." Krysta narrowed her gaze, focusing on the faces of the ancients. "Not some stellar phenomenon. A man!"

Myrddin's expression darkened. "He was once a man. Once a wizard. Now, he is nothing human—but he can be killed. When the time comes, take his essence without mercy. I assure you, he will give you no mercy if fortunes are reversed."

At that moment, a twisted, bitter laugh shattered the peace of the beach. Krysta drew close to her sha and her brothers on instinct.

"Old men, playing at games," came the cold voice Krysta recognized from her previous unintentional trip to this long-dead beach. "What chance have you against the power I've developed? I destroyed you once, and now, I destroy you again!"

A blinding, suffocating blackness fell over the six, like a giant velvet sack, dropped and tightened with a ruthless cord.

"Go," they heard the chorus of three say quietly. "With our blessings and strength."

With that, Krysta, Darkyn, Elise, Ki, Georgia, and Fari collapsed onto the floor of Darkyn's cabin, gasping, near to shrieking with the need for air and escape.

Akad was no longer next to them. He stood in the cabin's doorway, trembling. From outside came the nervous murmur of the large *pao* gathering—and another sound Krysta had never before heard.

It sounded like Chimera song, only raised in one long, endless, mournful wail.

Darkyn got to his feet, staggered, then righted himself and helped Fari and Ki off the floor.

"Krysta," he rasped, pulling her up as she fought not to scream at the sound of the crying Chimeras. "Take your brothers to the enclosure. Get the weapons there. You know what I mean."

For a moment, Krysta could only stand, staring into the golden depths of her husband's eyes.

The *Barung*—no, the ancients had confirmed it— *Barung* was making his final approach. There had been no time to plan an alternative to the solutions to the ancient rhyme. No real time to have a meaningful *pao*.

And now her sha was sending her to the enclosure with her brothers, which only made sense, since they were the most experienced pilots in the group of six.

But the rhyme…

"'Feed him on The People's blood,'" she whispered. "Darkyn, what are you going to do?"

She tried to sense the totality of his thoughts, but he was closing himself to her.

"No!" She raised both fists and pounded on his chest. "I won't leave unless you tell me you'll be here when I return!"

"I'll be here," he said in that rage-producing calm voice Akad always used.

"No," she said again, nearly choking on rising tears.

Darkyn's face hardened toward her. "If we don't have trust, we may as well fall on our blades now. You are a Ta's mate and a leader in your own right far before that. Hear me, woman. Take your brothers and retrieve the weapons."

Krysta stepped back, settling into the new feeling of rapport within the circle of her family. She felt no deception, but she didn't need those senses to trust her mate if she listened to her heart.

"Come," she said to Ki and Fari.

They followed her without hesitation.

As Darkyn, Akad, Elise, and Georgia turned to address the *pao* and to share with them what they had learned, Krysta led her brothers down the Uhr's orchard path at a run.

The normally blazing day-sky of Uhr was a dark, brooding menace, like a storm was approaching—yet a storm unlike any they had weathered.

"What weapons are we to retrieve?" Ki asked aloud, keeping pace just behind her with Fari as they ran.

"A special bow," Krysta allowed, trying to keep her mind off the sky and on the path. "And two deadly arrows."

Chapter Fourteen

"How can that massive space-cloud be humanoid?" Lord Gith's scorn was obvious, even with the sobbing backsong of the Chimera. The beautiful creatures stood like a golden-flecked rainbow of manes, tails and fur, gazing skyward near the distant end of the orchard. They had settled into a mournful dirge, which unsettled listeners more than their original sounds of alarm.

For the hundredth time in the last few stellar minutes alone, Darkyn wished for his double-axe. Though not a peaceful or proper alternative, the blade certainly would have made for a simpler solution. He forced himself to relax his tense jaw, to unclench his fists. His sensitive eyes studied first the incredulous face of the lizard slayer, then the changes in the skies over Uhr. How was it possible *Barung* had approached so quickly? Had he been quiescent and only waiting to identify the location of his most hated enemies?

The children and lineage of the men who defeated him the first time he rose to power. Of course. Of course! How could I not realize that? How could I not understand what would draw him here – and why?

"I scarce understand it," Darkyn said to Lord Gith as evenly as he could. "But apparently *Barung* was an ancient practitioner of native magiks, one who turned to evil and darkness many centuries ago. The forefathers of the races with psi-talents could not defeat him, but they were able to banish him and set into motion the plan we now carry out." He coughed. "With the gracious assistance of those more skilled at technology, of course. As you can all see, his approach has escalated. The crisis is upon us, and we must act now—as one people, united in our purpose."

One of the Kaeradi priests stepped forward, his sapphire robes billowing in the increasing wind. "'When *Barung* returns,'" he spoke-sang, "'six shall lead him home, blended from the triangle, joined by the stone.'"

A female in the Perth delegation joined him, lifting her voice to sing, "'Let loose the gentle innocents, for music soothes the shield. Feed him on The People's blood, and drive him to the field.'"

An imperial Bandu took the forefront of her group, and Darkyn recognized her as Queen Unk, one of the most formidable rulers in the fearsome history of that planet. "We are to understand, then, that the six have been blended from the original three psi-strong races, and are now joined through their relation to you." She nodded to the yellow stone seated in the center of his double-axe *pa* mark.

Darkyn nodded, feeling it best to keep his silence before Queen Unk.

She studied him for a moment, then gave what appeared to be a gesture of approval or acceptance, and stepped back.

"If Queen Unk accepts it, then so do we," the tiny Nostan commander announced in his piping soprano. He gazed at the Bandu queen adoringly from across the orchard path, causing the queen to pull back her purple lips to show her menacing dual fangs.

Conversation spread like ground fire through the *pao*. In minutes, the leaders had all acknowledged these truths.

At last, even Lord Gith ceased his meager protest. "So what is the plan, then, Ta of The People? How do your...*ancients*...mean for us to defeat this creature they loosed on us so long ago?"

"*Barung* is first and foremost bent on revenge," Darkyn replied. He saw the Perth warriors nod, and once more noted the fanatic, flinty gleam in their eyes. "We plan to use that to our advantage. The six of us, children and progeny of his greatest enemies, will draw him away from Uhr, toward the low-density area in space where the world of Perth died. Once there, we will have to contain him long enough for the energy-draining traps set by the ancients to destroy him."

"And how do we know these traps are even there?" Lord Gith's voice gained volume as he spoke. He raised a fist and shook it at the sky.

A Perth delegate, male, easily two heads taller than Gith and eerily like Queen Unk with his flowing white hair and purple tunic and breeches, stepped forward then. He leaned across the orchard path toward the lizard slaver. "Have you a better idea, OrTan? Do you believe your skull ships capable of destroying a force that has eaten worlds?"

"The traps are there," said Hoth, the Kaeradi peace chief. "We have been charged with the monitoring these many years, and we have done so. If *Barung* is led into the field and contained, he will be drained and crushed and returned to the universe as the space dust he should be."

Lord Gith seemed less inclined to offend the Kaeradi leader, and somewhat chastened by the Perth challenge. The lizard knew, as did everyone, that no force could stand against the attacking evil—that such slim hopes as the ancient traps were their only hopes.

Overhead, the sky darkened as if a true night were falling. Darkyn had never seen Uhr such a shade of gray, and he found it chilling.

"Brother," Akad said. "I will get the decoy ship you have kept hidden near the dryland basin."

Darkyn turned on his brother and put his hands on the priest's shoulders. "What do you mean?"

"You know what I mean," Akad said in his ever-calm voice. "No matter his appearance on the vision-plane, in the gray world above our consciousness, *Barung* is a primitive being. He will not follow the ships unless he tastes the blood they have to offer — unless he knows at gut-level his enemies are within his reach."

A glimmer broke through the darkness. Darkyn's heart began to hammer unpleasantly. The ships were coming. Krysta, Ki, and Fari had indeed been accepted into *Arcus*, *Calamus*, and *Telum*. It was only logical and right that their mates should join them as the seconds on board, that the six would be completed in such a fashion. He knew that, and yet, and yet—

"No, Brother!" Darkyn kept hold of Akad's shoulders. "I cannot lose you like that."

"You will not lose me. Our beliefs don't run in such a fashion." Akad smiled. His eyes crinkled at the corners, and once more, Darkyn could see his brother's eternal fatigue and burden.

"N-No," he stammered again, unwilling to turn loose his *a'mun* twin, to send him flying to such a gruesome fate. "This is my duty, my obligation! It's my blood *Barung* must take."

"You are needed in the circle, and you know it for fact now." Akad's deep brown eyes grew heavy as he glanced up toward the hovering *Arcus*, their Bow, with *Calamus* and *Telum*, the equally formidable Arrows hovering off either wing. "And I am tired," he admitted. "I have served two people with the fullness of my heart, mind, and energy for many stellar years. This is my fate, Brother. Your blood and mine are the same. Who else could tempt the *Barung*?"

"I cannot see this happen." Darkyn heard the dry wheeze in his own words.

And then hands were on his shoulders. Georgia and Elise.

"Step away from him," one of them said. Darkyn couldn't tell which. It was likely better that he didn't know.

"Escort Akad to his destination," Elise instructed the *Legio*. "See that his vessel takes off without incident."

The wolfish Kaeradi red-robes moved so swiftly Darkyn had no time to think, much less form a feasible alternative. In truth, he knew of no alternative, but he couldn't bring himself to embrace that fact.

Georgia turned Darkyn to face her then, so that he couldn't see his brother departing the *pao*, the path, and ultimately Uhr and the blessings and bounty of this life. He wasn't sure what to expect from her, but what he saw were hints and sparks of the ancient wizard who met them on the sands of the beach in the vision-plane.

"Get a grip," she said simply and firmly, despite the tears coursing down her cheeks, blending with the wild markings of her *pa*. "He's always right, your brother. We have our duties now, to Akad and to everyone else. Don't make me think I've greatly underestimated *you*."

From high in the darkening sky of Uhr, Guardian let out a wrenching cry. It rose above the infinitely sad song of the Chimera, above the restless, frightened murmurs of the crowd, above the growing wind and the distant but distinct thrum of the approaching *Barung*.

Darkyn felt like the falcon was screaming his pain for him, leaving him some sanity and dignity in this, the first moment he did not think he could bear.

He knew Georgia Tul'Mar was correct. The only course of action open to him now was to complete this task, and in doing so, honor the sacrifice his *a'mun* twin so freely made.

We have our duties now... Her words rasped against his mind until he found the strength to move, to head for the hovering *Arcus, Calamus*, and *Telum* with Georgia and Elise following close behind.

When he glanced upward, Guardian had departed. Teeth grinding, fists clenched, Darkyn kept walking down the orchard path, through the *pao* throng, though he knew his losses had increased.

The falcon had gone to Akad, to be certain his brother did not die alone.

"Time...for...grief...later," he told himself, and realized even Krysta would grieve the stubborn, jealous bird. They had found an accord as of late, the two women who had claimed his heart.

In his wake, Darkyn heard his warriors giving information and organizing the *pao* into groups. Those with psi-strength would monitor in the ways of the mind, lending whatever energy they could to the *pa* of the three ships, for as long as they could. Those with technological strengths would assist with communications and problem-solving as needed.

Those with lesser shares of either, they would speak to the gods, to the goddesses, to any favorable powers who might listen.

We have our duties now…

Darkyn stumbled.

Elise and Georgia moved up to support him, and he heard the call of his *hallas*.

Come to me, she said, in the patient, loving voice Akad would have used in the same situation. Only Akad had sealed off his mind and person, and Darkyn knew he would never again feel his brother's healing mind-touch, or the force of his embrace.

Come to me now, my love, my munas, Krysta repeated. *Don't forget your nature. You are made of stone, when need be.*

Darkyn became aware of Ki Tul'Mar and Fari in the link of six. They were offering a grudging sort of tribute, neither certain they could force themselves to do what Darkyn was doing — surrendering a brother for the good of the whole — no matter if that brother volunteered.

Even in his final choices, Akad unifies and spreads peace. Darkyn's statement dropped into the link, to be met with five gentle agreements.

And then he reached the spot below *Arcus*.

Krysta lowered the ship expertly beside him, and he stepped through the hull that would have opened only for him.

Keeping the ship steady with her mind was no easy task. Krysta battled her own grief and tears along with the increasing awareness of her sha's crippling pain. Ki and

Fari had equal difficulty, but Ki managed to bring *Calamus* to bear for Elise to board. Fari dipped down with *Telum* and retrieved Georgia shortly afterward.

On Krysta's command, the three ships moved up toward the turbulent orbit around Uhr.

Companel communications chattered in the back of her awareness, though she had no companel.

The People were trying to land all of the *pao* ships — but they could not.

Just as Akad couldn't take off, and Krysta couldn't lead her now-cloaked ships into orbit.

Something was blocking them!

A shield. Fari swore. *It's nothing of our making, and I don't believe it's being cast by The People.*

It's coming from...him, Ki confirmed, and Krysta knew he was using his formidable logic and new awareness like a laser probing tool. *It seems to be made of tangible emotion. I know that is not possible, but I sense discord. Unrest and misery. Somehow this beast has given energy to our fears and pains, and he is using them to hold us down.*

Of course, Krysta thought, cursing her own stupidity. *Most predators paralyze their prey in some fashion, just before they strike.*

"'Let loose the gentle innocents,'" Darkyn murmured, broadcasting the thought to all psi-adepts on the surface. Krysta felt him change the gating on his mind's energy to loan her more strength, to free her mind to make the call she wanted to make.

Please, she psi-sent immediately, calling up images of Chimera on Uhr and even on Arda, should any be able to perceive her. *Help us. I beg you. We need your song!*

211

Stellar seconds passed, then stellar minutes. With each tick of her mental clock, Krysta's heart hammered harder against her ribs. She tentatively reached for Darkyn's comfort, but he seemed seized by a distant stupor. But for the energy leaving the various gates of his mind, he was a million miles from their present.

What if they don't come? She pitched this worry for her mind alone. *What if – ?*

But she didn't get a chance to finish the thought.

A swell of high-pitched but amazingly smooth and pleasing music met her physical ears, coming even louder through her psi-perceptions.

The song had a timeless feel, and Krysta wondered if she knew it. She knew that was impossible, but perhaps the melody was archetypal. Universal.

Whatever it was, she thought it might be working. The unrest in the skies began to settle in spite of its malevolent intent.

She felt a ripple in the bleak energy holding *Arcus* hostage.

From Uhr's surface, the song intensified. A golden-white glow rose into space, accompanying the notes, swirling like the delicate but powerful sounds.

Companel chatter picked up. The People were finding holes in the shield that had dropped over the little moon. In rapid, organized fashion, they brought the *pao* ships down to the safety of the surface, setting the smaller ones down on the landing strip and the larger ones on the edge of the drylands where space allowed. Shortly, nothing would be in the air but the three psi-powered vessels, Akad's decoy vessel, and *Barung*.

The Chimera sang and sang, giving of their wondrous, guileless natures, and driving fissures into the dark barrier of discord and despair surrounding Uhr. No such emotions could withstand the joy and warmth of that simple, forceful song.

Steady, Elise instructed through their link, with Georgia's force of will backing her up.

Krysta narrowed her focus, forcing out as much of the psychic and technological noise as she could. *Arcus* felt like a part of her body and mind, moving at unimaginable speed in response to a single thought-direction.

"Darkyn," Krysta said aloud to her sha, who had settled numbly into the chair beside her. She offered her hand, and after a moment, he took it.

Useless platitudes about Akad drifted through her mind, but she discarded them. The best thing she could do was stand beside her mate, to offer him as much of her as she could spare and still fly the ship. This realization came to her easily, as many things about healing were beginning to come. They just...made sense. Seemed right. Like masterful shadings in a portrait, or the perfect addition to a collection. She could see the needs faster and more clearly with every passing moment.

Not bad for a mass murderer's direct descendent, she thought darkly.

Sister, he was an executioner. Ki managed to sound like a patronizing older brother even in such a maelstrom of activity. *He had a role in his world, and he played it.*

He enjoyed it, she countered. *He was dangerous.*

No, Fari argued. *He was efficient.*

Enough, Georgia snapped. *We'll argue about genetic stains later, okay? I think it's time to act.*

213

Krysta pulled her awareness back to the emptied orbits of Uhr. *Arcus, Calamus,* and *Telum* now flew alone, but for a refitted cargo ship a half-rotation to port. Further out, a now-condensed and streaking blackness arched toward them, moving almost too quickly to perceive.

And right above them, the Chimera song opened a massive fissure, wide enough to release her ships and Akad as well.

The evil is upon us! she called. *To me, Brothers! To me quickly!*

Ki and Fari responded with no questions or comments. *Calamus* and *Telum* streaked to her wing points, and she led them out of the barrier. Immediately, she extended the shield of *Arcus* to encompass them behind a wall of *pa.*

This had been the design of the ships' many makers, to create a host of weapons that would seem no more than normal space energy to the perception of *Barung.* If he scanned them, he would sense *pa,* but *pa* was everywhere, in all things, in various concentrations throughout any living galaxy or universe.

Barung would instead, they hoped, concentrate on the unnatural vessel escaping Uhr's orbit, the single unshielded ship. This would deflect his course to Uhr, and if Akad played his role well, aim *Barung* in the direction they wanted him to go.

As if on cue, Akad's psi-voice seemed to boom through space and time.

I am here, Barung. The son of your enemies, many times mixed. I have come to kill you as my ancestors could not. Do you dare to challenge me?

Instantly, the blackness slowed and changed course for the cargo ship. Akad piloted the vessel to the edge of Uhr's far-orbital space, well beyond the dark shield that sought to hold him back. Krysta realized the little vessel, though ramshackle in appearance, had been refitted for speed and endurance.

Another surprise for the Eater of Worlds. Another tiny advantage in a game of fractions and parries.

"You claim to know my enemies." *Barung's* voice sounded real, physical, and right next her elbow. Krysta startled, but kept *Arcus* from reacting only by sheer force of will—and the help of her sha, who seemed to have left his stupor. He was standing now, directly beside her, his presence like the strongest rock dead-center in a howling storm.

I know your enemies, the ones who banished you, Akad said, nudging his ship forward, leading the evil farther away from Uhr, and from Arda, toward the field. *I call you out in the name of Kaerad, and the warriors of the spirit. I call you out in the name of Arda, and the warriors of the mind.*

He paused, putting more distance between himself and Uhr, leading the *Barung* further into the desired field. Krysta eased her ships forward, overtaking Akad and positioning her tiny fleet in front of him, ready to drop their cloak at the right moment.

Akad dropped his final challenge then, and he did so with a perfectly-timed flair of rage and indignation. *You filthy, murdering bastard. I call you out in the name of Myrddin and Perth, and the warriors of the heart, who will always survive no matter your destruction!*

Space seemed to shake as *Barung* emitted a terrible roar. His essence changed size and shape, becoming a maw of unimaginable size. In the blink of an eye, he snapped up Akad's ship, then seemed to spit it free seconds later.

Krysta had an image of the vessel tumbling away through ripples and rips in time and space. The speed was lethal, if not the shockwaves of disturbed natural space. In seconds, the vessel disintegrated, leaving a shocked hole in the consciousness of Krysta, Darkyn, and the rest of the circle.

"For nothing," Darkyn said dryly, squeezing Krysta's hand so hard she thought her fingers might break.

"He had not the taste of my enemies," *Barung* murmured. The beast sounded petulant, almost like a child. "He was lying."

Krysta froze, mentally and physically. The pain in her hand echoed Darkyn's rage and profound sadness, mingled with utter frustration. She heard the confusion and stress of her brothers' minds, and Elise and Georgia. Then she heard Darkyn in quick communication with the psi-adepts back on Uhr. His hand released hers and passed over the stone in his chest, which now glowed a brilliant yellow — and she understood.

Akad was *a'mun*, born with no stone. Like most of the modern Kaeradi, he wouldn't have the full essence of a third of the trilogy *Barung* sought.

How easy it was for a grand plan to fail, to fall on such a tiny, trivial point.

Fractions and parries, Krysta thought desperately as the dark energy force grew yet again compact, and began to turn back toward Uhr.

"He was lying!" *Barung* roared.

Perhaps, came a steady, strong retort Krysta recognized, but couldn't place. *I, however, am not. If you would have a taste of the blood of your enemies, then try to take me!*

Who is that? Ki and Fari asked almost at the same time.

Krysta glanced at her sha, and the surprised admiration of his expression gave her the answer.

"It's Brand, your cousin. The one who killed Kolot." A shudder of hope took her, but she gathered herself quickly. "He must have been hovering in low orbit, in case we had need of him—he's of your blood!"

"And he has the stone." Darkyn rested his hand on his chest.

To restore my honor, to right my wrongs! Brand's psi-cry rang through Krysta's mind, and any with the skill to hear, as he streaked toward them.

Barung hesitated, but in the end, could not pass up the possibility.

He gave pursuit.

You have my blessings, cousin. Darkyn's mind-voice was heavy with pride and new grief. *Your honor is clean, and you die without wrongs.*

Brand's relief and determination felt as tangible as the dark shield they had broken through to escape into space, just before *Barung* swallowed the racing ship in one swift, brutal movement.

Krysta waited, breathless.

This time, the Eater of Worlds did not spit out his prey. Instead, he gave a satisfied growl of hunger.

Before he could turn back to Uhr, Krysta dropped the *pa* shielding concealing *Arcus, Calamus,* and *Telum.*

"We are here!" she shouted in her mind and aloud. "Do you think to take us so easily?"

They waited only long enough for *Barung* to identify them, to imagine how it would be to kill off the lines of his long-sworn enemies in a single coup.

Once more, space seemed to shake with his roar.

Krysta felt a charge of panic and determination. Doubling her focus on her ship, she pointed *Arcus* for her destination and began a flight faster than any she had known.

Ki and Fari rocketed behind her, so close and in such unison they might have been exhaust from her wings.

Barung bore down on them, a relentless wave of hatred and rage.

"Why do you run from me?" he asked Krysta. "Do you think I will let you keep the love and happiness you think you have found?"

Darkyn stroked her shoulder, helping her keep her thoughts clear of her fears. She was surprised how easy it was to ignore the bastard.

But then he turned his attack on Darkyn. "And you— how many failures can I count? I just killed your brother, Ta. You failed your *a'mun* twin, and lost him forever."

Krysta flinched as Darkyn stiffened, his thoughts ranging out toward that distant stupor she had felt when he first came aboard. She linked her arm with his, directed as much love as she could through their flow of energy, and worked frantically to keep flying the ship.

Do not fall into his trap. Fari's voice rose through their link. *My honest mistakes cost my parents their lives, and I thought they had cost me my sister. I almost gave up — but that is what evil and despair want. Hold fast, my new brother-by-marriage. Keep your mind on your shanna. Your hallas.*

Darkyn's grip on Krysta's arm tightened, and gradually, he brought himself back from that distant place of pain. Back to the present. Back to her.

Barung made the rounds, attempting to inflict doubt on Ki, on Fari, on Elise, and finally Georgia. It became easier to ignore him as their bonds strengthened.

Krysta expanded her perceptions, gaining an understanding of their location in space, in the "field" constructed by the ancients. In a sense, it was no more than a rudimentary energy fence, except that it had gained strength over the eons to have something like a life and consciousness of its own. Such was the way of all things of power, left to their own devices too long. They were inside the fence, streaking toward its core, at which point they would have to break their unity and head for the three points of the triangle the fence connected. From those three points, fates and forces of the universe willing, they would trap *Barung* where he hovered, unsure which enemy to pursue, and hold him until the weight of empty space crushed him completely.

They had moved so fast—unbelievably far, unbelievably swift! They were nearing the point where they would have to separate. Krysta felt loathe to do that, to let go of her family and feel them scatter to distant points in this desperate, nearly hopeless gambit.

She felt the comforting hum of *Arcus*, and wondered if the ship was trying to soothe her newest hesitations and fears. These fascinating crafts were something almost outside the range of possibility, just like defeating *Barung*.

With life, with pa, with love, there is nothing outside the range of possibility, Krysta, my sister of heart and purpose. I charge you with remembering this, now and always.

A sharp, stunned silence suffused the mental linkage of the six.

It was Darkyn who finally found his psi-voice long enough to ask, *Who said that?*

But they all knew.

The rhythm, pattern, and calm, confident presentation belonged to only one man: Akad of Arda and Uhr, priest and brother to them all.

Something tickled Krysta's cheek, and she knew before she reached up to catch the item what it was.

A single black falcon feather.

Krysta allowed the image to pass from mind to mind in their link before she placed the feather between her breasts like a battle amulet.

Ahead loomed the nexus where *Barung*'s past crimes would become his current doom. The site where Perth once stood, now an empty, psi-reinforced hole in space.

With one arm linked with her sha and one hand on the feather between her breasts, Krysta flew straight at that deadly hole.

Closer and closer.

She felt Ki's alertness. Fari's tenseness. The concern of Darkyn, Elise, and Georgia.

And behind them, all too close, she felt *Barung* and his terrible, murderous purpose.

With only fractions to spare, Krysta psi-shouted, *Now!* The force of her will mingled with Darkyn's support and strength pulled *Arcus* upward in a steep climb.

Calamus and *Telum* followed. Like arrows fired from their bow, they streaked away. Fari and Georgia headed for Earth in *Telum*. *Calamus* carried Elise and Ki toward

Kaerad. Krysta and Darkyn, charged with the hardest task but wielding the fastest ship, curved over the outer edge of *Barung*'s cloud of foul energy and shot back toward Arda.

Barung shouted and roared, but could not slow his headlong pursuit. His essence tumbled into Perth's dead space, which closed around him like a merciless web.

Krysta leaned forward, guiding *Arcus* on a clear path, trusting her solid knowledge of stars, planets, and large asteroids—and trusting the ship and her instincts for the rest. She hadn't dared fly this fast before, for fear of outstripping *Calamus* and *Telum*, but that was no issue now. She could feel the energies of her brothers receding, feel the smallest shimmer of what Darkyn must have experienced, separating from Akad with relative certainty that they would never be rejoined. She wondered at his strength to stand even that pain, and bore hers only with the warmth of her sha's presence.

"Fly," he whispered. "Fly, *hallas!*"

Chapter Fifteen

Space had become a blur of speed and trepidation for Darkyn Weil. He had been stripped of all roles now, past that of Krysta's sha and member of a circle of six who had taken on a task of utter necessity—and madness. He had no axe, no voice of authority. Nothing but his heart and mind and ready hands.

How could they possibly reach Arda in time? How could the other two make it to Earth and Kaerad?

With life, with pa, *with love, there is nothing outside the range of possibility...*

Akad's words repeated in Darkyn's mind as he glanced at the feather protruding from Krysta's jumpsuit. Once more, he felt a wash of wonder and awe. *Were you speaking from the grave, Brother? I saw your ship explode.*

With life, with pa, *with love, there is nothing outside the range of possibility...*

A riddle for a later time, but a riddle of hope, of potential.

He leaned into the ship's explosive forward motion. "How long?"

"Stellar minutes," Krysta breathed. She looked like a goddess in an artist's rendering. Her white-silver hair shimmered against her cheeks and shoulders, while her ample *pa* sparkled in the natural metallic gray light of the ship's interior. As it had before when she was aboard, Krysta's *pa* pulsed in time with the hull as Arcus hurtled through space. One hand remained between her breasts, on the falcon feather. Her other arm was looped through his, keeping them as close as they could be in this difficult and tense sequence of events.

His sense of the *Barung* remained bitter and sharp, like the pungent smell of death lingering in his nose and mind. The beast thrashed in his trap, sending out bolts of horror and gut-wrenching, poisonous emotional pain.

For now, though, it—he—was contained.

Darkyn's impressions of the two ships lessened with each passing moment, and somehow, he knew this was wrong. Using tricks of the mind long-trained by Akad, he re-gated the energy of his thoughts, supporting Krysta but also holding tight to the threads of connection to his family-by-marriage on *Calamus* and *Telum*. Georgia and Elise responded to his effort in kind, strengthening their bond with him.

Sexual energy flowed into the link from Georgia's connection.

Gods. The woman was sucking Fari's cock at such a moment! What would possess her — ?

Darkyn's thoughts broke off as his shanna's arm disengaged from his. She dropped her hand to his crotch and squeezed, simultaneously relieving and worsening the instant erection he developed.

"Be at ease," Krysta said aloud. "Having sex is a normal state of being for Georgia. She functions best when aroused. So does my brother. She's but following a true instinct to give them more power."

Darkyn considered this as Krysta continued stroking him through his breeches.

He ground his teeth at the pleasure and absurdity of the moment. "Given my fortunes of late, mating with you aside of course, you will tell me that frustrated arousal is my most powerful state."

"Actually yes, it is." Krysta squeezed and released, squeezed and released, bringing him further toward a place of absorption in her touch. "And mine as well, though less so since meeting you."

Careful to keep Akad's feather in her fingers, she lowered the zipper on her jumpsuit.

Darkyn groaned at the sight of her hard nipples, one sweetapple and one pa-silver, unfettered and awaiting his mouth.

"No, sha." Krysta kept her eyes straight forward. "For now, just look and enjoy while you can."

Her skilled fingers kept a broken rhythm on his cock now, preventing him from coming to orgasm. Darkyn clenched his jaw so hard his eyes narrowed. "And what, may I ask, is Ki's most powerful state—and Elise, his shanna?"

"Satiated," Krysta said without hesitating. "They've already come to orgasm once."

In his mind's eye, Darkyn saw the Sailmaster of Arda, piloting his vessel as surely and easily as Krysta, with his graceful, sensual woman bent forward in front of him, bracing herself on a shelf where the companel in a normal ship would have been. Elise was naked and flushed, and she still rode her sha's cock like a woman prolonging her own satisfaction.

"Life is less than fair at times," he growled, then realized he had enjoyed a few blissful seconds of distraction from burden, worry, and grief. In those few seconds, the power of his mind had increased. He was helping in the guidance of *Arcus* more, sparing Krysta's energy to aid in strengthening their psi-bonds.

His *hallas* was wise indeed.

And then the truth of Akad's last statement struck him.

I charge you with remembering this, now and always...

Krysta would be the one to remember such things, wouldn't she? It seemed a natural role for her.

The farther they got from *Barung* and from each other, the more difficult the overall energy drains became.

Krysta let go his throbbing cock, with his understanding but also his frustration. She placed a hand on the forward shelf of *Arcus*, and Darkyn knew she was falling into a more direct link with the ship. Her knees were shaking.

"We've entered Ardani space," she whispered as Darkyn moved behind her and wrapped his arms around her. He fondled her nipples, feeling the fires of her passion ignite beneath his touch. The nubs swelled and hardened, then swelled and hardened even more. He eased back on the pressure and teasing when he sensed her arousal beginning to overbalance her focus.

Darkyn found himself grateful that this journey would be so short, that they each flew ships that defied the normal space-time continuum. He didn't think he could bear for it to go on much longer.

And in the relentless theater of his mind, the Sailmaster's woman reached another orgasm. The Sailkeeper and his bride found a new position to enjoy each other while still attending to the needs of the ship. Georgia was leaning back across the forward shelf of

Telum, legs spread wide and red curls glistening with moisture from her swollen quim. Fari entered her with ease, holding her hips and pumping even as his arrow flew through the increasingly crowded space of Earth's solar system.

Darkyn groaned, then sighed. "Life is less than fair at times," he repeated as he rubbed his own cock against Krysta's ass.

Arcus began to slow, and Darkyn realized they were taking up orbit around Arda. He felt more than heard the ongoing song of the Chimera on the planet below, and farther away, on Uhr. It sounded like a welcome. It sounded blissfully, wonderfully like home.

In the distance, though, the bellows and shrieks of *Barung* were unmistakable.

And the fact that his thrashings were more effective.

He is beginning to break free, Darkyn psi-warned, hearing the edge to his own broadcast. *We must give energy to reinforcing the containment until the pressure destroys him.*

How? Ki's question carried both concern and frustration. *We are at maximum, all of us.*

There was a moment of stillness following the truth of his comment. Krysta sagged back against him, and Darkyn knew how tired she was. He cupped her breasts gently and kissed her neck, feeling the sweet sting of her *pa* against his lips.

The sting became a short, sharp burn as the hull of *Arcus* rippled, absorbing the Chimera song like a thirsty animal.

The boost settled into Krysta, and she managed to stand straight again. Darkyn kept his hands on her breasts, kept his cock firmly lodged against her ass.

Channel all the energy to me when I ask, she instructed suddenly, in a voice enhanced beyond what Darkyn expected. He startled, pinching her nipples in the process, and the flow of raw power over his fingers kept him from protesting her decision.

He knew instantly what she was considering, how she was thinking of drawing power from the ships, from the worlds at the triangle points.

This could kill you, hallas, he warned in a psi-voice pitched for her mind only.

She sighed and leaned back against him. *It could kill us all,* munas. *If so, then we all will have to die.*

Krysta's even tones made Darkyn understand he was in the presence of a spiritual force beyond his mate alone. It was what she called him, however, that focused his will and attention sharper than the point of a well-thrown lance.

Munas. *Made of stone.*

Yes. Just as she is hallas, made of fire. A perfect match.

He held his soul's mate closer, surrendering himself to her truth, her strength, determined to be stone to her flames. Determined to do whatever it took to help her, protect her, and destroy this evil that threatened them all.

One by one, Darkyn opened the gates to his consciousness full and wide, preparing for her call.

It came with a forceful, *Now!*

Reality left Darkyn in a harsh rush. He went blind and deaf all at once, and lost a sense of his body in the next instant.

The ships had disappeared.

He seemed to be…hovering.

Above.

But above where?

Not Arda, no. The space below was too vast. Like the base of a great galactic pyramid, with a dark hole, center bottom. A pit. A pit with something horrid and dangerous crashing against its walls and sealed roof.

On three sides of him, he could make out brilliant points of silver light, each connected to and feeding into the point where he stood. Brilliant white-silver flames shot up and down the connections, as if building them stronger, drawing them closer and tighter.

Darkyn found it difficult to keep his footing.

I am munas, he told himself. *I am the stone that anchors, the stone that doesn't burn.*

He then understood with a fierce rush of pride what — and who — those nearby silver-white flames were, in corporeal form.

A full awareness possessed him, and he felt all of his new family in their purest forms. Ki and Fari Tul'Mar had become the energy that kept them suspended in space, their support and power. Elise had become the strength of mind, the steadiness that kept them focused and in the same location. Georgia had become a halo of red fire, protecting them from any harm or disruption.

And then there was Krysta, the brilliance who used her infinite love to pull extra energy from their respective home worlds into the *pa* of their ships, and then pulled the *pa* of the ships into their very beings. From there, she had joined them by drawing on the true essence of each personality.

They had become a solid force of *pa*, directly over *Barung*. They were holding him in the pit of dead space, gradually compressing it more, and more still. Like their ships had been, the six were now unbound by conventions of time and space. They were now limitless.

What are we? Darkyn wondered. *Are we still human?*

For now, came Elise's bottomless response, *you are munas. Only munas.*

Respecting the instruction of their stabilizing force, Darkyn returned his attention to being the stone the other energies could use as an anchor point.

Sooner than he thought possible, the task was done.

Barung was trapped beneath the pyramid of energy they had created—but would the force of their will be enough to destroy him?

Darkyn felt grateful for the blood of Arda's first and strongest *Ord'pa*, flowing through the veins of Krysta and her brothers. There was, in fact, some place in the universe for righteous ruthlessness, and that place was right here, right now.

A bubble of silver light began to form around Darkyn. It expanded to be large enough to comfortably hold six people in corporeal form, and attached itself to the topmost point of the pyramid, directly beneath his feet.

Moments later, Darkyn began to feel his body again, though a faint electrical charge seemed to play along his skin. He realized he was naked. His *pa* hummed pleasantly, and the stone in his chest glowed brilliant yellow as it vibrated.

Elise and Georgia materialized next, also naked. Darkyn allowed himself a healthy appreciation of their beauty, so different, but neither less than the other. Elise had a classical shape, with the smooth, sharply defined lines of an ice sculpture. Her breasts, while not as full as

Krysta's, were certainly pleasing, along with the notable blush of her nipples. The shimmering blonde hair of her head repeated itself between her legs, and flames of *pa* seemed to lick every inch of her hips, thighs, and belly.

Georgia was flame to Elise's ice, with wild red hair on her head and thatch, and irregular vines of *pa* covering her body in random, bright patterns. Her nipples, large and round, and pulled to a point of arousal, approached the dark color of his shanna's gifts, but didn't reach it.

As he stared, filled with relief, more shapes began to materialize in the bubble. Three, exactly. Krysta, and her brothers.

Darkyn paid little mind to the men. His eyes were drawn to his woman with undeniable magnetic force.

As always, she was a splendid vision, even more so as she became whole in her naked splendor, *pa* shimmering in rhythm with the bubble around them. A new mark graced her chest, dead center between her breasts, and Darkyn recognized it for what it was. Guardian's gift— Akad's feather—only now in *pa* form, alive in Krysta's flesh evermore.

He wanted to hold her, taste the sweet wetness of her mouth, caress her nipples, bring her endless hours of pleasure some place safe, and quiet, and dark—three conditions they had rarely enjoyed in their short time together.

"What now?" Georgia asked, approaching Krysta close enough to stroke her shoulder.

Krysta took a slow breath and glanced down, through the floor of the bubble and the point of the tightly drawn pyramid. "We have done what we can. Now, we give what energy and strength we can to these bonds and wait for him to be destroyed — or defeat his trap."

"And what happens to us?" Elise's voice held no hint of regret or fear. Only wonder, and perhaps concern for her child.

"I do not know." Krysta's answer was weighted with burden, as Akad's had often been.

Darkyn started toward her, and realized Georgia and Elise had heard the same heaviness in her words. She needed them.

The six of them needed each other, and all the energy they could generate.

Before he could reach his shanna, Georgia and Elise had her cradled between them, kissing her neck and lips, running hands along her curves and rivers of *pa*.

A groan of need and desire filled the bubble, and Darkyn realized it was his own. Fari and Ki gave him small, uncomfortable smiles that spoke of kinship and understanding. Like him, they had erections of massive proportions.

Unlike him, however, they had both had relief many times over this day.

"I do not yet know how I feel about you," Ki Tul'Mar grumbled. "I will never know unless we survive this moment in time, which seems unlikely at best."

Fari agreed with a grunt.

Their meaning was clear.

Here and now, Darkyn could sample the pleasures of his family, his circle — and he should, for they might have a short time to yet know and enjoy this life. On the off chance they survived, the brothers, would make their decisions about him over time.

Darkyn didn't need a second invitation. He strode toward the women, focusing on Krysta, on her expression of relaxed joy at the caresses of Elise and Georgia. These women had enjoyed each other before, many times. They knew just where to pinch his hallas, just where to stroke her nipples and quim to draw out long sighs of pleasure.

He stood, holding his own cock, unable to take his eyes from the gathered loveliness.

Georgia kissed Krysta fondly, gently on the mouth, the differing shades of their lips mingling into one color as Georgia massaged first one nipple and then the other with long, flexible fingers.

Krysta moaned as Georgia kneaded her breasts, bringing the nubs to fine points as Elise, standing on Krysta's other side, kissed Krysta's ear and ran her tongue down the splash of *pa* on Krysta's neck.

Krysta had her arms around the women, squeezing their asses as she often squeezed Darkyn's cock.

Elise's hand drifted into the silvery thatch of hair between Krysta's legs and began a slow, sensual rub of her clit.

Darkyn heard the wetness move around Elise's fingers, smelled the ready musk of Krysta's arousal.

His hand tightened on his cock, holding back his own desire.

Let the monster rattle and scream in his prison at the bottom of this pyramid. Let him try to break through our energy field as we pour these passions, these truths into the bonds!

Beside the women, the Tul'Mar brothers gazed at their mates and stroked their own staffs, groaning almost in rhythm with the pleasure of their shannas.

Krysta tensed and gasped, and Darkyn felt the build of her first orgasm. His eyes fixed on her face now, on the closed, fluttering lids, the half-open mouth, sometimes brushed by kisses from the women pleasuring her.

She was so beautiful.

So beautiful, he said in his mind, directing the thought to Krysta, who received it with a new gasp and a shiver of joy.

You are close, hallas. Darkyn felt his own feral smile and squeezed his cock harder to keep his control. *Lips on your lips and neck, fingers pinching your nipples to aching points, that fine, graceful hand in your quim, dipping in and out of your wet center, pulling back to rub your clit over and over. Harder and harder.*

Krysta moaned low and long, thrusting her breasts into Georgia's firm grip, bucking against Elise's fast-moving fingers.

"Yes, *hallas*," he said aloud. "Come while I watch. Come screaming, and I'll make you scream again and again."

At this, Elise and Georgia shuddered with Krysta, both groaning. Georgia pinched Krysta's nipples harder. Elise stroked Krysta's clit faster.

Krysta came then, just as Darkyn instructed, with a low, satisfying scream.

She sank down between Elise and Georgia, her heavy-lidded gaze fixed on him.

Fari moved in almost immediately, spreading himself on the silvery floor in front of Krysta. Georgia straddled him. The sound of his prick sinking home in the woman's wet sanctuary made Darkyn ache to stride past him, push Krysta up against the wall of the bubble, and do the same.

Instead, he remembered his earlier lessons.

Fari and Georgia were strongest while fucking. Ki and Elise were strongest while satiated. He and Krysta—they were strongest while frustrated.

So we will keep our strength at its height a bit longer. As long as we can. Win or die. I should think this is the sweetest form of combat.

"Have you been fucked by two men?" he asked Georgia, who rocked back and forth, taking her sha's prick as deep as it would go.

She nodded and leaned forward, exposing her ass to Ki.

With a nudge from Elise, and a rumble of pleasure, Ki moved forward. Elise stopped him long enough to moisten his staff with her full, tempting mouth, then smiled as he knelt between his brother's legs and entered Georgia's ass with a firm smack of wet flesh and bollocks.

Georgia moaned, as did Fari, who was feeling the rush of her increased pleasure.

Krysta inched up on the bubble's far wall to better see Georgia in front of her. She seemed doubly aroused by Georgia's frenetic state. The redheaded beauty had her eyes closed, her arms braced against her husband's side. Leaned forward as she was, she was at Ki's mercy, and Fari, in turn, was at the mercy of Georgia's movement. Each time Ki slammed into Georgia's ass, she moved forward, partly unsheathing Fari's prick, then slamming back to take it deeper. Her breasts bounced and rubbed over Fari's *pa*, literally sending out sparks.

Krysta let out her own noise of pleasure, pinched her *pa*-coated nipple, and moved her free hand to stroke her own clit.

Wait!

She stopped at Darkyn's sharp command.

Elise moved over to Darkyn, stretched up on her tiptoes, and kissed his cheek. Her hand drifted down his *pa* to the stone in his chest, and he felt a surge as she touched it.

"Thank you for saving my life and my baby's life." She palmed his cock then cupped his balls, gently stroking and squeezing as he watched Georgia's hard fucking and beyond that, the increasing, explosive desire of his reclining shanna.

Gods, but this was sweet.

"You are more than welcome," he answered, but stopped her from pumping his cock. It felt wonderful, but it wasn't time.

No. Not yet.

"Go to Georgia," he told Elise. "Increase her pleasure."

Elise eyed him for a moment, then grinned and nodded. She moved over to the trio, knelt at Georgia's side, and kissed Ki as he pistoned in and out of Georgia's ass, then reached down to fondle his bollocks. This drove Ki to new heights, and he moved into Georgia even harder and faster.

With her free hand, Elise reached around Georgia's waist and easily found her clit.

Georgia screamed and came instantly, shuddering and jerking, but the Tul'Mar brothers held back, slowing their rhythm, then once more picking it up as Elise massaged Georgia's clit.

Behind them against the bubble wall, Krysta made fists and beat them against the unyielding surface.

"Georgia," Darkyn asked in low tones. "Have you ever been fucked by three men?"

At this, Georgia groaned incoherently, and Darkyn had his answer.

He could bring something to this circle, then, and he would.

Barung be damned. We will kill him, or we will enjoy the last moments of life like no people before us.

Keeping his eyes on his hallas, he strode forward, positioned himself in front of Georgia, and took her by the hair. She lifted her head, eyes glazed with pleasure, mouth wide for the task. Languid excitement was etched on every feature of her face.

When next Ki rammed into Georgia's ass, Darkyn thrust his cock into her mouth. Warm and wet and welcoming as he knew it would be — but his pleasure came from Krysta's throaty moans. Her nipples made peaks with no stimulation but what her eyes could give her, and the outflow of sexual energy rippling through the *pa* around them.

Darkyn could see her clit from his vantage point, it was so swollen. He had to grin, which caused Krysta to have violent, passionate thoughts.

Like Fari, Darkyn was a captive to the rhythm dictated by Ki — and Ki played his role masterfully, speeding up, slowing down, bringing them all to the edge repeatedly.

Georgia shuddered from orgasm after orgasm.

Ki finally thrust his fingers into his shanna's quim, and brought both women to orgasm at the same time he allowed Fari and Darkyn to come.

Darkyn gave no thought to pulling out. He knew Georgia wanted to swallow his essence this once, and he knew it would bring Krysta to the brink.

As Georgia collapsed forward, Ki pulled out of her ass, leaving her, for a time, to Fari's embrace. The Sailmaster turned his attention to cleansing his staff by rubbing it against the *pa* on his mate's hips. The air sizzled and crackled as the silver fire flowed to gently burn him clean—and then he pulled Elise down and mounted her, driving into her as if he had not just led them all in a prolonged session of pleasure.

Darkyn understood.

The lure of a soul's mate made everything else pale in comparison. These family joinings—they were but foreplay for the real thing. Planting one's cock deep inside your *shanna's* tight, drenched quim.

Darkyn moved between Ki and Fari and their mates, approaching his own.

He knelt between her legs, erection already at full strength again from just the sight of her beauty, from the barest whiff of her woman's scent.

Krysta lay against the side of the bubble, gazing at him with both murder and adoration in her eyes.

"I love you," she said. "Fuck me."

But she wasn't begging.

Darkyn loved that about her. Her strength, her command. Yet he knew—and he knew she knew—who held the power when it came to pleasure.

"I love you, too." He leaned down and bit one nipple, then the other. "Now spread your legs wider."

Krysta cried out and convulsed from just that contact, but she spread her legs wider.

Darkyn reveled in the feel of her soft, wet quim against his hard cock as he kissed her mouth. Her *pa*-coated bush made his staff tingle all the more as he pressed it into her folds, using the hard flesh to rub her swollen clit, letting the head barely enter her waiting center, then pulling it back as he once more bit her nipples.

Around them, the sounds of lovemaking intensified.

Krysta screamed in need and frustration, pulling his hair as he kissed her and continued to tease her quim with his cock.

"As I promised," he whispered against her ear, enjoying the snap of *pa* against his wet lips. "I'll make you scream again and again."

Below them, the *Barung*'s struggles became louder, more desperate, but he seemed an eon removed. This was the way to kill the bastard. Yes. With their love, their sexual energies, their strengths.

Krysta thought she might die if Darkyn didn't give her relief soon. She didn't want his fingers or his mouth, though both were quite skilled and driving her near to distraction as they danced over her nipples, her lips, her ears, and now and again her clit.

What she wanted was his cock.

Damn him!

He kept laying his erection against her, rubbing it up and down between her wet lips.

She came twice, little orgasms. Little tortures.

"What do you want, *hallas?*" he whispered. He rubbed his lips across her new feather *pa* mark, then sucked her coated nipple so rapidly, so deeply that she came again, this time shuddering as her clit rubbed against his erection.

Little tortures!

"I want you," she whispered.

Wrong answer, apparently.

Darkyn sucked her other nipple, pulling back just as she almost came again.

She pounded on his chest with both fists as he lifted up.

"I want your cock," she tried. "I want you to fuck me. Please!"

Also, clearly the wrong answer.

He rocked back, stroking his own shaft, yellow eyes penetrating straight to her soul.

"What do you really want, Krysta?"

Somewhere behind him, Georgia came with moaning fury, followed by Elise, but the sounds of wild lovemaking never stopped.

It was lovemaking now. Beyond recreation or simple pleasure. Beyond joining, even. Soul's mates were blending with each other, enjoying pleasures for what might be the last time.

Krysta blinked, then understood.

She felt herself smiling as she lifted her own legs, giving Darkyn a deeper entry when he chose to take it.

Gazing directly into his unsettling, fiery stare, Krysta yelled, "I want my turn!"

Right answer.

Darkyn leaned over her, bracing his arms beside her head, holding her still to look at while he drove his cock deep, deep into her aching, pulsing center.

Krysta felt her inner walls clench around him, felt him bury himself bollocks-deep, pull almost completely out, then bury himself again.

She felt like she couldn't get enough. Like she'd never have enough. Not now, not this day, not ever.

Her own moans of pleasure were all she heard, mingled with Darkyn's groans and the wet, slippery sounds of their complete joining. Their mingling of essence.

Krysta's nipples burned. Her lips throbbed as her sha, her munas kissed her deeply, all the while fucking her harder, faster, going deep then shallow—anything to increase her pleasure. Anything to make her scream.

As the heat built and built in her body, she did scream, repeatedly. The force of her orgasm felt like a lightning storm, striking every inch of her flesh. She rolled her hips yet higher, feeling Darkyn's jets of seed stream into her as he joined her, coming with a deep roar of male elation.

Before her body could even settle from that pleasure, new pleasures began. Elise and Georgia were suddenly there, sucking her nipples as Darkyn took her again.

Krysta plunged her fingers into their wet channels, delighting in the hot, silky feel, in knowing they took pleasure from her pleasure.

At one point, Krysta was certain her brothers had entered their *shannas* from behind, that they were all joined as one, sharing pleasure and energy in ways her mind scarcely understood.

All the while, she could see the eyes of her munas, her made of stone lover, eating her whole as he claimed her again and again, giving her all that he could give her.

She loved this man. Gods, how she loved him!

The orgasm that claimed her then was shared amongst six minds, multiplied twice over, then twice over again. The rush of energy was impossible to measure. Impossible to fathom. It rocked her body, making her wonder if she had become a shower of sparks, an explosion of stars lighting dark and faraway space.

In that instant of complete fulfillment, her expanded senses told her the moment of truth had arrived. *Barung* had taken such damage from their pleasure that he was desperate. He was massing his remaining strength for the last attack, live or die, crush or be crushed.

Krysta didn't want to surrender the moment, but the six knew the moment had passed.

As they got to their feet, trembling from exhaustion and joy muted only by the chance it was about to end, Krysta knew she had at least, indeed, had her turn.

Darkyn held her in his arms, flanked by Elise and Georgia, who held their mates just as firmly.

All of them looked down through the pyramid, at the black mass almost out of sight but rising quickly.

Here he comes, Krysta had time to say before space and life as she knew it exploded into pain and screams that had nothing to do with pleasure.

A fireball rushed at them all, despite their frantic joined efforts to thrust it back.

Krysta barely saw it strike the bubble, knocking Ki and Fari to the silvery floor. Only the women remained standing. The women and her munas.

And then Darkyn was between them and the fireball. He was throwing the women out of harm's way, Krysta included.

And he was engulfed.

Krysta's heart was engulfed with him. All of her senses seared. Her being screamed a denial.

The *pa* around them sucked inward, to her, to her alone.

An explosion took her full awareness, shattered it completely.

She had only a sense of drifting left.

A sense of endless drifting.

Chapter Sixteen

The day Darkyn Weil woke, he knew he was not on Arda, nor Uhr, nor any world he had seen before, even in vision.

He reached up, touched the yellow stone in his chest, and felt a reassuring vibration.

Not dead, then.

His axe was missing from his hip, but oddly, he didn't mind. His memories swirled and clashed, whispering of weapons far greater than those of the hand. He knew he was still a warrior, still a leader, but he also knew the meanings of both stations had changed for him, forever.

How, he couldn't yet say.

As awareness returned in full, Darkyn realized he lay on a bed of soft moss, so soft it might have been made from the finest trading silks. Golden leaves spilled from his body as he moved, and they, too, were softer than soft when he touched them.

As he sat up, he saw that his bed sloped down in a sculpted arc, coming to rest in verdant grass that had to be as silky as the moss. A single yellow orb hovered in the blue sky above him, bathing his skin with a softer, less intense warmth than he was accustomed to from big sun and little sister. All around this strange bed were tall trees with brownish-red bark and massive branches, lifting score upon score of golden leaves toward their yellow sun.

Occasionally, they rustled in a slight breeze, showing a glittery underside that reminded Darkyn of a gold version of *pa*.

Pa...

He glanced down at himself, trying to accept that he was alive, that his body remained attached to his mind. He saw that he was clad only in breeches, that his feet and chest were bare, and in places, slightly reddened.

He remembered throwing the women clear of the fireball, shielding them from the flames...

When he tried to stand, Darkyn felt a tightness in his back and knew he had scars from that decision. Many scars. He touched his head to find only bristles of newly-growing hair.

As he lowered his hand, he couldn't help but stare at his own flesh.

It was...silver.

Not in the crackling, sparkling fashion of *pa*, but yet silver and...flowing like *pa*.

My body has become like Krysta's hair, coated and fused, maintaining its true form and color, yet to the eye, silver-white and shining. My stone remains, yellow as always, and yet I know it's stronger. I could touch it and shake the foundations of a stone building, I think.

"Krysta," he said aloud, feeling the tears in his dry throat even as he called.

"Be at ease," said a voice from in front of him.

Darkyn squinted in the odd yellow sunlight to find a man standing at the edge of the sculpted mound holding his bed of moss.

"Yes," the man said. "Afternoon sun is bright here, even by your standards, only not as hot."

This man—he had black-black hair streaked with white. On Arda, he would be perhaps several hundred stellar years of age. Darkyn had the distinct sense this man was much, much older than a few hundred stellar years.

Questions swirled through his mind, but the only one of import was the first to his lips. "Where is Krysta? Where is my *shanna*?"

"Waiting for you in the House of Wisdom." The young-old man's voice carried an unmistakably light, amused note.

Darkyn had a sense of weights lifting from his chest. "She lives, then? She is healthy? Is she—?"

"Be at ease," the young-old man instructed again, this time with some sort of subtle binding in his voice. "Do not force me to send you back into trance. You have been sleeping long enough."

Darkyn found he couldn't speak, even if he wanted to. The man's command was like a spell, compelling him to silence until the fellow chose to lift it.

Slowly, cautiously, the man climbed the swell of the hill. Darkyn saw that he wore robes of sapphire, gold, white, and red, wound together in a way his brain had trouble perceiving. He looked like he might be Kaeradi, but Darkyn noted the absence of gloves.

"We do not wear gloves on Kaerad," the man said, making no pretensions about reading Darkyn's thoughts even though Darkyn hadn't sensed him doing so. "There are other protections here. You and I, we're kin enough that I could touch you without penalty, I think. Let us find out."

Darkyn stood as any man munas, made of stone as the fellow placed the tips of his fingers against Darkyn's temple. A pressure filled Darkyn's mind—and then he knew everything. All of the answers.

He saw in that brief moment how Krysta had channeled the *pa* of the pyramid and its bubble, driving away the fire that threatened to burn them to death. Forcing *Barung* back into the dead space of Perth, burying him deeper and deeper until the pressure crushed the last of his life force into stellar dust.

Ord'pa, she had been thinking.

Ord'pa, indeed. The executioner. Thank the gods.

Instinctively, then, she had sealed them all in their own envelopes of *pa* without even realizing her actions. The six drifted there, anchored around Darkyn, their most sorely wounded, until the ships of Kaerad and Perth and Arda came to get them.

By agreement of the *pao*, the Kaeradi took custody of the six and brought them to their home planet, where the healing sciences were most advanced. They were permitted the highest honor, that of a healing trance on an altar of their goddess, safely ensconced on the grounds of Kaerad's Council of Wisdom.

This mound was, possibly, the first place in the universe that had known man's presence. As such, the Kaeradi believed its healing force to be without limit.

More relief filled Darkyn. The other four members of his family were also alive, also well. He had been the longest in trance because of his burns, waking now, four long stellar weeks after the defeat of the *Barung*.

Much more information packed itself in Darkyn's mind. He knew the citizens of Arda and Uhr were eagerly awaiting the return of their heroes, and that Kadmyr, of all people, was serving as regent of both Arda and its rebel moon—even acting as Katryn's guardian until her parents were restored.

No wonder they are eager to have us back, Darkyn thought, remembering Brand's sacrifice with a pang of pride and sorrow. *He would have been glad to know the restoration of honor and faith in his family name was so complete.*

He saw also that the members of the *pao* who were typically at odds with one another had departed Ardani space without incident. He even saw that the Bandu consented to take a delegation of deliriously happy Nostans back to Bandu-Mother to reward them for their assistance in getting Brand's ship airborne against the *Barung*'s wicked shield.

"The universe may never be the same," Darkyn muttered, relieved to find his words again.

There were no pictures of Akad's fate, however, which filled Darkyn with dread—an emotion that made him weak enough to stagger.

The Kaeradi priest took his hand from Darkyn's shoulder. "The fate of your brother is complex, I'm afraid. His ship was flung into a ripple in time-space, and it exploded. Yet, those of us monitoring, those of us who withstood that burst of energy, had no sense of his life essence being lost. Once we returned to Kaerad, we set about studying—ah, yes. I forget the young have no use for tales."

Darkyn swallowed, feeling guilt at his impatience. Being so completely open to this priest was unnerving.

"We have determined that your brother is on Earth—no, no excitement, please. He came to rest on Earth in the Earth standard year 2800, more or less."

"More or less?" Darkyn sat right down on the ground. "You're telling me my brother is lost, what, some six stellar centuries in the *future*?"

The young-old man folded his hands, smiled down at Darkyn, and nodded. "Your falcon, too. Guardian, I believe her name is. They are both alive."

"Both alive," Darkyn said numbly, then felt the import and amazement. "Both alive!"

"One day, with luck and patience, we may be able to assist the two of you in communicating—much as Akad accomplished when he transferred Guardian's black feather into Krysta's care."

"Akad is alive—and he isn't alone." Darkyn felt his strength returning. "Guardian is good company, when she chooses to be."

His *a'mun* twin, the brother of his blood, heart, and soul, yet breathed, yet lived. One day, gods and goddesses willing, Darkyn might see his twin again. That hope seemed more than sufficient, for the time being.

Darkyn got to his feet slowly, feeling the weakness in his limbs.

"A few days of Kaeradi food, some exercise, time with your family, and you will be like new again." The priest smiled. "You have some scars on your back and shoulders, but even those may heal. *Barung*'s flames were not natural, the *pa* now infused in your flesh seems to be fighting against their damage. Come. I will take you to your woman. Your...*shanna*."

With surprising speed, the ageless man turned and headed into the red-barked trees. Darkyn followed after him, watching golden, glittering leaves swirl at his passage.

Pa infused in my flesh. In my very stone of power. Well. I suppose Arda and Uhr will get back six silver beings instead of the normal-toned creatures they sent forth. He let out a breath. *That, of all things, seems a small price.*

The path toward the House of Wisdom wound through endless trees, and a forest of enough beauty to rival those on his home world. He noted that there was a symmetry and perfection to most of what he saw, as if the plants and trees had been sewn on purpose—but instinctively, he knew they were not. This was simply a balanced world, a seat of great knowledge and healing. A place of wonder.

So why did he have a sense of unease, as if something were slightly off-kilter?

He found himself breathing harder than he should have as the young-old man at last led him out of the woods, toward a wooden structure of impressive proportion. Built in the shape of a five-pointed star, the House of Wisdom's points almost touched an outer ring of red and yellow flowering trees.

Darkyn's keen vision picked up activity in the windows of the center section, and near the large main door. His senses told him that his *shanna* waited there, and soon he would hold her softness against him and smell her soft, spicy scent. Bayflowers. The outdoors. Life itself.

"Krysta," he said to himself. "Hallas."

He didn't have to wait until he entered the structure. From the door came a shout of joy, and she was running toward him.

Even to his sensitive eyes, the changes in her were subtle. Where once *pa* had flowed and shimmered in great fluid patches, it now seemed quiescent, more under control — with no spaces between the patches.

Otherwise, Krysta was Krysta, but for a yellow robe with blue trim where her jumpsuit should have been.

Darkyn quickened his pace to meet her despite the persistent weakness in his limbs.

"*Shanna!*"

She fell into his arms, and when their flesh met, Darkyn felt an instant bolstering of his physical strength. Silvery energy flowed back and forth between them as their lips met.

Darkyn was aware of the oddity, but he didn't care. His attention was all for his beautiful mate, his precious hallas. He kissed her until he couldn't breathe, then kissed her again, wishing he could unzip his flesh and fold her inside him, never to be released.

"I was so afraid for you," he murmured into her ear, kissing the soft flesh, feeling the hum of her *pa* against his mouth. It didn't burn or sting.

"You're the one who slept for nearly a stellar month." Her laughter felt like salve on his scarred back, loosening his mind and emotions.

When he pulled back to look at her, he felt blessed.

"Ah." The young-old man swept past them, heading into the House of Wisdom. "You are rejoined. The healing is complete. Good. Good! Dinner is in three stellar hours in the main hall. Don't be late!"

Krysta held her *sha*, knowing beyond all knowledge that he meant more to her than anything ever had or ever would. Here, in his embrace, she was home. She would be home wherever she went with him, so long as he stood beside her.

My turn. Yes. He is my turn. I couldn't have asked for better.

"I love you," she told him without reservation. Her hands caressed his almost-hairless head, then found the scars on his back and caressed them. The marks of his bravery, his valor. The Kaeradi elders said the rope-like burns might be healed by the unusual concentrations of *pa* they all now bore—and if Darkyn preferred that, so be it.

For her part, Krysta didn't mind if the scars stayed. Another part of her lover's body to memorize with her lips and fingers. She rather liked him without hair, too, though she would love the unusual streaked mane when it grew back. The sensation of the bristles on her fingers made her wonder how they might feel on her belly, on her thighs.

In fact, the feel of his erection against her belly made her want to begin memorizing every new, sexy imperfection, here, on the steps of the Kaeradi motherhouse, but her more recent training gave her restraint.

"Come inside with me," she urged. "The others want to see you. Me, I'd like to get that over with so I can show you our rooms and have you to myself."

Darkyn's yellow eyes, almost the same shade of golden as the leaves on Kaerad's trees, captured hers. "Yes," he said simply.

The single syllable made Krysta's whole being hum with desire.

She kissed his cheek, feeling the delicious warmth of flesh and *pa*, then led him through the door of the House of Wisdom.

The greeting room, or main reception area for visitors, was as broad as it was long—and that was long. Easily four times the size of any room in Camford, save perhaps the Great Hall where banquets were held.

Ki, Fari, Elise, and Georgia were seated at the hearth of a quietly burning and smokeless fire when Krysta entered, but they stood immediately upon sight of Darkyn.

All the Kaeradi in the area moved away to tend their own tasks.

Krysta felt Darkyn stop behind her just as they reached the fireplace. Before even greeting his family, he said, "Now I know what's wrong. Do they have no women here? I saw none in their *pao* delegation on Uhr. I see none here, and I feel so little...how do I say it...well, feminine energy in the life force of this planet."

"It's a problem," Elise agreed. "But we're going to try to help them with it."

She came forward, wrapped her arms around Darkyn's neck, and kissed him on the mouth. When she finished, Georgia did the same. Both times, the soft hiss and crackle of mingling *pa* could be heard.

Krysta saw the look of nervous doubt in her sha's eyes as he glanced from the women to Ki and Fari.

The Sailmaster and Sailkeeper of Arda stepped forward, knelt, and placed their right fist over their heart.

Darkyn's eyebrows lifted from the shock of seeing the ancient Ardani gesture of total respect and fealty, typically observed only by *Tonna Kon'pa*, given to him by these men—of all people.

"Rise." He spoke the automatic word with a question in his voice.

Ki and Fari stood. Ki looked at Elise, then at Darkyn. "You almost gave your life to protect my *shanna* from a terrible death. For that, I can never repay you."

"Nor I," said Fari. "All we can do is give you our trust and respect, and our welcome into our family."

"And our word that Arda and Uhr will come to some accord that suits us all."

Krysta felt a lightness in her heart. This was as it should be, as she had so wanted it to be.

"Accepted," Darkyn said in his quiet fashion. "On all counts, and returned."

He slipped an arm around Krysta's waist. She pulled closer to him, loving the feel of his male body next to hers.

"The Kaeradi healers want to keep us another week," Ki said, seating himself on the hearth once more. "Though they will want the women to come back for different training sessions."

Darkyn glanced sidelong at Krysta, who snuggled closer to him. "I'll explain later," she assured him.

There would be time enough to discuss the fact that Akad's role would be filled—until his return—by not one High Priest, but three. High Priestesses, actually. That she and her sisters-by-marriage would be trained in the disciplines of old Arda, Kaerad, and Perth, in hopes of beginning a new and more holistic, unified tradition. And in hopes of keeping close to the basic rhythm of the universe, and preventing the dangerous isolation and arrogance that nearly destroyed Arda during the *Barung* crisis.

She'd also explain later about how their daughters (many, according to the far-seers of Kaerad) would spend at least one stellar year on Kaerad once they reached adulthood, to see if they might find a mate amongst the Kaeradi, who were indeed desperate for females. The breeding program established by the ancients to mingle the blood of the three worlds had upset Kaerad's delicate natural balance. Female births were at alarmingly low rates.

Sharing potentials in such a way seemed the least they could do, in honor of their rescue and healing after battling *Barung*.

Sharing potentials. Gods, Akad. If you could hear the way my mind talks now. The ways I sound like you.

The *pa*-feather, which had turned black against the silvery skin on her chest, tingled. Krysta caressed it.

Perhaps you can hear. With life, with pa, with love, there is nothing outside the range of possibility. I'll remember until you come home to tell me again.

Elise placed a hand on her belly as she spoke to Darkyn, telling him she was pregnant with a child conceived on the soil of Kaerad.

"They think I'm their *Ban'ania*, the mother of their future. That my son's, son's, son—and so on—somewhere down the line may save their planet. Hence my ever-present friends."

She gestured to the red-robed *Legio* across the room, seven of them, sitting utterly still in a straight line with their eyes trained on her. Krysta saw Darkyn's brows lift again, and knew that like her, he hadn't noticed them until Elise pointed them out. The wolfish guards were eerie that way.

Darkyn nodded, and Krysta felt his weariness—and his desire.

So did the other four. They smiled in that carefree way they had learned from the aged, experienced priests in the House of Wisdom.

"Where there are no secrets, there are few if any sorrows." Georgia intoned, then laughed at Darkyn's perplexed look.

Krysta took her mate by the elbow and led him out of the main room, promising to fill him in on everything. "Later. Later. When it makes a difference. For tonight, it doesn't."

"You sound like my brother," he noted as she led him into their spacious bedroom, to the edge of their large, waiting four-poster bed.

"Mmm," was Krysta's only answer as she gripped her wrap-around robe at the neck and removed it with one easy motion. Kaeradi had perfected the art of clothing— comfortable, durable, quickly dispensed.

Darkyn glanced at the yellow and sapphire fabric, now a puddle on the floor.

When he turned his attention back to Krysta, the weariness in his eyes had departed. She saw only hunger and want and loving affection.

He reached to the laces of his own breeches, loosened them quickly, and pushed them down past his swollen staff. She never even saw him step out of them, so quickly did he have her on her back, legs parted, pressing his hard cock into her quim as he bent forward to kiss her lips, then her ears and neck.

Krysta felt her *pa* flow and mingle with his as he circled his tongue around one nipple. Slowly, and with no sense of urgency, he pinched the other.

She groaned.

His hands felt like paradise, joining her skin and retreating, exciting her beyond measure. He brushed kisses over the feather-mark between her breasts, and each of these seemed to tingle against her clit.

Moving at the speed of the patient man he was, Darkyn ran his tongue down her belly, stirring the rivers of silver to new heat. Krysta thought she might combust, wondered if her *pa* could truly catch fire. His tongue plunged ever deeper, pushing the issue, tempting the *pa* to expand and swallow them both.

Krysta's heart hammered. Her throat felt tight and dry as all the moisture in her body headed down, down to where Darkyn teased the lips of her quim with his mouth. He kissed the apex, paused, suckled her clit until she felt an orgasm rushing toward her with the speed of a *pa* vessel, then paused again.

Before she could speak, he briefly kissed her clit again, giving her body-shudders.

Then he stopped completely, pulled back, and studied her with his intense yellow gaze. "Tell me, hallas, have we any reason to be at our strongest?"

"What?" The oddity of the question barely penetrated the sexual haze hanging over her thoughts.

It took her a moment to process. To understand.

To her awareness came the image of Fari and Georgia, making love as usual. They were out behind the House of Wisdom, just inside the nearest grove of trees. Elise and Ki had been making love all day. They remained in a satisfied knot, intertwined near the fireplace, discussing names for their unborn son.

"No," Krysta said emphatically, moving her hips to position his cock for entry. "We do not have to be strong. Absolutely not. Frustration can wait for another day."

Maddeningly, Darkyn didn't move, except to flick the hard ends of both nipples with his thumbs and forefingers. Exquisite shocks traveled the length of Krysta's body, making her quim ache so badly she thought about screaming.

"Perhaps we should...practice," he suggested. "After all, frustration, like any discipline, is an art."

Krysta lifted her head and let it drop on the bed. "Bastard. If you make me wait, I'll strangle you. I've waited long enough."

"An art form you have yet to master, I see." Darkyn gave her the first real grin she had seen since his waking. He allowed the tip of his cock to graze her agonized clit, making her jump. When she tried to move, he pinned her shoulders.

Still grinning. His yellow eyes filled with teasing and passion.

"Bastard. Bastard. Bastard!" She tried to grab his hair, but he still didn't have any. Stupid fire! "You heard the elder who roused you from trance. Dinner is in a few stellar hours, and we shouldn't be late."

"A few stellar hours. I see." Darkyn slipped his cock inside her quim, right where she wanted it, deeper, deeper—and then pulled it out. "I might let you come by then."

Krysta screamed at the top of her lungs, and in the light rapport she now kept constantly with her brothers and sisters-by-marriage, she heard the rich — though not at all satisfying — sound of laughter.

Enjoy this excerpt from
Cursed
The Legacy of Prator

Chapter One
Early Spring, 490
Prator Castle at Chapel Down, Scilly Isles

Eduard watched Ysbet stroll across the stone courtyard.

The princess drifted side to side, as if lost in some secret enchantment. Above her, clouds kept a lazy rhythm with her walk, and the sun made her black hair seem almost blue. No doubt she was headed for Prator's library.

The druids would be furious.

As usual.

Eduard resisted a smile.

The priests wished to ban Ysbet from the scrolls and books because she was impertinent and temperamental, and they claimed she didn't take care of the sacred texts — but King Roland forbade it. After all, who could stand against Ysbet if her will was fixed?

Her will, indeed. That and her intelligence set her far and above most females Eduard knew. Her rounded hips and jutting tits screamed *woman* instead of girl now.

Eduard blinked and gripped the hilt of his sword. His cock hardened, and he ground his teeth. Erections were not a proper response to the princess, especially from Prator's captain of the guards.

Just then, Ysbet passed several of the aged cooks. They shied from her, and one hissed and made signs of protection. The other muttered a single word.

"Custey."

Eduard fairly strangled his sword at that slight.

Accursed. Damned.

He had heard this most of Ysbet's life, from the older servants and those who still followed the druids. If King Roland discovered them disrespecting his daughter, he would have them stocked or flogged. But Roland rarely caught them, and Ysbet's mother Twyllian scarcely left the keep—and yet, somehow Ysbet endured. It was enough to tear even a soldier's heart, to see a woman so spirited, but so alone.

Woman.

His cock throbbed.

No! God's teeth. She's still but a child.

A child born of mystery, when Mordred and Arthur yet lived, and Camelot stood on the brink of disaster. When the Black Prince and his Saxon allies covered Land's End, camped at Camelford, barring escape to the sea.

Eduard knew the tales and remembered much, though he was only a boy when Camelot fell. Arthur's Men were poised for escape with Camelot's heartstone and Gawain's Roland as their future king—but Roland's wife, heavy with child, delayed the host. Then came a storm, with lightning striking like a god's hot wrath. Wind lashed the trees as Twyllian's babe came forth, stillborn, by rumor. But old magik roiled in that storm's heart, and a madman fetched the babe from doom.

Or so it was said.

The old ones believed Ysbet was a changeling. Some imp or faerie with evil purpose. Darker rumors held her to be the spawn of Mordred himself. On two things, the superstitious agreed: Ysbet was not of Roland's line, and Ysbet was not fully human.

As Eduard watched the princess all but vanish into the castle's open door, he wondered about the truth of those whisperings. And not for the first time.

Ysbet.

Could your magik have saved Arthur at Camlann, if you had been older?

And yet, foul Mordred perished by his side. With you, we escaped the Cornish coast, and Mordred's minions drowned in a great wave. It was as if Briton chewed off her tail to protect you and Arthur's Men. If that was not magik, then I have never seen it.

What has fate planned for you, Ysbet?

* * * * *

"Pendragon buried at Avalon these many years, and Mordred's best men drowned in his pursuit." Eduard's voice rang through the training stable beneath the clang of metal and grunts of bested men. "You would think such a loss of life would be sufficient to appease even the cruelest gods."

Ysbet squared her shoulders, and despite the impossible weight of the great helm covering her head, she nodded. Not that she agreed, and not that her opinion would matter if Eduard had the first clue who occupied the suit of mail before him. He always ignored her, even though she was a princess.

Because she was female. Because in her world, in her time, women were playthings. Arm decorations. A haven for hard cocks.

That thought made Ysbet shift inside her armor. She felt like a delicious secret, naughty in her disguise of metal, hidden in plain sight in a room full of half-clad soldiers. The thrill of deception mingled with the risk of discovery, stirring Ysbet to new levels of excitement. The soft, firm cloth of her gambeson, the quilted fabric shielding her flesh from the chain mail, rubbed without mercy against her nipples and her wet quim below.

Each move she made brought exquisite pleasure with a dash of pain, and her breath came in gasps. If she took but a few steps, she might come violently, right there in front of everyone.

To Ysbet, the conventions of her time bound her like the armor she dared to wear. If she had her way, she would break the rules. Any of them. All of them. And she would choose her father's guard captain for her wanton partner.

Ysbet had no sense that Eduard was "destined" for her by some prophecy or magik. And she knew he was far shy of perfect. But he was honorable and brave, much more the warrior than his father Andrus—and moreover, Eduard had a bright mind. The strength of his wit matched the might of his muscle, which Ysbet thought a rare match indeed.

All that remained was convincing Eduard they were fit for each other, and finding some way to circumvent ridiculous rules and laws about royal marriage.

Her extra senses and her rudimentary knowledge of roots and leaves might help her in these quests. Just like those skills had helped her choose today for her gambit, and brew a potion to further enhance the strength she had so carefully been training.

As Ysbet watched Eduard, the warm fabric gripped every area she wished she could tempt him to touch. He went about polishing his longsword to a wicked shine. His coal curls and impossibly broad shoulders reflected in the blade, along with the rush-covered stone floor of the training barn. Above them, rafters boasted hay and dust, and ropes holding straw dummies for sparring.

His Majesty's Captain, Eduard of Kent, had just dispatched such a dummy, and Ysbet had more than enjoyed watching his grace and fierceness. Not for the first time, she wondered if Eduard's chest might be hard to her touch. Like the metal of his breastplate. Like the smooth, polished firmness of the great helm beside his muscled thigh. And the bulge in his pants...

Spirit of the gods, what would he look like aroused? What would he feel like?

Though she had never known a man, she had imagined fucking Eduard hundreds of times. She had envisioned long, sweaty hours in the castle keep, tangled in the soft sheets of her bed while Eduard rode her like a man possessed. While he thrust into her until she cried out again and again. Her breath grew ragged, and the rubbing of the cloth became too much to bear.

Ysbet twitched as the heat of orgasm flooded her. The warmth grew as her eyes widened to take in the room full of men. Watching, but not knowing what they saw.

And what if they realized?

Wave built on wave while Ysbet gently rocked inside the mail to increase the pressure. She bit her lip, refusing to let go of her view of Eduard, of all the other soldiers so close by as pleasure flooded and ebbed, flooded and ebbed.

And then her knees gave, and she almost buckled under the weight of her armor. With a tremendous effort born of will, she steeled her muscles.

If I do not rein in my thoughts and my body, I shall fall and give myself away like some swooning maiden.

"Krell shows his foolishness, driving us like staghounds." Eduard's tense, deep tones caused Ysbet to shiver in the aftershocks of her climax. His words were like fingers, slowly working up her spine.

"Why would those Saxon beasts take interest in Arthur's Men with the mainland for bounty?" He continued. "We have naught for plunder but moss and shells, and shards of rock pretending to be a castle. Prator. What does it matter if this hovel holds a stone from Camelot? It is no prize for the taking."

Ysbet watched her reflection in Eduard's sword as she nodded. She held herself solemn and still, and as man-like as she could manage after such an explosion.

Her quim throbbed.

Already the fabric was back at work, stroking her clit while she clenched and unclenched her thighs.

The whole stable smelled of male sweat and the men's energy, and it was all she could do not to climax again each time she drew a breath.

"Mark me. Roland makes a fine sovereign, but with Arthur dead and Mordred's ghostly venom lingering in every eager ear, it is a cursed shame that Queen Twyllian fell ill before bearing a proper heir." Eduard snorted. "She's left us naught but a bitch pup for succession. How will a child the likes of Ysbet hold any alliance intact? Long live the king, I say."

Ysbet's pleasure sank like waterlogged petals in a river.

A stream of curses rose to her lips, rage mingling with her excitement like some dangerous wizard's draught. But she dared not speak her mind. She would save her epitaphs, store them like fine-tipped quarrels, ready to fire at Eduard at the first proper opportunity.

Bitch pup, indeed! And this from the stable's worst mongrel.

Her heart pounded beneath the ruby dragon covering her breastplate. Her birthright. The Pendragon coat of arms. Though in truth, she doubted her lineage. Ysbet was nothing like her mother or father. Nothing like her cousins, or the other women of the castle.

Ysbet fit with her kin about like a wailing wolf fit on a hut's hearth. She was restless. Different. Wild, and out of place. And so she studied in the libraries day and night. History and lore and ancient druidic beliefs. The allowed texts, and the forbidden. No one dared to stop her, though a few high druids muttered a single word when she passed.

Cursed.

She had been hearing that since her earliest recall, though she hadn't a clue why.

Cursed.

Some of the older druids would not cross her path. Which of course drove her father to a fine rage. If they had not been holy men, he would have killed them with his own hands. Ysbet chose to ignore them. Superstitious old gits. What did they know, anyhow?

When she wasn't ignoring fools, reading, sleeping, or practicing the arts of herbs, spices, and the little-known plants of the woods, Ysbet challenged her body. And thought of ways to be close to Eduard.

Take this excursion, for example.

It had taken Ysbet months of exercising, of lifting stones to take even a step within her armor—and the strength potion to complete the task. No woman she knew could lift a longsword much less wield it in full battle dress. She had never made it so far, fooled the pages and squires, even the knights and Eduard. This was her finest day, and she would not let his damnable mouth ruin her triumph.

Even as Ysbet stoked her resolve, a great crash silenced the constant murmur of the training stable. Stomps followed curses, and a scream ripped the dust in the air.

Dear One God of Arthur! Ysbet's heart pounded even harder. *Krell is coming! Why now, of all times?*

All thoughts of the cloth's rub on her body vanished. A great thrashing and crashing rose from the training yard that separated Prator's two keeps from the tumbledown training barn and sparring floor.

Ysbet straightened her shoulders once more, and placed herself in the most still and sturdy pose she could manage.

Krell would not know. He would not be able to tell that a woman wore the guard armor of Prator. The training master was not observant like Eduard. No. Krell was fire-tempered and quick to the blade, and if those traits were strengths, they were the only gifts Krell offered. Why her father trusted the likes of that mad Saxon mutt, Ysbet would never know—even if he was killing handsome for an older man—and even if he supposedly rescued her from an early death.

With another explosion of clatters and curses, the training master stormed into the stable.

Ysbet quaked in spite of herself.

Krell's unbound golden hair shone in the board-filtered sunlight, and Ysbet tried not to let her gaze linger on the training master's horrible scars. Two blazing red marks scored him like a herald flag, one on his cheek, the other across his chest. He boasted often of the battle that stole some of the beauty from his face, but remained silent as a post about the mark beneath his neck. Ysbet always thought someone had tried to run him through.

Tried, but failed.

Krell was not a man to trifle with, and not a man to lose in hand-to-hand combat. Nearly twice her age, he was like a sexy, fire-breathing older brother, and Ysbet feared his temper far more than the king who had worshiped her every step since birth.

As Krell stalked toward Ysbet, he surveyed his regiment, and to Ysbet's great horror, he began to count his soldiers.

Page and squire alike busied themselves at all manner of tasks, real or staged, clearly in hopes of avoiding the training master's attentions. Even Eduard was polishing his gleaming sword with a new vengeance, and Ysbet felt the want of something to do with her own hands.

Krell finished his tally and stroked his jutting chin. Ysbet allowed herself a wild hope that he would leave, but while she stared through the slit in her great helm, the training master shook his head and started his count again.

Ysbet groaned to herself. In a nervous pique, she clenched her fingers, and the gauntlets covering her hands pinched deep into her flesh.

"Oh!" she squeaked before she could stop herself.

Eduard's head whipped around. He stared at her with wide, dark eyes. Ysbet saw first amazement, then fear, followed by abiding fury.

The passion in his eyes nearly caused Ysbet's heart to burst.

"Get out," Eduard hissed. "You will have my head offered to King Roland in a basket!"

"Father has better use for his baskets," Ysbet whispered, still reeling from his heated glance. Somehow, she kept herself from moving. If truth be told, she could not move. Between her orgasm and standing so long in the weighty mail, her strength was fairly drained.

Eduard opened his mouth to offer more insult, but closed it. Ysbet's own wit and breath left at the same moment, for Krell had again stopped his count. The training master's hawkish blue eyes settled upon her. His lips twisted, and he pointed straight in her direction. "That one!"

Heat rushed to Ysbet's metal-covered cheeks. Krell would reveal her now, and Eduard, the king's captain, would be held responsible for her misbehavior in his training stable. Her father would fly into a fury, and likely have Eduard flogged for permitting the princess to put herself at risk by suiting for battle.

"To the yard," Krell growled.

Ysbet managed to pull herself up straight beneath the burden of the metal.

Walk. I must walk. The longer I can hold this charade, the less likely Eduard will pay for my folly with his flesh.

"Master!" Eduard's tone was firm but thin. "This—this—page. He was but suited so that I might test his metal. By no means is he ready for your challenge."

"Pah." Krell spit on the ground. "Pup's ready enough for what I've a mind to do."

The training stable went tomb-silent, and Ysbet feared breathing lest her panic rasp for all to hear.

"Why not me, Master?" Eduard stood with a cat's lazy grace and held his longsword high. "King Roland's new captain could fair stand a sparring match. We will make an example, for the younger amongst us."

"The boy." Krell's voice was deadly quiet. As Ysbet tried desperately to choke back her terror, the training master waved his hand by his ear like he often did when he was angry or otherwise emotional. "The boy, and the boy alone. Carry him to the yard, if ye must."

Eduard hesitated, but Ysbet knew he had to defer. Krell was the training master, and his authority was absolute. Even the king's captain dared not stand against him, for on Krell, life depended. The master's hand guided the hands who raised swords beside Eduard. The master's fingers checked each inch of the captain's armor before a battle. A twist of a bolt, a shift of a plate, and Eduard would be dead with none the wiser. Only a foolish soldier would deny his training master's whim.

"Sit down," Ysbet whispered to Eduard. She took a step toward Krell, but the effort of guiding her cumbersome body nearly staggered her.

"Have ye naught better to do?" Krell roared at the nearest knight.

The knight almost fell on himself as he seized his sword and busied himself with a straw dummy. The other soldiers scrambled back to tasks in similar fashion, and Ysbet found herself quickly ignored. She was left alone to struggle toward the half-crazed training master, but Eduard's dark eyes were undoubtedly searing holes in her backplate.

The very thought of Eduard's intense gaze pushed her forward. She was no fainting blossom like the serving wenches he saw fit to bed and then dismiss. She was a head taller than each of them, to be sure. And she was nothing like her mother, Queen Twyllian, who fainted at insects and the slightest startle. Eduard seemed to have no time for such women.

Eduard seemed to have no time for anything save his precious swords. Perhaps he might find interest in a female of strength and skill...

About the author:

Annie Windsor is 37 years old and lives in Tennessee with her two children and nine pets (as of today's count). Annie's a southern girl, though like most magnolias, she has steel around that soft heart. Does she have a drawl? Of course, though she'll deny it, y'all. She dreams of being a full-time writer, and looks forward to the day she can spend more time on her mountain farm. She loves animals, sunshine, and good fantasy novels. On a perfect day, she writes, reads, spends time with her family, chats with friends, and discovers nothing torn, eaten, or trampled by her beloved puppies or crafty kitties.

Annie welcomes mail from readers. You can write to her c/o Ellora's Cave Publishing at 1337 Commerce Drive, Suite 13, Stow OH 44224.

Why an electronic book?

We live in the Information Age—an exciting time in the history of human civilization in which technology rules supreme and continues to progress in leaps and bounds every minute of every hour of every day. For a multitude of reasons, more and more avid literary fans are opting to purchase e-books instead of paperbacks. The question to those not yet initiated to the world of electronic reading is simply: *why?*

1. *Price.* An electronic title at Ellora's Cave Publishing runs anywhere from 40-75% less than the cover price of the <u>exact same title</u> in paperback format. Why? Cold mathematics. It is less expensive to publish an e-book than it is to publish a paperback, so the savings are passed along to the consumer.

2. *Space.* Running out of room to house your paperback books? That is one worry you will never have with electronic novels. For a low one-time cost, you can purchase a handheld computer designed specifically for e-reading purposes. Many e-readers are larger than the average handheld, giving you plenty of screen room. Better yet, hundreds of titles can be stored within your new library—a single microchip. (Please note that Ellora's Cave does not endorse any specific brands. You can check our website at www.ellorascave.com for customer

recommendations we make available to new consumers.)

3. *Mobility.* Because your new library now consists of only a microchip, your entire cache of books can be taken with you wherever you go.

4. *Personal preferences are accounted for.* Are the words you are currently reading too small? Too large? Too…**ANNOYING**? Paperback books cannot be modified according to personal preferences, but e-books can.

5. *Innovation.* The way you read a book is not the only advancement the Information Age has gifted the literary community with. There is also the factor of what you can read. Ellora's Cave Publishing will be introducing a new line of interactive titles that are available in e-book format only.

6. *Instant gratification.* Is it the middle of the night and all the bookstores are closed? Are you tired of waiting days—sometimes weeks—for online and offline bookstores to ship the novels you bought? Ellora's Cave Publishing sells instantaneous downloads 24 hours a day, 7 days a week, 365 days a year. Our e-book delivery system is 100% automated, meaning your order is filled as soon as you pay for it.

Those are a few of the top reasons why electronic novels are displacing paperbacks for many an avid reader. As always, Ellora's Cave Publishing welcomes your questions and comments. We invite you to email us at service@ellorascave.com or write to us directly at: 1337 Commerce Drive, Suite 13, Stow OH 44224.

Discover for yourself why readers can't get enough of the multiple award-winning publisher Ellora's Cave. Whether you prefer e-books or paperbacks, be sure to visit EC on the web at www.ellorascave.com for an erotic reading experience that will leave you breathless.

WWW.ELLORASCAVE.COM

Printed in the United States
35500LVS00003B/55-291